DAY and KNIGHT
The Case of Missing Things

BETTE GUY

Author Bette Guy
www.betteguy.com

Published in 2013 by
LONGBOTTOM PRESS

Interior layout and cover design
by Publicious Pty Ltd
www.publicious.com.au

Cover images: © korvin1979 - Fotolia.com
© Leonid Tit - Fotolia.com

Catalogue-in-Publication details available
from the National Library of Australia

ISBN: 978-0-9874860-0-4

Also available in ebook
ebook ISBN: 978-0-9874860-1-1

DEDICATION

To anyone who's ever chased a dream, and
caught it, and been pleased they did.

ONE

I raced down the hallway, burst into my bedroom, threw off my beanie and collapsed onto the bed. I was quivering with excitement. The thrill of the hunt. Having taken my considerable weight off my feet I lay back and listened to my heart booming like I'd just completed a marathon. Arms outstretched, eyes goggling at the white pressed metal ceiling of my nineteen-thirties weatherboard cottage, I felt well pleased with myself. The glare from the high wattage bulb swinging low on its metre- long cord began to hurt my eyes. I shut them tight and relaxed into the mattress. Memo: *Replace all bulbs with the less emphatic eco-friendly type.* My new career had begun. My first Case. Not that it was all that brilliant a job, not by world standards, but I'd done it okay. Hugging my legs to my chest I rocked back and forth, like a cockroach flipped on its back. My form of exercise. Sure beats running on the spot.

I flipped open my eyes and was struck by the number of spider webs hanging across each corner of the three metre high ceiling, each gathering dust as well as flies. Spiders have patience and perseverance, something I had to acquire. *Memo: Clean up the spider webs. Soon.* I usually worked on the principle of never doing today what could be put off until tomorrow. Lucy Knight, my best friend, held to a similar homespun philosophy, although being both street smart and vigorous she's far less naïve than me. She wasn't always that way. At primary school she clung to me like a leech, so that's what I called her. The name sort of stuck.

When I confided to her about my dream of becoming a

Detective we both knew no way could I join the Police Force. A criminal record for a start. Nothing bad, just a few petty crimes. Worse, I'd been known to rave on about the need for scrupulous integrity, which doesn't go down too well in certain workplaces. I'd also frequently voiced the opinion that dobbing in people should be a capital offence. As for the planting of evidence, I reckoned that should carry the hung, drawn and quartered variety of punishment. So, having both a criminal record and an idealistic version of integrity, I had little chance of joining any branch of Her Majesty's Service. So I'd have to go private. Not that I'd ever sold all that much dope. In any case the law had changed since then and I hadn't touched anything too illegal for around thirteen years. I never did discover who kept dobbing me in. No honour among thieves, not like in the really old movies, not even like in the nineteen-seventies, when hippies automatically closed ranks against the law.

Luckily, I'd managed to save the fifteen per cent deposit for my cottage out of the 'gifts' people donated in exchange for weed. Problem was, once mortgage papers were signed I needed a proper, regular income. Apparently banks want loans repaid on a regular basis. Something to do with their profit margin? To become a bonafide home owner and a fair dinkum Private Investigator I needed to make lifestyle changes. So, I'd changed. A few years back I was an easy catch for a macho, mean spirited, drongo. A few months of uncontrollable lust saw me trapped with a violent no-hoper, both of us selling dope to make the rent. He had three kids that I was supposed to look after every other weekend, which meant treks to the beach and so sand in every orifice; rainforest walks, so loads of blood sucking leeches and endless boring conversations with kids who hated me. Plus putting up with him and his mates. Lust is one thing, what it leads to is another. No way was I going to fall for that again.

Gathering the evidence had felt real good, although total satisfaction was a bit premature. I hadn't yet shown the client what I'd come up with but it was basically what she'd asked for. Any man who cheats on his wife, especially when they've got kids, deserves to be thrown out of house and home.

Contemplating my new lifestyle, I sat up, rubbed my eyes, stared around the bedroom that was eighty five per cent owned by the bank and opened up the curtains to greet the rising sun. It was the pale red of a cool spring morning. Surfers would be cruising the coastline checking for the perfect wave. Street cleaners would be driving home after the night shift. Workers would be on their way to stack supermarket shelves and some people would be returning to their own beds, each one witnessing the new born sun promising, as it always did, the unknown, possibly the unknowable. Life, during the dark hours, was filled with the unexpected. I was going to like night work. Not that I had any more night jobs lined up, or even daytime ones. Clients weren't exactly falling over themselves to employ me, yet life suddenly had a fringe of brightness around it. I felt so stupefied by my own success I thought of calling one of those Reality TV shows, to put my name down. But I changed my mind real quick. The need for humiliation never was high on my agenda.

I headed towards the kitchen, the neighbourly magpies raising their confident greetings to the new day. Soon a whole community of birds would be stridently saluting each other as they exchanged gossip about their predictable lives. Truckies too, high on stimulants or recent sex at the last Truck Stop, would be doing the same thing as they raced between Sydney and Brisbane with their perishables. Carbon footprints are big when you live half way between two capital cities, each hundreds of kilometres apart.

Swinging my legs like John Wayne in *High Noon* I strode into the kitchen, the dregs of the adrenalin rush slowing. I felt satiated yet restless, like after good sex. Unfortunately, sex, good or otherwise, had become somewhat of a rarity. According to the medical books, thirty eight wasn't old, yet most men seemed to want chicks half their age. *Memo: Check out fitness centres again.*

I'd checked out every gym in town at least once. They all looked like hard work. And for what? Losing a few inches around the hips? In my case around everything, but shit, I am not obese. Not according to my mirrors.

I put on the jug and piled Arabica coffee into the pot. At that point I didn't give a shit about what size my hips were, or even when my next shag would be. More important was the next Case, whatever and whenever. Hopefully something mysterious and money making. Fame-making would be even better. How many adulterous husbands did I need to spy on and photograph before getting my big break? Sure I expected to start at the bottom, the easy, less important Cases first but surely it couldn't be too long before I was dealing in real crime, real missing objects, real missing persons, real murders. Real murders? Murders! Who was I kidding. Okay, so I'd been watching a lot of TV cop shows.

Slurping down my morning mouthful of caffeine I laughed at my naivety. As if to agree, perched on its favourite eucalypt branch, a kookaburra joined in. Still, Fate had dealt me a decent card. Fate, a good word to cover coincidence, chance, destiny or whatever. God's Will sounded pretty inadequate for the twenty first century.

It was down to Fate that I'd been at Lucy's party that night. It was Fate made me so stupid drunk I said yes, yes, yes, to taking on my first Case. It wasn't Fate exactly that made me good with a camera. I'd been taking photos since I was a kid but it was Fate made my dad send me the decent Canon for my thirtieth birthday. Lucy's party had been the usual sort, wild and noisy, one where everybody drank too much, ate too much, talked too much, smoked too much and, depending on how things went, shagged too much.

Anyhow, I'd soon downed a few glasses of red and chomped my way through truckloads of food; pizza, cheese and bickies, 'funny' cookies, stuffed olives, sliced gherkins and tiny cherry tomatoes rolled in nasturtium leaves. I rounded all this off with a couple of Mars Bars. Things were becoming hazy. No bloke had offered himself up and I hadn't seen one worth sacrificing myself for but then, around midnight, he appeared, the man of my fantasies, casually leaning up against a cupboard Lucy had scored at an Op Shop. He was thirty something, pale face, eyes like amber, muscled body and short blonde hair, the surfer look without the tan. He held a second glass of wine, presumably for someone else. I moved in. He beamed the kind of smile I'd kill my grandmother for. If she was still alive that is. I sidled to his side, in what I imagined to be a sexy manner, though my alcohol filled legs kept collapsing, totally spoiling the effect. I made a grab for him.

His name was Mathew. I told him my name, which he didn't seem to believe. I was blatantly rubbing myself up against him when an irate redhead breezed in from nowhere. She took one look at me and snarled, her face hard as any marble masterpiece. The slits that served as her eyes dared me to stay clinging to him. It was a scenario out of my teens. I'd lost all those rounds too. I posed, sullen. She whirled me round, breathed heavily into my face, she must have eaten the whole tray of garlic stuff and told me the man was hers. I spat out the words before I'd even collated them in my brain.

"Oh, so he's a paying customer of yours, is he?"

She stepped back as if prodded by a Taser. If looks could kill I'd have been dead, cremated and scattered unceremoniously over some extremely unsanctified ground, such as the Council Dump. Surprisingly, her voice changed to sultry and sarcastic.

"Sorry, darling, am I walking on your patch?"

Her scarlet lips pouted. Her eyes squinted with the power of the conqueror. She'd clearly got her High School Certificate in both English and Psychology. *Memo: Check out psychology text books.* She curled up the corners of her mouth. Sign of a sadist, according to Lucy, who was well informed on such matters. I clenched my fists in preparation. She pulled herself up tall, around half a metre above me and moved in. I was ready, emotionally if not physically. I yelled with the bravado of an eight year old facing off with his four year old sister.

"Come on, then! Do your worst."

Out of the corner of my eye I could see Lucy, black leather-clad legs astride, arms folded, cat grin on her face as she watched and waited. I knew she'd be there for me. All the same, I was shit scared. The woman moved her hands over Mathew's backside then smiled at him, sickly sweet. I waited for her to take a crack at me but she simply turned and walked away. Perhaps she'd seen the threat on Lucy's face. I was well and truly miffed but at least I hadn't been humiliated. I shouted out the only lie I thought would provoke her.

"For your information, I'm not a hooker, I'm a private investigator!"

It was not only a lie, it was a beauty of a lie. I knew it, Lucy knew it, probably the whole world knew it but, too late, it was out there. My heart soared with the strength of impotent aggression yet all she did was stride off into the cool night air, dragging Mathew beside her. I huffed and puffed, circling the furniture, then perched myself on the arm of the black leather sofa. I gulped down the glass of red Lucy shoved under my sulking nose, which eased my ego out of bottom gear and into second. I dropped into the sofa beside a couple of blokes doing unspeakable things to each other. There's a limit to what should be done in public. *Memo: Check if what those two were doing is possible without being double jointed.* I pointed to the bedroom, which they occupied within seconds. Lucy plonked herself down beside me. Linking her arm through mine she snuggled up, her head against my shoulder. We're best friends, me and Lucy.

"Really Flab, a private investigator? You could have chosen something easier."

She called me Flab on account of my insatiable desire for all things fatty and sweet, resulting in size twenty clothes and the inability to run without everything flapping. Dawn French had a lot to answer for. I shrugged.

"Easier?"

"It can be dangerous."

"So?"

"You don't even have a gun."

"I don't reckon on using a gun."

"So you stand there and let a crim blow you away?"

"No. I run like the wind."

Lucy roared like a firecracker on New Year's Eve.

"You? Run? What all eighty-five kilos of you? All at once?"

Tact was not one of Lucy's better traits.

"I can get fit."

I can also lie when necessary.

"Besides, there are other ways to escape."

"Such as?"

I had to think seriously for a few seconds.

"If I find myself in a dangerous position I'll make sure there's a decoy. Someone to steer them away from me."

"And who's fucking stupid enough to do that?"

I stared hard at her. She stood up.

"Oh, no, you don't. No fucking way!"

I suddenly felt evil, and liked the sensation. She shook her head at me.

"You, Holly Day, are wicked!"

"You, Lucy Knight, are my best friend and protector."

After two bottles of red the matter was settled. I was going to be the best Private Investigator on the north east coast and Lucy was going to be my off-sider, if and when required. Not that either of us actually believed anything either of us was saying at that particular moment in time but it felt like a positive move.

In the real world, I'd done market research for around fifteen years: government departments, non government departments, small businesses, corporations and, occasionally, political parties. I became good at my job, basically because I came up with the results the client most desired. I'd moved from market research to investigator, not that big a move. After the first Case, a successful operation, I considered myself fully fledged. Well, not quite fully fledged. I wasn't licensed, and my only qualification in the art of detecting came from watching TV shows and movies and reading thrillers. I'd had no practical experience and no authority to carry weapons of any sort. Yet, out of the blue, at Lucy's party, a sad, middle aged woman had asked if I really was a Private Investigator. Having described myself as such, very loudly and very publicly, I felt obliged to agree with myself. Besides, I wanted to be one.

Turned out her husband was playing away from home and she wanted sufficient evidence to take him to the cleaners. *Memo: Isn't that what the Family Court did?* Anyhow, we agreed on a fee and she wrote down the address of the other woman who I had to photograph with the erring husband. As he usually got home around two a.m. we figured he left his girlfriend's place about one thirty. In a country town it's easy to get from any point A to any point B in under half an hour. Plus, at that time of morning there'd be no traffic problems; the odd cop car, a few homeless people bedding down for the night, people exchanging hard drugs for hard cash and drunken youths certain they were enjoying themselves. A few days later she phoned me to confirm I'd take on the job. How could I honestly refuse?

I drove to the house in question and parked my nineteen sixty-six, burgundy Valiant Station Wagon across the street. I sat and waited. And waited. He must have been on Viagra. Patience was something I still had to cultivate. Three a.m. came and went. I shivered. Contrary to the tourist brochures, some nights do get cold in this sub tropical region. At a quarter past four the front door opened and out they stepped, him buttoning up his jacket, her holding a pink, silky slip as clingy as Gladwrap, against her anorexic body. The lovers hugged passionately. Shit, was I jealous at the thought of all that sex. The goodbye took several minutes. A great photo opportunity. I raised my camera and clicked rapidly. They were too busy with each other to notice, though briefly

I wondered what he'd do if I was spotted. Beat the shit out of me? More than likely. But they were well occupied. I replaced my outdated camera with an outdated cam recorder I'd bought second hand and gathered five glorious minutes of evidence. He walked down the path to his car. She swept back inside. I pulled my beanie over my forehead and sank down into the seat while he drove off. It was a few minutes before I could breathe easy. I was back home by five a.m. expecting to nod off quickly. I didn't. So there I was, listening to the dawn chorus and drinking brewed coffee, a PI virgin no more.

After changing into my pink bunny rabbit flannelette jammies, I snuggled back into bed, emotionally and physically exhausted. *Memo: Check if flannelette is simply fluffed up cotton. Who does the fluffing up? Low caste Indians or high cost machinery?* Newly wakened magpies vied with the kookaburras to praise the rising yellow hued sun. A couple of red and green lorikeets, stoned early on nectar, trilled briskly from the red bottlebrush. The faint hum of distant trucks scurrying along the highway filtered through the bedroom curtains. They were familiar sounds. I'd lived in this town all of my life. My breathing slowed, the excitement eased, the self satisfaction slacked off and I began to settle into the rhythm of sleep. I had completed my first Case. It would lead to bigger and better things. Who knew what might turn up at Lucy's next fateful party?

TWO

A loud knock jolted my mind from dream to reality. I squinted at the tick-less clock. Who the hell could it be at that time of the morning? Way too early for Lucy and if anything had happened to my dad, they'd have phoned first. So, who was it? The knock came again. Reluctantly I grappled with the journey from bedroom to front door, cursing the noise as it became louder with each step.

As I flung open the door the fierce laser light of the 10 a.m sun dazzled my eyes, more or less blinding me. I blinked, trying to focus on the shadowy hulk outlined against the backdrop of sky and trees. I leaned forward.

"Yes?"

The voice was gruff and threatening.

"Hand it over."

I raised my eyebrows high.

"Hand over what?"

"The fucking camera!"

So that was it, the camera. My brain slowly whirred into action. He wanted my camera. But who was he? Wrong size for the adulterer. So.

"What camera?"

The man stepped closer. I smelt his anger. I moved back, willing my knees not to buckle. He stood tall and straight, a youngish posture but his voice sounded older.

"The fucking camera you took pictures with earlier."

Gazing up at the block of masculinity I felt like a five year old confronted by the bogey man. *Memo: Dispose of the pink jammies.* I played the innocent card.

"What are you talking about?"

He leaned his broad shoulder against the door jamb, his face remaining in the shadow of his baseball cap. *Memo: Get a baseball bat for future protection.* I attempted to shut the door but his leather boot was already half way over the threshhold. A muscled arm shot out and grabbed me. *Memo: Learn to run!* He yanked me around and pulled me towards his hard body. I tried to shout. Nothing came out. He twisted my right arm up against my back. That time I screeched. He rattled his command into my left ear.

"The camera. Get it!"

My capacity to think rationally was diminished by the pain.

"What do you want with my camera?"

He hauled my arm a ratch higher.

"Nobody takes pictures of her without her say so, right?"

The clue. He was worried about her, not the errant husband. He spun me round and lifted me off the floor. I flailed my legs about in the idiotic hope of kicking him in the shins. I missed completely. The heroine in a movie I'd seen made a success of the same move. Clearly I needed a good Director and a better script. The man's response to the attempt was to whack me. I groaned. I was running out of sound effects. And where was Neighbourhood Watch when I needed them? He was getting angrier by the minute.

"Just shut it and get the camera!"

I breathed out the obvious question.

"You're squeezing the life out of me. I can't move."

As if he hadn't cottoned on to the fact he slackened his hold and I swung my arm into its rightful position. The blood raced to put a stop to my pins and needles. He immediately pushed me, sending me careering down the hallway, his voice rasping against my jangling nerves.

"Get it! And no tricks, right?"

I half turned to sneak a proper look at him. Big mistake. He thumped me in the back. I so wanted to fight back but cowardice had set in.

"Any tricks and you'll get more than you bargained for!"

Making my way to the bedroom I thought it weird how he wasn't coming with me. He obviously hadn't weighed up whether I could escape out the back or whether I'd come back with a gun, or even the one golf club I owned. *Memo: Change the golf club for the baseball bat. Better swing.* Pity I didn't have two identical cameras so I could bring him the wrong one. Shit, my evidence was going to disappear. I thought I'd try and calm him down. Best thing to do with nutcases, apparently. After first trying to make them laugh. He didn't look like the laughing type.

"I won't tell anybody what you look like."

What a wicked lie. I wondered if the woman was waiting for him outside. For a moment I was tempted to escape via the back door but then I'd never know where and when he'd jump me. The great thing was, he hadn't mentioned the camcorder, so in spite of the shock, from which I was quickly recovering, I was feeling lucky. *Memo: Buy a lotto ticket. Could be my lucky day.* His powerful voice echoed around the cottage.

"Hurry up!"

Neighbourhood Watch was obviously deaf, if not still alseep. I peeped out to check the intruder couldn't fully view me then pushed the camcorder far under my bed. Then, with camera in hand, I strode boldly back to the waiting bundle of muscle. On the way I half heartedly snatched at the golf club. I'd used it a few times when religious salesmen came to the door. I'd only had to wave it in the air and off they'd rush, smiling wanly, out of fear or pity, not sure which. Not that I intended to wave it at him, it just made me feel braver.

For some reason the hulk didn't quite understand my innocent intent. Soon as he saw the club he took one giant step towards me and, growling like an injured grizzly, smashed his fist right into my nose. I shuddered with the shock, toppling backwards. Shit, it hurt. Incoherent kaleidoscopic patterns raced like maddened amoeba before my eyes. I understood his intent alright.

"I told you, no tricks!"

I thudded to the floor like a full sack of flour and watched with horror as blood, my blood, gushed from the smashed cavity. It splattered against the eggshell blue wall then slid artistically down to the polished floorboards. I lay in a crumpled heap. He stared down at me, as if baffled at how I'd got down there. Then he picked up the camera and ran out, slamming the front door behind him. The car engine was already revving. She'd been waiting. For a few seconds I lay there not quite sure whether to cry. I hadn't felt that stupid since a ten year old had beaten me at Pool.

Scrambling to my feet I shuffled my way to the bathroom, pressing the sleeve of my jammies against the afflicted nose. Trails of blood followed me to the bathroom, where I threw myself under the shower for a couple of minutes before easing myself into navy track pants and a bright red T-shirt. Checking the injury in the mirror I looked like I'd done ten rounds with Mohammed Ali. The sight was hilarious but I wasn't laughing.

Ten minutes later I'm chugging my Valiant to the Emergency Department. Amazingly, I found a parking spot right next to the entrance. *Memo: Tell the world about this tiny miracle.* At the counter a critical eye swept over me, quickly coming to the conclusion that I wasn't likely to die for at least twenty minutes, so a doctor wasn't needed immediately. A swathe of forms was thrust into my free hand, the other one left to comfort my injury. I ticked every illness I'd never had, as well as the few I had. Who was going to check the nonsense anyhow? Under 'Allergies' I wrote 'Hospitals'. The critical eye was not amused. I was told to sit and wait. For another miracle, I presumed.

While Public Hospitals offer a brilliant service, approaching death is the only way to zip to the top of their waiting lists. Eventually, everyone in the waiting room who was expected to die, had, and so my name was called. A doctor, distinguished by his swagger and his stethoscope, glided towards me with a deferential nurse beside him. He gazed at the offending injury with the intensity of a god working out what had gone wrong with his creation. He poked and pressed. After five minutes of this callous exploration I asked for a painkiller. His huff would have halted a marauding lion. Had I, in my dazed state, asked for a line of cocaine to snort? Not much chance on Medicare. It was the nurse who explained.

"No painkillers yet. In case you need anaesthetic. It is not safe."

Not safe? My dad's eighty year old sister, Auntie Gert, had spent six decades handing out painkillers, aspirin, to all and sundry and they were all safe. Okay, so most of her friends were dead but that was pure coincidence.

Both doctor and nurse walked away, leaving me clinging to the sides of a bed only a size eight could lie on with any dignity. By contrast, I was a large flab on a small slab. I checked out the décor. Blue walls with bottle green trim. Colour blind painters? The background noise of clanging stainless steel, squeaking shoes and whispered commands was annoying but as the only screams of terror resounded from the Maternity Ward I felt it was okay to stay. I was tempted to mention the shoulder tendons the attacker must have ripped but the nurse floated past, oblivious to the pain. Shit, the attacker! He could go back for the camcorder if the woman had by any chance noticed me filming. I had to get it out of the cottage. I'd phone my cop brother, Pete. He could do it while off-duty. I punched in the numbers and waited. When he answered he was brisk.

"Yes?"

"Pete?"

"Who is this? Oh, Holly, you. Is it important? I'm in the middle of something."

I was miffed. He always treated me like I was a normal member of the public.

"You're always in the middle of something."

"I'm at work, sis."

"I just need something picked up."

"Your old crock broke down again?"

Do I mention the hour?

"Somebody hit me."

"Have you reported it?"

The formal response continued.

"Did you get a good look at him? I assume it was a him?"

"I don't want it on the record."

His voice rose a few degrees. I could imagine him sitting up straighter and having a finger poised over his computer keyboard.

"Really? You're not in trouble again, are you?"

"Why do you always think the worst of me?"

"I don't. I just wondered if it was… him again."

"Oh, never mind."

"I need to know exactly what's happened. Time, place, description of attacker."

"Do you have to play it by the book every time?"

"Oh, yes, sis. Believe me, I do."

"Well, let's just forget it."

"No, wait. Are you hurt bad? Shall I send somebody round?"

"A couple of hours rest, I'll be fine."

"Are you sure?"

"As I said, I don't want it on record."

"You should be pressing charges, sis."

The pain was getting to me as well as the irritation with a baby brother who lived only for his job.

"Will you stop being a cop and behave like a brother for once!"

"Hey, sis, that's a bit much."

"Is it?"

"I'm only doing my job. And if you…"

I clicked him off. What did I expect? We'd never been close. He was only ten years old when mum died. It always felt like he'd blamed me and not the cancer for her death. And after, when I'd turned into a brat, he never tried to help. Even when I got into trouble he distanced himself from me because he wanted to join the police. In a way having no sibling to rely on pushed me closer to Lucy. She'd do anything I asked of her. I'd call her. Mind, the hour could be a problem. Easing my mobile out of my trackies I flicked up her number. She answered with a purr. I suspected she was in the middle of something exciting.

"Who is it?"

"It's me. Holly."

The purr was replaced with a growl.

"Flab, what the fuck do you want at this hour?"

I checked the watch I didn't recall putting on.

"It's eight thirty."

"A.m?"

"P.m."

"It's not morning?"

"No."

"Fuck."

I knew she'd be mad. I needed her help.

"I'm in hospital."

She threw back a taunt.

"You're not fucking drunk and incapable again, are you?"

I was well and truly miffed.

"Some man's broken my nose!"

I heard her relax.

"Is that all?"

"It hurts! And I need a favour."

"I don't fix noses."

Under other circumstances I would have appreciated the joke.

"I need you to pick something up for me. From under my bed."

"Some good gear?"

She sounded more interested than she had a right to be.

"Don't be an idiot. I gave that up years ago. So did you!"

She sighed with the panache of a bi-polar sufferer.

"What is it then?"

"A camcorder."

She laughed.

"You into something sexy I don't know about?"

There was nothing sexy Lucy did not know about.

"Five minutes of evidence. My first Case. I need it for the client."

"Is it that important?"

"The bloke who attacked me might break in and get it. Then, no evidence. Then, no Case. Then, no pay. So will you do it?"

The pause was palpable. I heard a whisper in the background.

"Have you got somebody with you?"

I sounded like a jealous lover. She chirped back, sharp as a whipper snipper.

"Flab, if I'd been in the middle of shagging somebody, no way would I have answered the phone!"

I knew this to be a profound truth.

"So can you go over. Soon. Like, now."

"My feet are already on the fucking carpet!"

"Thanks. Keep it at your place til I get out of here."

We each had a key to the other's place. In case of emergencies.

"Good luck with the nose job!"

She was laughing. Resembling a pulverised boxer was no laughing matter for me. I'd just clicked down the cover of the mobile when a pair of freshly sanitised hands snatched it off me. The nurse glowered.

"These are not allowed in here. Switch it off."

I took it back, switched it off and wedged it back into my pocket. I pondered on how I'd made a right mess of my first Case. Mind, I was on L Plates. I couldn't be too mad at myself. Then, without so much as a 'How ya going', I was wheeled down a dimly lit corridor that led to who knew where. Hell, maybe? Not wanting to see any instruments of torture I closed my eyes and concentrated on Mars Bars and a big glass of the best Red. I hardly felt the cannula go in.

THREE

The nose healed quicker than my ego did. I accepted the subtle modification to its shape without remorse. Only once did Auntie Gert peer closely at it, before shuffling off and mumbling about the dangers of cosmetic surgery. I didn't want her telling dad about her unfounded suspicions so I bribed her with a pink satin cushion. She's addicted to the colour. She and her house overflow with all things pink: cushions, curtains, slippers, crockery, prints, nighties, knickers, bras, rugs, toys, bedcovers, blouses, cardigans and anything else that took her fancy. Easy to buy for.

It turned out my client was satisfied with the camcorder evidence. I asked to be paid in gift vouchers, being as my ABN hadn't come through. I hadn't applied for it, so not an actual lie. I wasn't even licenced. She still offered to recommend me to other people. On my way to the shops to spend my fee I was confronted by a tall middle aged man in a grey striped suit, white shirt and blue tie. He halted right in front of me, blatantly grabbed my wrist and twisted it. It hurt. I had a flash back to the Chinese burns I'd received from Billy Harrington in primary school. I'd been wary of him too. Glaring at me with steel blue eyes the man nonchalantly asked if I was in contact with Giselle Knight. I had no idea where Lucy's mother was and why would I tell him if I did. He peered down at me, threatening me with his silence. My nose flinched in remembrance of the fist. He thought it was fear. There was that too. When in doubt, play the innocent.

"Giselle who?"

He gurgled a laugh which caused the hairs on the back of my neck to shoot up.

Sweat trickled between my breasts, its most frequented place when I was either shit scared or boiling hot. I tried to ease my wrist from his grip. He retaliated by pressing his fingers even tighter. I groaned. Charade or not, he was having none of it.

"You are Holly Day, are you not?"

That floored me. It was bad enough him knowing of Giselle but what a shock him knowing who I was. He smirked with tight lips and patted me on the head, like I was his pet dog. I wished I was. I'd bite both his hands off. Or his balls. Instead, I threw him a very human look of contempt, which only broadened his sneer as he let go of me. The final remark was tossed over his shoulder as he marched away, victorious.

"I will catch up with you later. Count on it."

My knees started knocking and my hands trembled. He was a complete stranger and yet I had to find out who he was. Like any half decent investigator, I immediately asked questions. Of myself in this instance. Was he connected to the man I'd photographed? Or to the 'other' woman? Or to the man who'd clobbered me on the nose? How did he know Lucy's mother? Worse, how did he know me? I licked my wrist to ease the soreness. Calmer now, the hairs on the back of my neck lay themselves flat. It took a brisk walk back to my Valiant before my heart stopped pounding. I whistled pathetically all the way. When I was little dad taught me the song about whistling a happy tune to hide being afraid. A lesson in bravado. It suddenly occurred to me that over the past few days I'd acquired the trappings of a Private Investigator; being followed, being threatened, being thumped, being scared shitless and being intrigued by strange events that left me with a mystery to solve.

The thing was, how to become a properly licensed investigator. I'd checked the phone book and my mate, Brian, had checked out appropriate websites. There were already heaps of PIs covering my area, several of them being franchised ventures. Most were either into insurance fraud, debt collecting and adultery, or big stuff to do with 'security', in all its guises. I didn't want cases big on violence, big on guns or big on drugs, not yet anyhow. I'd prefer taking on jobs like missing people or even missing objects. Lots of people go missing; men running from the law, women running from men, men running from other men, children running from parents, parents running from children and old people running from Old People's Homes. I couldn't blame the old trying to run from those places. I'd also thought there'd be a big line in finding people left money in a Will who didn't know about it. They'd pay real good. I might find somebody really rich, or really famous, or both. Maybe I'd become rich and famous myself. If, that is, I solved a Case important enough to be on Twenty Four Hour World News. The stuff dreams are made of. *Memo: Read that book on the meaning of dreams.*

I did own a gun. It was hidden away. I'd never used it. I didn't particularly want to. I had used my dad's .22 rifle a few times, which I fully intended keeping in the Wagon when I was on a Case. An offence, yes, but far better than being dead. I'd once used it to kill a mad dog, the canine variety. Mind, if no probing questions were asked about the species of the mad dog it might be thought of as the human variety. Great for street cred.

Years before I'd snuck the rifle out of dad's wardrobe, got some ammunition from where it was hidden in the shed and me and Lucy thumbed a lift up the mountains to play. It was mostly when we were in Year Ten. We frequently wagged school. Lucy knew this man who delivered stuff up to Nimbin. I knocked countless tin cans off countless fallen logs strewn around countless Native Forest floors. Lucy was hopeless at taking pot shots but she was already so good at martial arts she'd have given Bruce Lee a run for his money. So I'd never boasted about being what I considered a crack shot. One morning we'd met this weirdo. An old hippie. He came across us in the bush and straight out asked if I would shoot his crazy dog. Just like that. He'd been very insistent. Naturally we thought he was a loony but I was at that age when showing off was a life challenge so I said I would. The poor dog let out a blood curdling howl as it comprehended its fate. The man, clearly crazy as his dog, waved for me to shoot.

Overly confident of my skill, I raised the rifle and fired. Disaster. The shot went through the dog, rebounded off a massive eucalypt and nicked the man's leg. He gasped with the shock and hopped around before dropping to his knees. Lucy and me were scared shitless. No way could we fetch help. That meant police. It meant dad getting real angry with me. It meant a prison sentence for sure. The man snagged at his bloodied pants and sunk to the ground. Laying spreadeagled, staring up at the canopy of trees he moaned and swore loudly. I was sick to the stomach. He was going to die on us. I rushed over, leaving Lucy to fathom out how to get me off a murder charge.

"I am so sorry!"

The man struggled to sit up. He was unbelievably calm.

"It was an accident. My stupid fault for asking a...you, to use the rifle."

He was I guessed going to call me a stupid girl. I heaved my already over developed chest.

"I...I could have killed you."

"True but you didn't."

The man stumbled to his feet, swaying dangerously in the process. He went as white as a sheet. He was definitely going to die. Hippies must die too. My mind raced. What next? How to explain if the cops came. Who was going to call them? We sure weren't. What about my integrity? I had to make some sort of an effort.

"You need an ambulance?"

"It's just a graze."

Cowardice made me want to believe him.

"Are you sure?"

He nodded firmly yet kept pressing where the wound was. He peered at me.

"What's your name?"

Shit, he was going to report me. Lucy was by my side.

"Maggie Smith. That's her name."

A grin spread across the hippie's face. Is that what happens when people are about to drop dead?

"Yeh. Right. My names Harry. Forgot my last name."

"And I'm Holly. Holly Day."

Lucy heaved a loud sigh.

"Holly!"

I'd felt honour bound to tell him my real name. He hadn't laughed.

"Are you sure you're alright?"

His smile remained.

"Sure. Not every day a man gets shot by a hol…i…day."

His laughter was etched with a groan of pain as he limped closer.

"Look. I'll be fine. And Cocktail was old and in pain."

"Cocktail?"

"On account of the cocktails I gave him."

Drugs I assumed.

"He'd gone a little too crazy. I wanted it to be quick and easy for him. Couldn't make myself do it. Seen too much trouble with guns."

He pointed to the rifle drooping from my hand, his voice low and wistful.

"Too many deaths."

I hadn't known what to say to that. Was he telling the truth about guns? Had he once killed somebody? Had he been in some war or other? I guessed I'd never know. He handed over ten dollars, picked up the dead dog, carried it off into the bush and limped out of my life for what I supposed would be forever. There I was, at fifteen, killing a helpless animal. I never told anybody about it, and Lucy promised to keep quiet. Such a long time ago and yet the appearance of the stranger had somehow reminded me of Hippie Harry. That's what I'd named him. Did the stranger have anything to do with the dog incident? Did he know Harry? Did Harry know Giselle? Did the stranger know I'd killed the dog? If so, how? Questions, nothing but questions. My nerves had been stretched to breaking point and I needed to find answers but was I up to it?

For a start, did I really need a gun for the work I intended to do? How much work would I get? Enough to pay the mortgage? Mind, if I got short of cash I could always bum meals off Auntie Gert. She'd got into nutrition in a big way since the talk down at the Community Health Centre. For an eighty year old she sure was sharp. Apart from being addicted to pink she couldn't resist gossip, a useful asset for any investigator. According to her machinations with the Internet, there was at least one gene devoted to addictions, which could explain her addiction to pink and mine to all things fatty and sweet. I wondered if Giselle Knight had been born with that gene. She'd apparently been hooked on drugs since the nineteen seventies. Back then the proposition of an addiction gene would have been laughed out of court.

I was musing on this while waiting for Lucy to turn up with the info on becoming a PI. She'd picked it up from Brian's place. He was brilliant on the internet. Me, I hated computers. I figured one day I'd get eaten by one.

Lucy breezed in with the usual bottle of red and several Mars Bars and a bag of calorie heavy cookies. Unlike me, Lucy exercised off her intake. It had been raining all morning and she shook herself like a longhaired Retriever before parking herself in a chair. Her black leather Tote bag spilt a pile of printouts onto the coffee table, some of them dropping onto the carpet. I gaped.

"How much is there?"

She chuckled.

"Fuck, Flab, this is only a fraction of what's on the Net."

I sighed loudly as I fetched two glasses and poured. I wondered whether to mention the stranger who'd asked about her mother but Lucy was going through a relatively fragile stage, breaking up with her latest. Lucy got through men like I get through chocolate bars. Like all other addictions men are rarely good for a woman. So I kept the information for later. *Memo: Ask Lucy, when the time is right, if she knows where her mother is these days.* I took a seat and gazed at the pile of papers.

"Is all this just about being a PI?"

"This is just the bits about getting a licence and a gun!"

"I told you I don't need a gun."

I didn't mention the one I had or the .22. Lucy shrugged and sipped at her wine.

"You'll need something to defend yourself with."

"I have a baseball bat, a six inch blade, a capsicum spray and my brains."

"You'll definitely need a gun then."

I chomped into a chocolate bar and began sifting through the website material. It read like most bureaucratic shit. Massive complicated paragraphs made up of words only found in a Thesaurus when one simple sentence would do. Lucy snatched up a couple of pages.

"Hey, listen to this, its fucking hilarious."

I'd never heard her use the word hilarious before.

"This business specialises in Surveillance, Factual Investigation and Mercantile. What's mercantile?"

"Industrial espionage? Stealing ideas from a business. That sort of thing."

"Like spying on McDonalds?"

"Similar."

I wasn't convinced she had a clue. She shifted forward in her chair and continued reading. *Investigation involves the confirmation or denial of a suspicion and observation to establish a fact.*

That was stating the bleeding obvious but I let her go ahead. *'Our Private Investigation firm covers fraud and sexual harassment'*

"Where were they when I needed them? *Illegal activities.* Well, that's got to be right…and drugs."

"I don't want to get into drugs."

"No. Best not to."

Lucy's eyes filmed over with sadness. She must be thinking of her mother. I was glad I hadn't mentioned my confrontation with the strange man. I poured another glass. She settled back in her chair. As she crossed her legs the black leather pants crunched like cellophane wrapping. As a best friend Lucy was a rare, well packaged, gift. She continued, her voice soft with disbelief.

"Listen to this crap. *'We have intelligence driven people locators.'* What the fuck does that mean?"

"They employ clever people to find missing people."

Lucy shook her head, a floppy Retriever once more. *"We use instinct and experience to investigate public and private indices'* Indices?"

I reached over and wrenched my one and only Dictionary off the shelf, disturbing a couple of years dust.

"Indices…. Shit, it isn't in. It must mean indicating."

"It says it's an effective tool to find missing persons."

"Good for me then."

"Is somebody lost?"

How to explain that most people are lost, one way or the other. Auntie Gert would have understood. She could be real profound. I guess profound came with the wrinkles. I snatched at a sheet of paper I'd spotted.

"Missing things. That sounds like my kind of Case."

"What I want to know is do people stupid enough to get themselves lost, fucking deserve to be found?"

"Depends what they've done. Besides I don't have a licence yet, so in theory

I can't find anyone."

"I know someone who could get one made up for you."

"One what?"

"Licence. It would look so fucking good you'd never tell it was a fake."

"A fake!"

I'd pretended to be shocked but I was real interested.

"If, hypothetically, I wanted a false license, how much would it cost?"

Lucy grinned and stood up.

"Hypothetically, not all that much."

I could hardly enquire any further in case she rushed off to order me one.

"Without a licence, I can't get paid, not officially. Not as a taxpaying business."

Lucy perched herself on the arm of the chair and kissed my head.

"You, Flab, are so naïve. It's easy. If you know the right people."

Lucy was bound to know the right people. I felt her firm biceps pressing against my floppy ones as she pushed home the point.

"What you do, Flab, is you set your Bank Manager up as a charity. All payments go into that account, which of course he's holding for you. He takes a small cut."

I was genuinely amazed.

"You are joking."

She stood up, fetched the bottle and poured me another.

"It could be arranged."

"Not with my bank manager, it couldn't."

"You'd be surprised."

"But it's illegal!"

"You'd be fucking amazed at what lawyers can get fixed."

I gulped down the wine and pondered on the theory. It would mean bypassing all that bureaucratic stuff and what harm would I do, if I was just finding missing people and things. I was struggling with my conscience when Lucy flung herself in front of me with a triumphal jig.

"You're seriously considering going for my plan!"

Integrity meant I had to deny it.

"Forget it! …Let's read up on this.'

We both sat down and in solemn silence went through papers explaining how to obtain a Masters License, an Operator License and power of entry requirements and a hundred other boring regulations. It was depressing. Yet I had to get licenced some day because I needed to be legit to cover myself insurance wise. I could meet up with some nasty people. While Lucy would be capable of disarming six torturers in thirty seconds, me, I'd buckle at the first electric shock to wherever. Lucy came up with what she termed a solution.

"You'll just have to become an amateur sleuth."

"Do you mind."

"An amateur with a professional attitude. And fee structure."

That didn't sound so bad.

"Short term. Until I'm able to be fully licensed."

"You could still give the charitable bank manager a go."

"Lucy, it's a criminal offence!"

"A girl has to make a living somehow!"

"I may as well go rob a bank."

She jumped into the air, frightening the shit out of me.

"That's the best idea you've had in years! Count me in."

I forced myself out of the comfortable sofa.

"This is not helpful."

"No. What we need is more food and more drink."

We strolled down to the local cafe and gorged ourselves on pizza and garlic bread and three café latte's each. We sat back, bellies full, satiated with our private thoughts. Was she thinking about her lost boyfriend or the mother she hadn't seen in twenty years? I was thinking about the stranger and whether that was a mystery I could solve. If I did attempt to, where would it lead me and to what.

Later we watched yet another episode of my favourite amiable cop show, *Midsomer Murders,* with its old solid houses, its old solid detective and its old panorama of solid dialects with characters, both innocent and guilty, preyed upon by the ponderous leading actor, Detective Chief Inspector Barnaby. He was certainly not supposed to be an amateur sleuth, and yet I'd often worked out who the villain was before he appeared to. But then he had to stick to the script.

FOUR

I'd always been slightly envious of Lucy. She was a size ten for a start, had a figure any celebrity would die for, eyelashes that flapped rather than fluttered, biceps thick as a full grown carpet snake and a kick that would boomerang a Sumo wrestler to Tokyo and back. One sexy lady. Men loved her. Okay, they didn't stay around too long but that only bothered her for a couple of weeks. She was never all that bright but she sure was street smart, with as many contacts as a bent cop. Like me, she'd never had children. We both reckoned on waiting for Mr Right, if such a person existed. At our ripe age it had to happen soon, our use-by date hovering ever closer. I just hoped we didn't go for the same man. *Memo: If my knight in shining armour ever turns up, hold on tight.*

Lucy worked three days a week for a solicitor, which left her plenty of time to help me if I needed her. Her main task seemed to be the shredding of anything vaguely resembling legitimate evidence, which she managed with the alacrity of a parliamentary secretary. According to Lucy, her boss, Paul Diston, had a pack of clients with very dubious morals. Some had criminal records going way back. She showed me what she was wearing for the interview; the lowest top ever created, the highest skirt possible and shoes with outlandishly dangerous high heels. She'd have swaggered in, sat down, crossed her legs, flapped her eyelashes and beamed unfathomable sexual promises. The job would have been hers in fifteen seconds flat. She earned good money too. My most interesting job, the market research one, was good practice for a budding investigator. I had to ask questions, sort fact from fiction, filter out the crap, digest seemingly inconsequential fragments that often led to the desired outcome, stick to a plan and, most important, gain people's trust.

I'd only had one more Case since the cheating husband. A mother, driven frantic by her imagination, wanted me to find out what her fifteen year old son, Michael, was up to. For three Saturdays in a row I faithfully followed him from his home to town. Each time he squatted under Callam Bridge with the same bunch of mates, conjured up a bottle of spirits, poured the contents down his throat, fooled around, moved rapidly on to vomiting, finally sank into a heap and after a short rest, straggled home to his worried mother, no doubt having a fantastical story to explain the state he was in. For me it was as boring as shit but then I wasn't swigging alcohol nor was I fifteen. I took over twenty shots with my new fangled Digital SLR, courtesy of the insurance company. His mother was relieved to have evidence to face him with. No idea what she was hoping to achieve. Few parents permanently prise their kids from their friends because basically it's against the law of Nature. My own dad had done his best to get me away from Lucy, a bad influence he reckoned, but there we were, thirty odd years later, still the best of friends. Funny thing was, mum took a real shine to her. She'd be proud of us both if she was still around. I'd felt a bit sorry for the boy I followed, which was wrong. Emotional involvement was not an asset for a PI. *Memo: Toughen up! But how?*

It was after one of these Saturday night excursions that Lucy turned up on my doorstep unexpected. I'd just got myself a glass of red and switched on the TV. She wasn't using her key so naturally I collared my baseball bat when I heard the racket at the door, before staring through the newly installed peep hole and letting her in. She threw herself down the hall then flung herself onto the sofa. Before I'd finished barricading myself back in I could hear her sobs echoing round the cottage. Lucy crying? She couldn't possibly have broken up with yet another man already could she? Maybe she'd got into an argument with a cop? Never good news. I just hoped she hadn't fallen in love again. Unrequited love for Lucy meant me living through a cyclone for at least a week.

I waltzed as nonchalantly as possible into the living room and looked around. No wine, no bag of goodies, just one drastically sobbing friend. I figured it was bound to be something trivial, like she'd missed out on a pair of shoes in a sale, or some hairdresser had explained how hair loses its natural shine once a woman hits forty. Really serious stuff like that. I switched off yet another re-run of *Midsomer Murders,* still trying to work out how there was anybody left alive in any of the villages. Memo: *Get all the DVDs out and count the population, both dead and alive.* It would be interesting to learn the survival techniques of the English upper classes. What was the trick? Should I count the number of ten bedroomed houses? Or knives in the kitchens? Or washing lines? Or hidden cellars? Or maybe the walled gardens held a clue? Shit, I was getting carried away. I had to concentrate on my friend.

Her tears had been downgraded to a grizzle, though having gone on for ten minutes it was a real worry.

"Can I get you anything?"

This bought on an exaggerated groan.

"I'll make coffee then?"

The groan grew louder. I was running out of ideas so I strode into the kitchen, my ears pricked for any lessening of the sobs. After shedding two buckets full of tears Lucy called out.

"Flab!"

It was the cry of a whale in distress. A size ten whale. I pulled back my shoulders and walked in, coffee just made. Lucy's mascara-streaked face gazed up at me, her lips trembled, her hands reached out for me. Instinct told me to run. Too late. I was pulled into the seat beside her. She moved in close. Shit, she wasn't in love with me, was she?

"Are you… in love again?"

"You think I'm fucking crazy?"

No need for a reply to that one.

She clung to me. She began to cry again. I found myself wiping the tears off her leather pants. Maddening. She grabbed my hand and squeezed it so tight I winced. I tried to look her in the eyes.

"Are you in bad trouble?"

It would have to be something really bad. Normal trouble she shook off no problem, apart from finished love affairs. She heaved a loud sigh. I sighed less loud and recalled the time she'd helped me through my worst nightmare. Three yobbos had raped me. I was fourteen. I knew who they were but they threatened to punch up my dad if I told on them. By that time mum was ill and dad had enough on his plate. I'd limped home and phoned Lucy. She said no point in going to the police as every boy I'd ever had sex with would be counted against me in court. At that time there'd only been one sexual encounter, a pathetic one at that, but I couldn't admit that to my best friend. She judged everybody by her own activities. The men thought they'd got away with it but one by one Lucy picked them off and, already proficient in martial arts, she gave them a good going over. They spent time in hospital rather than in prison. Poetic justice, like the revenge in that movie *Girl with a Dragon Tattoo.* Some bastards deserve it. Comforting, having Lucy as my minder. Now it looked like I was hers. The sobs changed to a sniffle. I stroked her hair.

"Tell me what's up. Please?"

Her puppy dog eyes turned their gaze up to me. No words.

"Do you need a doctor?"

She shuddered. I thought the worse.

"Shall I call the cops?"

This bought the reaction I'd been waiting for.

"It's mum."

Considering the stranger who'd recently stopped and asked me about Giselle it was too weird a coincidence. Lucy hadn't seen her mother in years, not since she'd gone up north with her no-hoper drug dealer friend.

"What's happened?"

"She's in hospital."

I guessed Giselle would have been in and out of hospital a few times. Rehab. I asked the obvious question.

"Another OD?"

Lucy's response was swift and loud.

"She's had a fucking heart attack!"

"Shit. Is it…. bad?"

"So they say."

She stared ahead of her, the pile of dirty crockery in the sink in clear view. *Memo: Wash up first thing.*

"You've been up to see her?'

She nodded. I probed.

"How about her …you know, the bloke?"

"He'd scarpered. The mailman found her. The door was open. She just lay there, clutching her chest. She could have died."

"But he saved her. Got her to hospital. That's good."

I wasn't so sure it was a good thing, considering Giselle's lifestyle. There was genuine bewilderment in Lucy's eyes as she turned to me.

"Her place had been stripped bare. No furniture, no painting stuff, no clothes, no nothing. The fucking bastard must have took it all."

"Not much of a surprise."

Lucy stood up and paced the room, a caged animal, her eyes now dry, her lips wet and drawn tight, her arms folded across her chest, her voice thick with resolution.

"The thing is, it was fucking amazing. Where she lived. The house."

Her mother, a remnant of the hippie era, a product of the nineteen seventy-three Aquarius Festival, had been holed up in the mountains around Nimbin for almost two decades. She'd stayed on after the Festival and lived first in some man's Kombi, then a tepee, then a banana packing shed and, once she was sort of settled, in decommissioned dairy bails. She'd shown us over her abodes a few times, as soon as dad let me go with her. She'd hitch a lift down, pick us up and hitch a lift back up for the three of us. Then it was a case of walking, or squatting on the back of a Ute or inside a Kombie, until we'd reached her living quarters. Shit, it was fun, all that bumping around and the laughter and the flashing past of trees and the whizzing around dangerous bends, sometimes missing other vehicles by centimetres, the sickly smell of dope clouding our minds and the sun shining in through the windows. Back then the sun seemed always to be shining, even when the mountains were filled up with mist.

Giselle lived for years with rusty old corrugated water tanks and outside dunnies, usually nothing more than a hole in the ground. She bathed in gentle flowing creeks and cooked on open fires and viewed life through the haze of kerosene lamps and smoke. She'd started her journey with drugs soon after arriving there and hadn't stopped since. Not as far as we knew. Mother and daughter hadn't contacted each other for a couple of decades. Wherever her mother was living, the cost of her drug habit would mean it was likely to be a dump, or at least, very basic. Unless she'd got clean, which I hoped for yet doubted. Lucy spoke soft.

"I couldn't believe it. The place."

I could but didn't like to say so. She stopped pacing.

"It's massive, Flab. One of those McMansions! Close to the river. Unbelievable."

It sure was unbelievable. Property prices up at Noosa were real expensive. She stared out of the window.

"And she owns it. All paid for. Years ago. I checked."

For me there was only one possible answer.

"They must have got in with some gang. Bikies?"

There were plenty of them with connections to drugs in this region. Lucy hinted at a smile.

"I guess."

We were both assuming Giselle was still an addict. She sat

down and stared at the blue and green rug I'd bought at Ikea last year. It made me realise my choice of colours was thankfully more varied than Auntie Gert's obsessive pink everything. Silence seeped through the room as I recalled the stories Giselle told us as teenagers, before she went away, before she became totally enslaved by heroin. Of her paintings, of her alternative lifestyle, of her seemingly endless number of boyfriends, of her hopes for the planet and everything living on it. Maybe now, with this heart scare, they'd dry her out for good. First, she had to survive the heart attack. I stretched myself out. What to do?

"Another coffee?"

Neither of us had finished the first. I waded off to the kitchen unprepared for her next comment.

"The house, it's worth two million fucking dollars!"

Had there been anything in my mouth I'd have choked on it. To me it was proof that Giselle had got in with a syndicate of some sort. No way was I going to question Lucy's fact finding mission but shit, two million dollars. Taking in the coffee I sank back into the sofa and sipped the boiling caffeine. Lucy hovered over hers and solemnly pronounced her diagnosis.

"There are drugs that can cause a heart attack, do you know that?"

I did know that. I also knew they sometimes produced only the symptoms. It depended on what the heroin had been topped up with.

"Is that what you think happened?"

"It would need a fucking expert to check it out. Who'd bother anyway when she's a long term druggie?"

This made complete sense to a natural born cynic. Her observations working in a solicitor's office had served to increase her cynicism. She was certain half the clients ought to be in prison and they weren't. I had to be rational.

"Surely the cops will look into it?"

"Are you kidding? Why would they care?"

"But why would anybody try to kill her?"

The threatening stance of the stranger flickered through my mind. Lucy stood up, spilling some of the hot liquid down her front. She didn't flinch.

"It's a fucking stupid idea. Somebody trying to kill her."

"And why now? All these years. Easier to give her a plain old overdose."

Placing the mug carefully on the table she sighed.

"That's what I can't work out, Flab. Which is where you come in."

A warning bell peeled in my head.

"Me?"

The eyes, toughened by her mother's condition, glared at me.

"You're an Investigator. Investigate."

I had no intention of investigating murders, successful or otherwise. No way was I ready. I heaved myself up and fathomed the best escape route. Lucy cut across my thoughts.

"You've got to do it."

Being emotionally tied to my best friend meant there was no escape. *Memo: Avoid Lucy's wild parties like the plague. Or next time agree to being a hooker, anything other than a PI.* She put her arm round me which only increased my panic. She was going to dump the whole caboodle at my feet.

"There's something else."

Shit. A honey drop glistened in her widened eyes. The trap was set.

"I found some of her old diaries, hidden behind a pile of plastic bags under the sink."

A distraction. What a relief. Giselle's diaries could be interesting, to us, to the cops. Better still to a film producer.

"Have you read them?"

"Fuck Flab, I only found them yesterday. There's over a dozen! And it's more scribbles and numbers than writing."

My heart missed a beat. This could be more interesting than a possible attempted murder, which I'd happily leave for the cops to sort out. A mystery that might need solving.

"Could be it's some sort of code."

I imagined myself sitting on the verandah surrounded by old code breaking books. I could almost smell World War Two and Enigma, the code breaking machine. I conjured up details about drug deals, names of punters, dealers, drop off points, cash transactions, overseas syndicates, the Asian triangle, where money was laundered and by whom. Dates, times, venues. Blood rushed to my head. The diaries could provide the sort of evidence criminals would kill for. Cops too. The bent ones, so they could be destroyed. Depended on how high up the ladder the miscreants went. A hot thrill raced through my entire body. I just had to walk about. This could be a real investigation. It could make world news. I could become famous. On the other hand, I could end up in the concrete foundations of some Gold Coast block of units. My hands were suddenly clammy. Even so, I longed to set my eyes on the diaries.

"Do you have the diaries with you?"

A withering look was thrown my way.

"You think I'm fucking crazy?"

I raised my eyebrows. She glared back.

"Besides, there's something more important."

Now what.

"Mum wants me to find out who my father is."

The bombshell sent my previous level of excitement plummeting like a shot cockatoo. Here was I eager to discover drug barons and money laundering and all kinds of corruption and Lucy wanted me to find some bloke who hadn't a clue what his sperm had produced. I was well and truly miffed. I moaned loudly. She ignored this.

"She wants me to know, in case she…you know."

The heart attack must have finally pricked Giselle's conscience. She'd never bothered all these years to discover who'd fathered her daughter. It seemed a hopeless proposition to me. I feigned interest.

"There might be clues in the diaries. Names and such."

"Mainly initials."

"So how am I supposed to sort out the one man who's your actual father out of the hundreds your mother slept with?"

Lucy turned her anger on me. A rare event.

"It wasn't hundreds! She exaggerated when she told us. We were so fucking stupid we believed her!"

As teenagers we'd certainly been impressed by Giselle's alleged sexual exploits. Maybe she'd lied about the quantity as well as the quality. Most women I knew only lied about the quality.

"Even if it was only a dozen men, it was way back in nineteen seventy-three!"

There was a quiver in her voice.

"We have to find out, for mum's sake and for mine. In case she...you know...dies soon."

Odd how Lucy suddenly wanted this information, even if it was for her mother's peace of mind. At school she didn't give a shit about who her father was. She imagined him to be whatever she wanted him to be. Some years he'd been some businessman, rich and famous. Others an Oxford Don. Or a brilliant explorer. The one that hung around the most in her mind was that he was a famous rock star. Anything her imagination could conjure up she floated the story, which changed according to her age and her mood. Facing reality was not high on Lucy's agenda when it came to a father. I was less than secure in the idea.

"Are you sure you want to know?"

She marched to the kitchen swinging her hips with the rhythm of all of our ancestors .

"She's my mother! And she wants to know who my father is! End of story."

She hung her head over the sink waiting for the calm to restore itself.

"We all know I was conceived during the Aquarius Festival at Nimbin. That's a start, isn't it?"

She was right. It was a start. Where all investigations begin. Where it might end up was anybody's guess. I'd be chasing the truth, or a version of it, that was all. Beginning, middle, end. No way could I fix this outcome like I used to fix my market research projects. The prospect scared me. It was going to be a real challenge finding the father out of the possible dozens who'd shagged her mother up in the misty mountains all those decades ago. But then I always did like a challenge.

"I'll give it a go, right? But I can't promise anything."

She hugged me with fervour.

"Can I stay the night?"

How could I refuse? Sad to say I wasn't expecting a knight in shining armour to clatter up my path, break down my door and ravage me, lovingly of course.

"You can stay any time you want."

She already knew that but it was good, her asking. After settling her down in the spare room, I made for the bathroom, pondering, as I cleaned my teeth, how the hell I could get DNA samples from every male who'd gone within cooee of Giselle at that Festival. Half of them would likely be dead. All the same I couldn't wait to get my hands on the diaries.

FIVE

Lucy's mother had led a seemingly wild life. My own mum's life had been cut short by cancer. I was fifteen when she died. Me and dad coped differently. I turned into a loud brat, he slipped into silence. Auntie Gert moved up from Sydney to save us from ourselves and each other.

It was on my twenty first that he told me the truth, after he'd got drunker than I was. Mum had got pregnant to a married man, dad came to her rescue and made an 'honest woman' of her. They decided to migrate to Australia. He'd accepted me as his own. They grew to adore each other. I'd never wanted to know who my real father was. Mum was mum. Dad was dad. I was Holly Day, their daughter. Now, out of the blue, I was being asked to find out who was Lucy's birth father. I'd never told her about mine. No point. Sometimes not telling the truth is not exactly telling a lie. Politicians used that idea all the time.

Giselle was ill and could possibly die. I felt the pain of that possibility for my friend. Far back as I could remember her mother had been a painter. Before she moved up north, me and Lucy saw heaps of her work. She worked like a maniac once she started on a picture. Her ancestors were supposedly Spanish gypsies. Giselle certainly had the looks; long, dark, curly hair, black eyes that beamed seduction and olive skin so silky she'd have made a living in beauty ads. She dressed in bright Indian cotton skirts and loose drawstring gypsy tops. Beads and bangles dangled from every part of her body. She danced barefoot a lot. When she had to wear shoes it would be Chinese black slippers. She kept a copy of *Mao's Little*

Red Book for years. *'It is impossible to swallow an entire banquet in one gulp,'* was one of her favourite Mao sayings. We'd sometimes see her shooting up. Whether watching her inject herself or brush her hair I was fascinated by her long slender fingers. They were neither stained by living nor roughened by time. They moved with the flowing rhythm of her soft laughing voice. She was a true hippie; idealistic, full of hope, shamed by regret. If she was going to die, she'd had a good innings, for an addict.

We were heading north in the Valiant, its familiar steady chug comforting to us both. The hospital had phoned. Giselle had taken a turn for the worse. Lucy sat silent beside me, letting the scenery pass without comment. Not a word about the first wattle blossoms of the season lining the highway, nor the usual excitement at ospreys circling above tall gums or rosellas flittering their way from nectar to nectar. It was strange having her so quiet, her straight blonde hair scraped back into a ponytail, her nostrils flaring like they were sniffing out the future and her lips a pale pink slit in her face. She looked like a little lost girl. I'd never loved Lucy more.

I brightened myself up by pressing hard on the accelerator and imagining the once familiar smell of Giselle; patchouli mingled with cannabis, an earthy mixture that tingled nostril and genital hairs alike. She was a fantastical mystery to us both, a hippie living on heroin, mung beans and sex. That was our misinformed take on her existence. Once she'd been part of a caring hippie commune, now she was alone and possibly dying in a hospital. Back in the nineteen seventies tree hugging hippies were always good for a laugh. It was no laughing matter now for Giselle.

Outside the hospital I parked the Valiant, with its size and the maneoverability of an army tank adding to the difficulty of planting it in the tiny space. I only scraped the paintwork off three cars. No one stopped to take my number. No doubt they were arriving for or departing from patients, ill or worse.

We walked in silence along corridors clearly created by someone whose fantasy was to design mazes. Once in the ward we were greeted by a doctor who appeared to know about Giselle Knight. But a straight answer on her condition was avoided like the plague. Even more annoying were the conspiratorial stares the staff gave each other.

It was some shock, seeing her for the first time in twenty years. She was pale, her face twisted with pain. They'd have given her medications, which may or may not be easing her withdrawal symptoms. Her eyes were duller than I remembered, though a defiant sparkle remained. Her hair lay in ringlets over her shoulders. Her fingers, long and gentle as I recalled, clung to the bedcover as both me and her daughter took smiling steps towards her. Lucy kissed her on the cheek and sat on the bed. I nodded a greeting. Tears were held in check. Giselle closed her eyes. Lucy took her hand. I held Lucy's hand. Silence ruled. After half an hour Lucy suggested I take a break.

I strolled out into the comforting warmth of the coastal town. Pink hibiscus exchanged Morse code conversations with each other. Bangalow palms bristled their fan shaped leaves in the slight breeze. Lines of grevilleas, imprisoned in tubs, seethed in the sun, their heavy sprays of yellow flowers waiting for lorikeets to relieve them of their nectar. The smell of salt and fish drifted in from Laguna Bay. Cottonwoods and eucalypts scented the air with a sense of well being, adding to the atmosphere of coastal living.

Walking fast and whistling softly I ignored the tourist traps of food and souvenirs and only absentmindedly snorted in the artful aromas of coffee simmering, brewing, percolating and dripping from the hearts of attentive baristas.

After looking around for a shop where I didn't have to queue for ten years to be served, I turned yet another corner and there it was. Not a pile of scrumptious Mars Bars but a painting that was strangely fascinating. It was in the window of a charity op-shop, opposite to where I'd been bought to a halt. The picture beckoned to me like a motionless spruiker, drawing me in to view it at close quarters. A child's pink plastic tea-set was on show next to it.

Auntie Gert would love that. The painting was the Surreal style, a landscape of reds and greens with a blue heeler dog squatting in the corner, with its eyes made of tiny pieces of sapphire blue glass. I'd seen a few similar works by Giselle when I was young. It had to be one of hers. I looked closer and there in the bottom right hand corner was her familiar mark, G. K. No date. What an amazing find and what a coincidence!

I waltzed inside, stepping past a vast expanse of second hand everything. I picked my way past the neat rows of carefully hung items and the untidy baskets full of whatever. *Memo: Check what clothes under size twenty I've got to donate.*

Central to this bustling capitalist metropolis was a glass display cabinet on top of which sat a cash register of the older type, with two women, also of the older type, hovering behind it. Several of the louvre doors on the changing rooms clanged merrily back and forth, some customers clearly on the poverty line, others clearly not.

As I approached the counter, the two old ladies, both with matching grey hair and similar facial wrinkles, hopped out from either side of the counter and met in the centre. They stood motionless, their grey skirted hips slightly touching, their lips simultaneously parted in a wicked smile as their hands, clasped in front of them, twitched in anticipation. I felt I was about to be inducted into a cult by their meet-and -greet party. The pair looked the same, dressed the same and moved the same. They could be twins, sisters certainly, a CWA version of Tweedledum and Tweedledee. Two pairs of eyes flickered over me from the top of my head to the tip of my toes. Was I being valued as an item for sale? The pair had an aura both sinister and servile. They gazed at me. I shivered. I'd seen dad give mum that look just before chopping the head off a chook.

Simultaneously, the women, side by side, step by step, moved towards me, their eyes twinkling like mirrors reflecting the sun. They beamed a strange wisdom, as if they knew something I didn't. I stood my ground. I was an investigator after all, I had to investigate. What had they got in store for me apart from the painting? How much was the painting? Was it certainly one of Giselle Knight's? Who had donated it? Grinning like an ape I asked if I might look at the painting in the window. The reaction was immediate. The two old ladies stared hard at my face, then at each other; then, simultaneously nodding their heads, they took another step towards me. I refused to run. One of them touched my arm lightly and spoke with the intensity of an oracle.

"We knew you would come, my dear."

I was stunned by the pronouncement. I forced a smile, my jaw aching immediately. The other woman followed up with an even more unnerving statement.

"And my dear, the weather is perfect for it."

I'd already sussed out that it was best to humour the insane. Better get some practice in. I'd be bound to meet a few in my new line of work. Mind, they didn't look the kind of women to tell jokes to. They'd probably never laughed in their collective lives. I relaxed my smile.

"Whow. If you say so."

Tweedledee looked me over again. Shit, they could have been procuring me for a Sheik's Harem.

"You, my dear, are also perfect."

The ladies waited patiently for my response, so I did what any sane person would do. I stepped back and pointed to the street outside.

"They say the weather is always perfect up here."

They were as bewildered as I was. They frowned, turned to gaze at the street beyond the world of the charity shop, then returned to look at me. One spoke, quiet as a mouse.

"No, no, my dear, we have been waiting for both you and the weather to be aligned."

"That's why we put the painting in the window today," the other added. "So that you would be drawn here."

I wanted to hare it out of there but the picture was what I'd come for and so I pointed to it. Without another word they walked, in tandem, to the window. I followed. The one I'd christened Tweedledee leaned her large rounded body to the front of the display and gingerly pulled out the picture. She passed it to Tweedledum who held it as if the paint was still wet. As we all walked back to the cash register Tweedledum whispered confidentially in my ear.

"I can understand why it has taken so long to sell. It was waiting for you."

The other nodded in agreement. I presumed that somewhere, not too far away, there were a couple of straightjackets waiting, one for each of them. As if clicked into action by a mechanical device, they stepped back behind the counter in perfect harmony. Laying the painting on the glass top in unison they asked if twenty dollars was a fair price. I nodded and offered up the note. Tweedledee took it from me but it was Tweedledum who placed it in her pocket. The cash register she'd avoided was prior to computerisation. They too were very prior to computerisation, by around five centuries. Back then they'd have been burned at the stake. Yet, naturally for an investigator, I felt curious about them. Weirdo's? Probably. *Memo: Read up on witches and all things weird.*

Both of them began the task of wrapping up the purchase, totally ignoring a young girl swaying at the counter under the weight of an armful of clothes and bric-a-brac. Then it hit me. The pink tea set.

"I'd also like the child's pink tea set in the window."

Four hands halted their wrapping. Then, with a silent agreement, Tweedledum marched off to the window to collect the prized possession. At the same time Tweedledee calmly finished off the wrapping, sticking the paper down with about twenty metres of tape. Before the tea set was placed on the glass counter, Tweedledee asked in a voice that rang with perceptible joy.

"You do know the artist then?"

Another bolt from the blue. I was taking no chances.

"Well I...Er.. I was wondering if you knew the artist?"

By this time Tweedledum had returned and had heard the question. She signalled, via mental telepathy or whatever, for the question not to be answered. Both ladies stared first at the parcelled picture and then at me. The voice was low and steady.

"I am afraid we cannot say if we do or do not know the artist."

Tweedledum continued, as if to improve the explanation.

"Once there is a change in the weather, it may be different."

There was something deeper than I understood going on. There must be a connection between them and Giselle, or at least with her paintings. But what? Probably nothing substantial. Two old ladies selling me a painting and I was reading what into it? I was reading a lot into it. Crazy or not, the pair were not letting on. I made a grab for the painting while handing over five dollars for the cute tea set.

I thanked the elderly women and was half way across the room when I turned round. They were huddled together, eyes on me and whispering earnestly. The young customer, now fully stretched out under her unpaid for pile of goodies, was overshadowed by a rough looking man who grumbled that he only wanted to pay for one overcoat. His pleas fell on deaf ears. He shuffled out of the shop, wearing the coat. The young girl eyed his escape jealously. I held the painting above my head and shouted to the old ladies.

"A good artist, hey?"

One of them instantly shot back the reply.

"Yes, we think she is a very good artist."

Immediately her hand flew to her mouth. She glanced at her companion. In return she was given a glare that would have stripped paint off a thrice painted cedar door. Before either of them could say or do anything else I made my exit.

It was good to be back in the real world, certain I'd escaped from something, or from somewhere, or from someone. For no apparent reason I began to hum the song, *Lucy in the Sky with Diamonds*, feeling as high as a kite, without the need for LSD. Tweedledee had referred to G. K. as a She, and an 'Is' not a 'Was.' So, they at least knew of her. A connection well worth investigating.

SIX

We needed to stay on at Noosa for a few more days to see how Giselle went.

She was seriously ill but was being well cared for. There was nothing more we could do but wait. Lucy spent most of the time with her mother while I snooped around.

Lucy had given me the key to her mother's mansion so naturally I went over. According to the mailman Giselle had lived in the house with her man for around fifteen years. Before that was anybody's guess. Maybe the comfy cells of the Brisbane Correctional Centre. There was no clue to who the man was.

I let myself into the house. The foyer was almost the size of a football pitch, with a row of pseudo Greek statues leading to numerous other rooms. The whole house was a blinding splash of white and stainless steel. It reminded me of a TV show set in a mortuary. Lucy had searched the place and come up with the diaries, but what she had missed was a single blonde hair attached to a scrap of lemon myrtle soap. Definite DNA material. In a plastic bag it went. I'd send it to a private company that analysed samples, once my old school mate, Brian, had found one on the internet. As a teenager he'd been a virtual fuckwit yet he'd turned out to be a deadly technology expert. I'm too impatient to be a browser but Brian scours the Internet for whatever is required. The DNA possibilities of the hair provided a tiny piece of a jigsaw that could take some time to put together. But it was a start.

I drove back to the CBD, parked the Valiant in a loading bay and put a 'Visiting Doctor' sign in the windscreen. There had to be a tiny chance there was one doctor in town who prefered a beat up classic car like mine to the latest Porche. Surely. Coffee shops clustered the pavements like whores vying for customers, with their pungent smells and fashionable swirls. Still hungry for answers, I stepped down a narrow laneway. The lane was off the tourist track. There was a mixture of hairdressers, el cheapo stores and empty shops displaying huge 'For Lease' signs. One of the shops had the sign 'Art Gallery' swinging high above its doorway. A bit out of the way? Unless it was an artistic brothel. I peered through the window into the dimly lit interior. A solitary man stared up at a lonesome oil painting. His stance and his expensive, yet ill fitting suit, gave him the air of a con man. I'd met a few of his kind when market researching. His body language yelled 'Do not trust me' but my curiousity had been aroused.

I stepped inside. Art Nouveau Grecian Urns preened themselves close to the shop front. The single painting hung on a burgundy coloured wall. The proprietor turned and assessed me, just like I'd done to him. I suspected we were equals in the murky world of deception. He called my bluff with a cheesy smile, which I immediately wanted to wipe off, preferably with a sledge hammer. He padded his way towards me. 'Beam me up Scotty', was my first thought. He manufactured yet another smile and spoke with a terribly British educated accent.

"Good morning, Madam. How may I be of assistance?"

Before giving me a chance to reply he waved his hands around the room.

"As you can see, Madam, we have more or less sold out. There are the Urns. Nouveau Grecian of course. "

I shook my head to reject them. I moved to the oil painting hanging close to the burgundy velvet curtain that separated the showroom from the back. The price on the painting was two thousand dollars. The one I'd just bought for twenty dollars was far superior. I'd already decided to hang it over my bed. The man noted my feigned interest at the framed work.

"A new artist. Not a very good one I am afraid but we all have to start somewhere."

"How true."

I moved towards the velvet drop. Immediately the man was right beside me. I felt his body quiver. For a second I wondered if my honour was at stake, then I remembered my honour had disappeared twenty four years before. All the same, his presence made me shudder. He laid his hand gently on my arm. I held my breath. He beamed, graciously, like a butler taking a visitors coat.

"That area is for staff only, madam."

The voice was emphatic. He didn't want me out there. An excellent reason for me to see it. Time for action. I bent over, took in an enormous breath and groaned, loudly. He tapped my shoulder.

"Madam?"

I went from groan to moan. Much more effective. Then I covered my mouth with my hand and gagged. He was glued to the spot in bewilderment. I forced out the words.

"A toilet. I need a toilet!"

Still he didn't move. Shit, was he thick or what.

"I'm going to vomit."

I stroked my stomach lovingly. Usually I get mad at the size of my stomach but the flab was proving positively useful. I gasped.

"Morning sickness!"

He came out of his dithering state. Taking my elbow he steered me towards the back but stopped us both just in front of the velvet partition. Raising his voice to an abnormally high pitch he spoke in slow deliberate tones.

"Customers are not actually allowed to use the private toilet."

He was warning somebody. After the briefest of delays he led me through the curtain and along a narrow corridor, off which several rooms with their doors wide open were situated. The first was filled with partly packaged paintings of various sizes. According to the labels heralding their destinations there was a big overseas market for what was stored there; Hong Kong, London, Amsterdam and New York City. I was pushed on. I gagged a few times to keep up the pretence. In a smaller room at the end of the hall white cardboard boxes, each approximately twenty centimetres square, were stacked on shelves. They smelt of thick glue, the kind kids used in Primary School for sticking everything to everything else. Hong Kong seemed to be the port of call for all of those objects.

Finally, I was steered to a door that he opened and into which I was shoved, politely. I clanged up the toilet seat and did a pretty good impression of vomiting, retching and moaning, at appropriate intervals. Shit, I should have won an Academy Award for my performance. Mind, after attending Lucy's parties I'd had a lot of practice at vomiting. *Memo: Next party get Lucy's drinks analysed down at Health and Safety.*

I was steadily retching when I heard a motor start up just outside the tiny window. I stood on the toilet and squinted hard through the tiny crack in the right hand corner of the pane. There was a green Kombi van driven by a man wearing a brightly coloured Tibetan wool hat pulled low over his forehead. I desperately tried to see the number plate but the U turn flicked it out of view. I almost fell off the toilet when I saw who was in the passenger seat. It was Tweedledum from the Op Shop. Or maybe Tweedledee. Was I being followed? If so, why? If not, what was she doing there? Was this another connection between Giselle's old home and her new one?

The Proprietor coughed loudly. If I'd retched anymore I'd have vomited for real. I stepped down and flushed the toilet. Wiping my mouth with toilet paper I threw open the door. The man, bless him, looked anxious. His eyes moved to my stomach which, with the amount of flab I was carrying, could easy pass for a six month pregnancy. He sighed loudly. Maybe he'd expected me to drop the baby in his toilet. I wobbled effectively back to the showroom. Seeing a chair I quickly sat down.

"Can I rest a while?"

I pointed to where we'd just come from.

"You carry on if you're busy."

Shit, I was pushing my luck.

The man cocked his head towards the lonely oil painting.

"If you like this one I can do it for one thousand. Your gain, my loss."

Making people part with their money for art was an art in itself. Me and Brian once had a stall down the market. Last year of High School. We needed cash. People were paying big money for bits of plastic rubbish on the next table, then squabbling over paying fifteen dollars for some hand crafted art work. Pathetic. Brian got so angry that by noon he'd had enough and ran around giving stuff away. He was definitely on something stronger than I was. Rampant youth. Those were the days.

The stuff he gave away was brilliant compared to the painting I was now being offered. Hands behind his back the man swayed back and forth, his eyes reverting to the back room on every drop of his heels. He was nervous. About what I'd seen? About the man and woman who'd been in the Kombi? Could they be axe murderers? Art thieves? Whatever, something fishy was going on. I made a tricky attempt at standing. Very convincing. He stopped his rocking and took his chance.

"If madam is feeling better?"

A hopeful look passed over his face but I wasn't finished with him.

"Did you have a financially successful show?"

He chirped up, taking a renewed interest in me.

"Yes indeed. Very rewarding."

"A particularly special artist?"

He hesitated. I raised my eyebrows and grinned cheekily. That got him.

"The artist has a special following, yes. Special collectors, you understand."

I did not but I nodded ferociously, a look of calculated candour on my face. He took the bait.

"You are a collector?'

"I certainly am."

Not a lie. I collect anything that's pink, for Auntie. I sighed deeply.

"Most everything is so...so.."

I paused as if needing the right word. I did. It came.

"So, boring. I am looking for something financially rewarding, long term of course but also something, em...different."

I had no idea what I was talking about but it sounded like I did and he lapped it up.

"You must let me have your contact number. A mobile number is all we require."

We? So there were others involved. The Tweedledee pair? I almost whispered the question.

"The white boxes?"

"Ah, those. All sold I am afraid."

"They are 'different'?"

I hadn't a clue what I was guessing at. The man laughed hard.

"Indeed, very special ones, madam. Very poplar with our East European clients. Splendid pieces, if I do say so myself. Not one of the eggs is the same."

"Eggs?"

My mind dashed off to some place in my memory. Easter eggs? Boiled eggs? Rotten eggs? He explained.

"As in Faberge."

"Ah, of course. My memory. Dreadful. It must be the hormones."

Shit, I was getting good at telling whoppers.

"We do our best to please our clients, madam."

His self satisfied smile meant he'd sensed I knew more than I did. I sensed I was digging a hole for myself. The Kombi couple could be back any minute. He carried on, oblivious of my ignorant guess work.

"They have become very collectable, madam, especially for, how shall I say, for the peculiarly discerning buyer."

"What current prices are we talking?"

It was a blunt ask but he grasped it in both hands.

"The Eggs. From a few thousand to around twenty thousand. A valuable investment, as I am sure madam understands."

I held back the huge gasp that gathered in my lungs. He continued with the pitch.

"Of course, this selection of eggs is all accounted for and the paintings, well they have been sold also. But, if madam has a particular painting, a favourite she especially desires, a purchase can be arranged. Anything. For a price."

A painting I desired? I couldn't tell a Margaret Olley from a Dame Nellie Melba. *Memo: Check out art books.* I played the fool with the only famous painting I'd heard of and giggled coyly.

"I always especially desired the Mona Lisa."

The man clapped his hands and joined in with the giggling.

"Madam aims far too high. Even for us."

For us. He was definitely not in it alone. The hole was getting deeper. I changed tack.

"This show, this artist you represent, do I know him?"

"It is actually a Her."

This time I couldn't hold back my gasp. To cover my lapse I turned it into a response to the imaginary baby.

"The baby. Kicking. I think it might be a her too."

"You have not been scanned?"

Shit, he wasn't as ignorant about babies as I thought he'd be.

"I like surprises."

I figured I was about to get a bigger surprise than I'd bargained for when he went for his inside pocket. He'd sussed me out. I was asking too many questions. He smelt danger. So did I. He was going to pull a gun on me. I gauged the distance to the door. No way could I run faster than a bullet. No way could I run fast, period. I waited for the climax of my life, which looked like being a bloody one. My eyes stayed on the pocket, sweat pouring between my boobs. After a few seconds of silent panic I saw it was no gun. I felt a right idiot as he took out a small notebook and a pen. I grinned and sank deeper into the chair.

"Madam's contact?"

I was in real shit. Back to the essentials. I gagged and began to make a run for the toilet. He followed me, fast.

"Madam!"

I locked the door behind me and did another great acting job. His voice sounded too close for comfort.

"Is madam alright?"

No way could I squeeze through the small window even if I could break it, so I quietly stepped out, once more wiping my mouth. I stroked my stomach.

"Do you have children?"

He visibly shuddered at the thought. I knew where he was coming from.

"Indeed not."

"Ah. Look. I feel rather unwell. I really must go home and lie down. I will be in touch."

"Very well, madam."

With that I shook his clammy hand and walked out. The clear blue sky was such a welcome contrast to the dim claustrophobic gallery that I almost shed tears. Gulls circled overhead, shrieking a signal that food was being scattered down by the fish and chip shop.

The man, who hadn't given me his name or asked for mine, had referred to the special artist as a 'she'. It could certainly be Giselle's work being shipped off. For big money? Did that mean she was a famous artist? All these years me and Lucy never knew. But then, we'd never watched art programs on the ABC. Had Giselle's live-in man organised to sell her work for his own profit? He could have got her out of the way by administering drugs to falsify a heart attack, or perhaps it was supposed to be a lethal dose? Too risky? As Lucy said, who'd give a stuff about another druggie dying.

I sat on a low brick wall and told myself to stop jumping to conclusions. Giselle might not be the innocent I had thought her. Before her heart attack she could have known what was going on.

She could need the money. Maybe she was being threatened and wanted to escape to another life in another country. That took money. I was, as usual, letting my imagination run riot, but wasn't too worried. That's how investigators are supposed to be.

I retraced my steps, fascinated by the discovery that one of the Tweedledee women was in the Kombi. Was there a strange connection between Giselle's old abode near Nimbin and her mansion at the beach? What part did the two old ladies play?

Deciding to cleanse both body and mind I drove to Perigian Beach, changed into my swimmers and stepped lightly into the water. Reasoning that the life savers didn't deserve having to drag a body my size out of the water I dutifully kept between the flags. I didn't get much body surfing in but I dog paddled a lot, battling waves an enormous one metre high. Kids of course swam out into the depths. Smart arses. I felt totally refreshed when I walked out onto the pleasantly warm sand. I convinced myself I'd used up enough calories to eat three Mars Bars.

While drying off, I sat and watched the gulls circling before they dived for food scraps. Ever since the Aquarious Festival had people circled Giselle, feeding on her creativity and her vulnerability?

Sure I wanted to find out who was Lucy's father but I was suddenly keener to get to the bottom of the art stuff. The diaries could give clues to both mysteries.

SEVEN

I was happy to be back from Noosa but after the weird things that went on up there, with the gallery and the old ladies, I reckoned I should retrieve the gun I'd hidden up in the roof. It was a hand gun, a Beretta, easy to carry in my shoulder bag. I'd obtained it for protection. My ex could be violent. The gun was an old model yet serviceable, as far as I knew. Climbing up the ladder to get into the roof was not such a problem. Getting my body through the manhole was slow going. It was darker than expected up there and while heaving myself up I put my hand on the crackly discarded skin of a carpet snake. I hoped the snake hadn't mistaken my small Beretta for a big rat. Gingerly, I continued exploring. I felt the bulk of the gun and flicked aside the blanket it was under, almost choking on the dust. The gun looked smaller than I remembered, yet it felt good in my hand. The ammunition was in the shed, somewhere. I edged my way back down the ladder. It was hard to believe that the small weight I was holding was, when loaded, a lethal weapon. It was like being in a movie. At least I wouldn't have to do thirty takes, though maybe life should be like that. Thirty goes at getting it right.

I was just putting back the ladder in the garage when I heard a tiny scraping noise. Had Lucy forgotten her key again? Was it from inside or outside the cottage? Whoever it was, they were restrained about it. No banging on doors, no smashing of windows and so far, no beating up of bodies, specifically mine.

I stepped inside, via the back door, and peered through the dimness of the cottage. Dusk was closing in. I'd been longer up in the roof than expected. No lights were on. I crept down the hallway, stopping at each doorway to listen, gripping the impotent gun in my hand. The noise came again, gentle yet persistent. Maybe an escaped prisoner. Though Grafton jail had been closed down. Was I scared? Too right. I fondled the Beretta and edged my way back down the hall. I was miffed there could even be an intruder. I'd put two hundred dollars on credit card for security stuff. True, half of it was pretend. Fake video cameras, signs that told lies about security patrols and locks so cheap a three year old could break them. Tin cans tied to long pieces of string stretched across paths, back and front, might have worked just as well. *Memo: Check what a static guard costs.* I'd read about hiring a security guard who'd hang around on a semi-permanent basis. Shit, if I could afford one of them I'd rather spend the money on a toy-boy.

Suddenly there was a loud clatter, followed by an indecipherable expletive. It sounded like it was from outside, by the bathroom. My heart beat resentfully fast. Then came a scraping noise. A two ton rat? Lots of macadamia plantations in the region meant lots of very big nut-loving rats. A noise again. I'd had enough. I leaned against the wall, breathed deep and prepared myself. I tossed the gun onto the table. Useless without the ammo. Then changed my mind and picked it back up. If it was one of the weirdos I'd met up at Noosa, the mere sight of a Beretta might make them run. Could it be Giselle's live-in man, who'd seen me snooping round the mansion? Did he suspect Lucy had given her mother's diaries to me? Did he think I'd deciphered the codes? I could be in dire danger. *Memo: Stop watching old movies.* I wished Lucy was with me instead of being up at Noosa. By now she'd be out there windmilling her arms and legs, flattening the would-be assassin with a karate chop. No blood, just pain.

I flipped open the bathroom door and flicked on the light. Outside the window a voice shouted.

"Get out of there, you hoon!"

I recognised the voice. It was Auntie Gert. What was she doing out there? Her shadowy face was concealed by the air freshener on the window sill. The window was open a fraction. A wrinkled, sun spotted hand was hanging onto the window edge. The voice shouted again.

"I will call the police!"

I stood on the stool and pushed the window up higher. Our noses almost touched as I peered out. The shock on her face was about the same as mine. She gawped, mouth open. Not a pretty sight. She didn't have her teeth in.

"Auntie Gert!"

She stared at me, wide eyed.

"Holly?"

"Auntie, it is you, isn't it?"

"Who do you think it is, Harrison Ford?"

"What are you doing?"

"I had a feeling one of those crooks would try and break into your place while you were away."

"A feeling?"

"Us old people do have them, you know."

She squinted at me.

"Are you sure you're Holly?"

She hadn't got her glasses on.

"Yes. It is me."

"I was worried they might have stolen some vital information."

I stepped onto the floor.

"Better get you inside. Wait for me."

"I got up here, I can get down."

"Wait!"

"Hey, I'm the wise woman round here, right."

"Whatever."

I dashed outside. We almost collided as I skirted round the corner. She was standing on a clump of white daisies, wearing her pink calf length flannelette nightie, over which was a pink woolly dressing gown which matched her pink fluffy slippers. I steered her into the kitchen. She wiped her forehead.

"I think I'm having a hot flush. All that talk of Harrison Ford."

"You're too old for hot flushes."

Memo: Read up on the menopause. Again.

"I'll never be too old for Harrison Ford."

How could I deny her that dream.

"Of course not."

"I was worried for you, Holly. That Giselle woman used to mix with all sorts of riff- raff. You could be in danger from her druggie gang. Bikies and such."

Auntie Gert watched the TV news every night. Bikie gangs were on it a lot.

"I don't think she has a gang."

"I was worried. Anybody could break into this place."

"They did. Well, you did. Or you would have done."

"You didn't answer your phone. So I thought I'd investigate."

"Investigate? You're eighty years old!"

She glared at me, insulted.

"Did she tell you who Lucy's father was? That Giselle?"

"She doesn't know."

"I bet she does."

Shit, it hadn't occurred to me that Giselle might be telling porkies. But why would she? Nevertheless, a seed of doubt had been planted in my mind. I'd taken for granted I was being told the truth. So had Lucy. I needed to think that one through.

"I'll take you home."

"I drove here, I'll drive back. Thanks all the same."

I hadn't noticed her car out the front.

"Where's the car?"

"A few houses down. You do that so's not to alert the criminals."

Auntie Gert was a fully paid up member of Crime Stoppers.

She peered at me and wagged her finger. It was easy to imagine her flying through the air on a broomstick.

"Of course, if the key had been where it was supposed to be, then I'd simply have come in through the front door."

"And given me a heart attack!"

"Don't be silly."

"Home time, Auntie. Sorry I didn't let you know I was back. I just got busy."

"You young ones. Always busy, busy, busy. You don't gain wisdom by being always busy."

I smiled. She was right. Shit, she was always right. I thought of the pink tea set.

"Wait there."

I strode into the bedroom, routed around in the wardrobe and bought out the bag it was in. Her eyes sparkled mischief.

"Will I like it?"

"You will love it."

That satisfied her. As soon as she was gone I whizzed outside, put the ladder back, removed the wheelbarrow she'd been standing on and put the key back under the rock. I'd sort out the ammunition in the morning. Back inside I poured myself a large glass of red and chomped on a Mars Bar. Sinking into my comfort zone in front of the tele I pondered on the idea that Giselle did know who the father was. But then, it was a stupid idea. Why would she lie about it? Maybe there were more pieces to the jigsaw than I'd imagined. What would Inspector Barnaby do? What I did, I expect. Pour another glass of wine and ponder.

EIGHT

I've always suspected my baby brother Pete had inherited the family's crazy genes; he'd proved me right. At thirty six he was getting married for the third time. It was a worry, although at the time the biggest worry for me was what to wear to the wedding. I had nothing suitably glitzy that fitted me and no way could I buy a second hand outfit for it. Some woman would loudly introduce herself as Geraldine Basildon-Dangar, the previous owner of the said outfit. Shit, I'd have to shoot myself. Or her.

Touring all the boutiques in a fifty kilometre radius took all day. At the last one I found something red, shiny and tight, with a Lucy-style plunge neckline. It made me look sexier than I'd done for over a decade, so naturally I bought it. Bang went a month's mortgage repayments. The fabric clung to my flesh so tight I almost turned myself on. Plus, I figured that if I kept on the move, my flab wouldn't settle in one place long enough for it to be all that noticable. I had to buy shoes to match. Red, with heels that rivalled the Eiffel Tower. Also a large hat to cover my unruly hair until I lay down and I sure intended being laid down some time that day. That's what weddings were for.

I'd not met Pete's latest bride. The wedding came out of the blue. Her name was Marina de Rossi, her Italian father being a businessman with projects all over the country. In other words, a rich bastard. She was a size ten, so I'd never really be able to aprove of my sister-in-law. Her classic ivory gown with a voluptuous shower of silk and lace made me green with envy. What it must have cost would pay off half my debts.

At the reception there was enough food and drink to satisfy a Melbourne Cup crowd. The best man, Mario, was her first cousin and like her, dark everything, which meant he'd have lots of dark body hair. Shit, evolution has moved on. Yet even at a distance I could see how he turned on the charm. Every woman he met, young or old, gazed and drooled, even though he had a blue eyed blonde bimbo stuck to his arm. Neither of them wore a wedding ring.

As I swallowed my fifth vodka it dawned on me that Pete was marrying into a Catholic family. He hadn't been to church since he'd screamed the protestant church down when the vicar dribbled water over his head. Had Pete sold his soul to the Pope? At least his bride had a rich daddy. Some girls have all the luck. Mind, she was marrying my cop brother so there'd have to be something wrong with her. Maybe there was something missing from the top paddock.

The day of the wedding was dry and ten degrees below hot. A great spring day. An eight piece band played retro music, making half the crowd sway with nostalgia and the other half rush off to vomit. The free flowing alcohol wouldn't have helped either group. The reception was held in a hectare size garden. The huge Marquee was kept in place by dozens of ropes and pegs, giving it the appearance of an unwieldy sailing ship about to escape its moorings. Flowers of every shape, size and colour were plopped into huge vases and placed in strategic positions. A blue heeler sat still as a statue at one end of the lawn, guarding a set of pseudo Greek Urns like the ones I'd seen at the gallery. The dog eyed everyone with distrust. So did I.

A proper church ceremony made the marriage proper, in the eyes of somebody's god, somewhere around one o'clock. Two hours later everybody, including me, was totally pissed. I was draping myself over a chair doing my best to appear sexy when a man strolled over and started feeling me up. He was a foul smelling zombie so I aimed a knee at his groin. I missed. Made no difference; he tried to plant his mouth on my lips. I pushed him away. He forced himself closer. He was getting the better of me when suddenly he was picked up and thrown to the ground. A bouncer had arrived on the scene. I stared in disbelief as my attacker scrambled to his feet and lurched towards the other man. The knockout came quick. He crumpled onto the well-mown grass while I was pushed unceremoniously into the chair.

"What do you think you were doing?"

Shit, was I miffed. Who did he think he was? I swayed on the seat and hiccupped loudly. Then I realised it was Mario, the Best Man. He towered above my thumping head. I lifted up my eyes but they only got as far as his trouser zip. I giggled, imagining the contents behind the zip. Mario rubbed his knuckles. *Memo: This man is not afaid to stand up for a woman.* He put his hand under my chin and lifted up my face. Shit, he was fabulous.

"You okay?"

I formed a smile as weak as my knees.

"You saved my life."

"Not exactly. He has a problem with alcohol."

"So does half of Australia."

He smiled as he took in my condition.

"You need strong black coffee."

"Three sugars."

"We'll see. Come on."

He took me by the hand and I wobbled beside him, my stiletto heels sticking in the soft earth at every step, which meant he had to drag me along. He ran out of patience.

"For heaven's sake, take off those shoes."

So forceful!

"These are the most beautiful shoes I've ever had."

"It is not as if you are the bride!"

So much for the charm. I extricated my feet from the shoes, almost falling over in the process. He pointed a fatherly finger at me.

"Do not move!"

He even sounded like my father. Steeped in alcohol, I stayed where I was, sighing with pleasure as I watched his bum rippling as he strode away. In his outfit he looked like a waiter. Was he a waiter? Did he wait for sex or take it whenever the urge took him? The way my lower regions were tingling I frankly didn't care which. I focused on the garden; tall palms flowing to the rhythms of the wind, pink tipped white magnolias puffing out their scent and clumps of primitive native grasses with mauve spikes robustly stretching towards the sky. Magpies and noisy miners gathered scraps of food from the ground while a squawking yellow tailed black cockatoo circled effortlessly in the skies above.

It was a good place to be, until I saw him, the stranger who'd known mine and Giselle's name. His appearance sobered me up quick smart. He was standing beside a marble fountain on the other side of the garden. Next to him stood a pretty boy, gazing up with the adoring eyes of a newly acquired lover. Been there, done that. Their bodies touched lightly. Spying me, the stranger had the nerve to offer me a grandiose wave. I quickly turned away. Mario arrived back with the coffee.

"I have only put in one sugar. You are sweet enough, are you not?"

The charm was back. As for the body hair, well time would tell. He watched as I sipped the hot liquid gingerly.

"Drink it up."

What was he, my keeper? I pointed to the man and his friend.

"Who is that man?'

"Who?"

I pointed again.

"Him."

"Oh, him. His name is Martin Stanford-Smythe."

"What's he doing here?"

"He is a guest."

"A guest?"

"Of the bride's family."

"Of the bride's family?"

"He is a business colleague."

"Business colleague?"

"Please stop repeating what I say. What about him?"

We were both getting annoyed with the questions. Nevertheless, I needed to know.

"What kind of business?"

Mario stepped back.

"Ah, I see, you're concerned for your brother's welfare. What kind of a family he has married into."

"You could say that."

"Marina is a part of the De Rossi family. De Rossi Constructions; housing estates, government buildings, nursing homes, that sort of thing. It pays them to have an MLC as a friend."

"An MLC?"

"A politician."

"I know what an MLC is!"

Mind, I had no idea what the initials stood for but who does? Mario's face had taken on a vacant look, he'd drifted off some place.

"Tragic places, nursing homes. Like hospitals. Being entirely dependent on other people. I would hate that."

A black mark. Mario sounded like he was a loner. I needed to make sure.

"You don't like to depend on people?'

He stared at me, eyes wide, back from wherever his thoughts had taken him.

"I tried it once. Once was enough."

Calm and anger tumbled together. Sad.

"And the blonde?'

I pointed in the direction of the temporary dance floor. The blonde was dancing with the bride's father. Mario grinned.

"She is an occasional lover. Very useful at times."

I wasn't going to let him get away with that.

"I have one of those. Like you say, very useful."

I lied with such ease. His grin dropped to a smile.

"Glad to hear it. I have Best Man duties to perform. But I shall return."

He gave me an Army style salute and moved off.

"Don't get lost. I will be back. Okay?"

I nodded eagerly, like some slut grateful for the attention. Straight away I could have kicked myself. Soon as he was out of sight I made for the drinks table. Martin's lover boy barred my way. He had provocative cupid lips. I could see why the much older Martin SS was attracted to him. He wore a white T shirt under a grey suit, a clone of the one Martin wore. He eyed me thoughtfully.

"Can I fetch you a drink?"

I shook my head and tried to side step him but he outdid my every move. A proper little dancer.

"You are Holly Day. Martin wanted me to meet you."

"Why?"

"Who knows darling but whatever Martin wants, I oblige."

"Is it worth it?"

I was being bitchy but I didn't care. He was confident.

"Oh, yes. Very much worth it."

His eyes narrowed as he looked me over.

"Darling, I have no idea who does your hair but they should be hung, drawn and quartered."

My hat must have fallen off when the zombie was doing his thing. I wondered where it was.

"Oh, very mediaeval."

"So is your hair, darling. You should let me do something with it."

"I'm setting a new trend in unruly hair."

He laughed. I joined in. He held out his hand.

"Jack Kitson, Martin's latest acquisition. Under no illusions whatsoever. I work with your brother's new wife."

"She's a hairdresser?"

"God, no. She owns the salon, a string of them, in fact, right across the country. One or two abroad, as well. Won several awards. Wonder you haven't heard of her. But then you wouldn't have, would you."

His turn to be bitchy.

"She also has an import/export business. A very busy lady. I do so hope your brother realises he won't be seeing very much of her."

"He's made his bed.... She must be very rich."

He evaluated my jealousy.

"You cannot earn much at your game."

"Game?"

"You have a car over fifty years old!"

They'd done their homework.

"It's a collectors car. A classic."

"A classic piece of crap."

How he must amuse Martin. He kept going, with what he'd no doubt been commanded to say.

"What is it you call yourself? An amateur sleuth? How positively nineteen fifties. To match your car?"

Shit, what else were they privy to? I felt the sweat trickle between my breasts onto my new red bra.

"As it happens, I'm in market research."

He giggled like the schoolboy he'd been a couple of years before.

"You know what, darling, I like you. You are feisty and nowhere near as stupid as I was led to believe."

"Is that your man's summation of me?'

He was about thirty years younger than Martin. The bitch in me rose to the surface.

"At least I never cradle snatch."

At this he roared with laughter so high pitched it caused Martin to turn his gaze on us. I blew him a kiss and stalked off, picking up my shoes as I passed the table.

The confrontation had cleared my head. I made my way to

the back garden. The De Rossi family had to be multimillionaires and my brother had married into it. The thing was, why had they let him into the family? He was just an ordinary cop. No great influence, as far as I knew. He'd never seemed bothered about promotion. As a high powered businessman De Rossi would already have lobbyists in all the important places. So what did they need Pete for? Shit, I was getting paranoid. There is such a thing as plain old love. Isn't there? I wandered back, just in time to catch sight of the newly weds dashing down the winding steps, hand in hand, eyes shining. It sure looked like love. I yelled and waved like crazy.

"Have a wonderful honeymoon!"

Pete turned, winked at me and pulled his bride round to wave to me. She beamed as new brides tend to do, then mouthed a thankyou. Then they were off.

They were going on a Pacific Cruise. Rather them than me. I once got sea sick on a floating restaurant. I kept waving my goodbye, along with everyone else, as the happy couple raced to their waiting limousine, which soon drove off, crunching down the gravel driveway.

A firm body leaned against me. A soft kiss was blown in my ear, turning the existing tingles into a roaring fire. I turned round to face Mario. There was concern in his voice.

"I thought you were lost."

I smiled, coy as I could manage.

"I wanted to wave the happy couple goodbye."

I also wanted to ask him more about Martin SS and Jack Kitson but that could wait. It was Pete's day and, with any luck, Mario was going to make my day. As we leaned against the pseudo greek columns I thought of mum and dad on their wedding day. Dad kept the photo of them outside the Registry Office on the sideboard. Mum didn't show as being pregnant with me. Shit, she'd have loved to see Pete so happy with his beautiful bride. His first wife or third, it wouldn't have mattered. Tears welled in my eyes. Mario gently held my face in his hands. My body trembled as he pressed hard against me. We kissed. No tongue but all the better for it. He steered me towards one of the limos parked round the back. Once inside we wrenched off our undies. It was good I'd worn my sexy red ones. Every pore of my body clamoured for his touch. As he came down on me I succumbed to the romance of the moment. No Viagra needed in this long, sleek robust vehicle. He took me places I'd forgotten existed. So what if I never saw him again? So what if I hated myself next morning. I'd live with it.

NINE

Idid hate myself the next morning. Too old for one night stands? Still, great sex though. While still intoxicated at the remembrance I phoned Lucy, who was up in Noosa. She scoffed at my rapturous descriptions.

"Listen, Flab, he'll fuck you for a few short weeks then piss off to fuck somebody else. That's what men do."

I bit my lip. Having his body for even a few short weeks would be nothing short of heaven. I decided to take the conversation down another path.

"Leech, I've been going through Giselle's diaries. They're mostly filled with trivia and coded initials but..."

She interrupted.

"I fucking know that."

"A sort of code."

"I fucking guessed that."

I heaved a sigh.

"And get this, one set of initials is mentioned right from day one of the Aquarius Festival"

"So, you've found my father already?"

"Not exactly."

"So what you getting me all fired up for?"

"I've found out who the initials stand for. I think."

"Flab, he's not some fucking no hoper, is he?"

"He's a politician."

"Same thing."

"Leech!"

"Last thing I want is for him to be a fucking politician!"

She was in one bad mood.

"Leech, I can only investigate. Whatever comes up, good or bad, that's it."

I was getting angry. Lucy remained belligerent.

"So he could be this pollie, or a no hoper, or a scum bag?"

"It's too early to be sure who he is, or what he is. But, yes, any of those things."

I continued like a practised deceiver.

"Mind, the initials, the man who's name I think I know, well, he wasn't a politician back then."

"That supposed to make me feel better?"

I considered telling her about Martin Stanford-Smythe but thought it best not to overload her brain. Change of subject was called for.

"So, when are you coming back home?"

"Depends on how mum goes."

"But she is improving?"

"Sort of."

"What do the doctors say?"

"Nothing that means anything."

"But if you're coming home?"

"Like I said, Flab. I'll be there when I'm fucking there!"

I paused to give her time to apologise. Me, her personal detective treated like I was some shit gofer at an abattoir. I heard her breathing deep. I couldn't wait any longer. I raised my voice half an octave.

"I'll catch you later then. Take care Lucy."

"Lucy?"

She was wary when I called her by her proper name when there was just the two of us.

"There's nothing you haven't told me is there?"

"Nothing that's really significant."

This could be a lie or it could be the truth. Too soon to tell. Her voice was slow and deliberate.

"You sure?"

"Yes."

She hesitated. Then it came out.

"Sorry, Flab. You're doing your fucking best. If I can help in any way."

A gift, duly accepted. I needed to make things better.

"There is something you can do while you're up at Noosa."

"I hope it's interesting. It's as boring as rat shit up here."

To think, tourists paid hundreds of dollars a day to stay in the same boring as rat shit town.

"It won't be boring. Promise."

I yet had to think of something to make her feel good. I was her best friend. Her and me sort of belong together, like caramel and chocolate.

"I'll give you the details in a day or so."

"Don't you forget."

"Ciao."

"You too."

I replaced the phone in the charger, wishing I could recharge my body just as easily, not to mention my brain. I showered and poured myself into black stretch jeans, an aquamarine T shirt and added my turquoise and silver Indian drop earrings. I'd decided to drive up to Nimbin to check out the area. I wanted to visit where people had done all that free love and drugs stuff back in the seventies. It might help.

Nimbin, up in the mountains, surrounded by State Forests, has been known as the cannabis capital of Australia for around four decades. Most marijuanah was being grown hydroponically, much to the indignation of the older hippies, who prefered the natural way. Drug gangs used bushland, their own blocks or national forests, anywhere large quantities could be hidden. The law was using infra red to seek out their plantations, but enough was apparently being missed to keep the business ticking over. I had no idea if the infamous magic mushrooms had made it to the endangered species list. I'd never bothered with them. Why risk nausea and hallucinations when the same effect came from watching Parliamentry Question Time. I didn't need my perceptions changed that much.

The drive up was uneventful, apart from a van careering all over the road until I overtook it. Driving into the village I slowed down to the speed limit and cruised down the main street, taking in the famous rainbow painted shopfronts with their weathered facades and rough street furniture. To the tourist, Nimbin must look the same as the image preserved by the myths of the Festival. Business, for both legitimate shops and illegal dealers, had grown exponentially, brisk and beneficial to all. Real estate prices had boomed. So much for the hippie dream of escaping suburbia. It had come to them.

Old timbered buildings, weathered by age and purposeful neglect, straggled both sides of the street. Houses dribbled along roads further out, leading to farmland then up to the native forests. Most were the weatherboard variety, built in the few decades before the area was rediscovered by newcomers. Recent years had seen a trend in parcels of land being subdivided into an acre or so, with houses of brick or stone or aluminium sheeting proudly denying any relation to the bigger town subdivisions. Hobby farms were a dream of the intellectual class who proposed to play their part in saving the world by using solar panels and tank water and enviormentally sound septic systems, all at a greater cost than the original hippies could ever have afforded. Some parcels bordered rough country before sweeping up to the higher peaks.

Nimbin used to be a quiet nondescript village, then along came the Aquarius Festival, which changed everything. Quite a few participants stayed on to start multiple occupancy communities. Some had kids, some sent them to school, some remained kids themselves. The local settler families, mostly dairy farmers or wood loggers, tolerated the newcomers and vica versa. The hope for perpetual love, peace and harmony had been rekindled worldwide after Woodstock. An alternative lifestyle sprouted from the hope. The horrors of the Vietnam war became a focal point for protesters, along with the logging of old growth forests. Having witnessed Giselle's community lifestyle, when Lucy and me were teenagers, I admired it but could never live it. Me dig a vegetable garden? Me stand in front of a bulldozer to save a tree? Me, milk a goat, or worse, a cow? Me, no flush toilet? I think not. Not after the initial excitement, which generally lasted no more than thirty six hours.

Soon as the Valiant was parked behind the main row of shops I stepped out and breathed in deep. The air smelt different from that closer to the coast, a quintessential mixture of misty mountain air and hazy thought processes. I was after clues to what had happened back in the seventies. I had no idea how many of the original hippies were still around. Most would have moved on. Many would have died. I was seeking a tangible connection between Giselle's life back then and her life since she left the region. Walking up the main street I had to concede that my chance of finding immediate evidence about Lucy's father was that of a snowball in hell. Thirty nine years had passed since then. Great if I could have jumped back in time. Where was *Dr Who* when I needed him.

I put in my order at the Mecca Café and sat down at the hewn timber furniture that squatted in irregular lines from the counter to the pavement. The place was cluttered with men between twenty and sixty, although with faces as rugged as the furniture, any assessment of age can be misleading. Hair was mostly darkish and matted, with a few dreadlocks sprinkled about. Everyone seemed to be smoking some form of intoxicant, legal or otherwise. I'd heard that the war in Afghanistan meant top quality hashish was harder to come by. The chatter was vociferous, amiable and interspersed with explosive laughter. Most hugged jackets to their chests. It gets cold up in the mountains, at least until the sun breaks through the mist. Tea, or coffee, with cakes, were consumed with relish at each table, where groups of four to six sat lounging and yarning. It was late breakfast time, even though it was already eleven a.m. Nobody bothered me. I bothered nobody.

In the street a few old cars trundled up and down. Tourists, both local and international, wandered about, gazing at the old buildings and their contents. Any lasting visible signs of the Aquarius Festival or the Hippie lifestyle were hungered after, a legend to be relived through the camera lens and a decorative bong bought as a conversation piece for 'back home'.

A tour bus roamed past, side panels painted in bright rainbow colours. Halting opposite the cafe it poured out its contents, mostly young backpackers. A few oldies stepped down with less ease but with similar outfits, only larger sizes. I could empathise with that. Soon, sales of various substances would happen down the alleyways, to the mutual satisfaction of all concerned. It was a well known fact that almost all visitors came for the white hippie experience, which frequently included cannabis. Few enquired about the aboriginal tribes that for thousands of years lived as sole occupants of the country.

I flicked myself into a comfortable position as my tea and cakes arrived. Gorging on the profiteroles I opened up one of the diaries. I read again the entries made by Giselle about the people she was with, and peered once more at the elusive initials. Was Martin SS the father? He could have had sex with girls too. Why had he stopped me in the street and asked after Giselle? How come he was at my brother's wedding? Suddenly, I saw the man who I was sure had bashed me on the nose. Surging with anger I swivelled myself round and yelled out to him.

"Oy! You!"

He turned towards me, recognised me, and took off like a race horse, a flash of black shorts and white T shirt. Before I could extricate myself from the bench he'd sprinted out of sight. I followed fast as I could but was gasping for breath after only a hundred metres. Shit, I was so unfit. Sweat poured off me. My calves screamed pain. Once he'd slipped around a corner I sidled back to the front of the café. The occupants gazed at me, laughter rippling quietly. I pulled back my shoulders.

"He broke my nose!"

Only half a lie. He'd fractured it. No chance I'd catch him. I bent over, hands on my knees, panting like a long distance runner. Graduallly my heart rate dropped to near normal. I stood upright, flicked back my hair, smoothed my shirt over my jeans, pulled my bra straps into their correct position, restrained my bladder from emptying itself and accepted that I was well on my way to becoming an ancient monument. *Memo: Get fit. Very fit.*

Walking back to my table I tried to retrieve some kind of dignity by pointing in the direction of the escapee.

"Some blokes can't be trusted, hey? I said I'd pay what he asked."

The customers turned away, unconvinced. I returned to my cold cuppa. I'd check out the attacker later. Somebody would know who he was. I opened one of the diaries. The constant reference to Martin SS meant he had to be important. How come he'd lost touch with Giselle if he'd been important to her? Where did the nose breaker fit in, and was he connected to Martin? Were those two old ladies from Noosa mentioned anywhere? What would Giselle have called them? OL1 and OL2? Probably not Tweedledum and Tweedledee. I scoured the diary for anything that resembled a reference to them. Nothing. Maybe in another diary. Suddenly, a voice boomed out from behind me.

"Hey, Harry!"

I looked up to catch a man in his thirties, dark skinned and dishevelled, hurrying to the exit, his khaki army bag flopping against his hip. He called out again. Everyone's attention moved to the street outside the cafe. An old man half turned, in search of the voice. He'd been making for a grey early model Toyota Truck. The voice yelled even louder.

"Harry, you old dog!"

The apparent owner of the name, dressed in old navy jacket, baggy moleskin pants and heavy leather boots, crossed the road to meet up. My heart missed a beat. He walked with a limp. It couldn't be Hippie Harry, surely. Not after all these years. I asked a couple of the men and they confirmed, with schoolboy laughter, that yes, that was Harry and yes, he was still more or less a hippie. I slammed shut the diary, packed my bag and moved out into the street. The truck was driving off with the thirty something man in the passenger seat. I strained to get the licence number but my eyes, not being one hundred percent, missed it. *Memo: Get eyes checked. Am missing important stuff.*

So, after all these years Harry was still around. Did he ever get another dog? Did he use it to test his cocktails? What a chance for my investigation! I pondered on whether Harry might be Lucy's father. He could be. One way or the other I had to find out. His DNA would be pretty simple to get.

On my way back to the Valiant I twice brightly refused an offer of Weed. Twice I said I had enough already. Twice I lied. I had better things to do with my hard earned dollars. I made my way to the Hemp Embassy. They'd be a positive mine of information on who was around from the Festival days. Whether they'd pass any of it on to me was a moot point. After all, I could be a cop, or a criminal or worse, a journalist. If it was Hippie Harry he'd have known Giselle Knight for sure.

TEN

Surrounded by primitive scenery I drove slowly up the dirt track. Monstrous gums stretched up through mist, air roots dangling, reminders of an evolutionary survival technique. Shiny invasive vines threaded their way up and over everything. Dank slimy mulch covered the forest floor and turned dark rocks into slippery imitators of dirt. Hippie Harry's block bordered Nightcap National Park which to the uninitiated, like me, smelt of menace.

I'd been told where Harry lived and although instructions were vague, possibly on purpose, I reckoned I was on the right muddy track. About a kilometre in, clumps of smaller eucalypts stood dark and despondent on either side of the old logging road. I half expected hobgoblins to ogle me from behind trees. Though if I had met anything it would most likely be a Bikie checking on a cannabis crop.

Round a bend, through a narrow gap in the forest, I viewed the slate blue rocks of a mountain side glistening in the damp air, water drops glistening with rainbow coloured clarity. Tolkien country. The Valiant chugged and lurched and skidded, as dictated by the depth and viscosity of the soil. Small rocks, made slippery by moss, made the going slow. At last, I came to the boundary marker. Four lines of barbed wire stretched across my path. A hand painted sign warned trespassers to keep out. So much for love, peace and harmony. I had no idea how far in his living quarters were. Then I saw the stake, half hidden by an overhanging branch. Strands of barbed wire were attached to it and it in turn was hooked to a neighbouring tree. I opened wide this bush gate, to allow the Valiant to pass through.

I was treading my way back to the Wagon when I felt the cold barrel of a rifle pressed against the back of my neck. There was no mistaking it. Shit, had I stupidly stumbled on a massive cannabis plantation? I swallowed hard, desperate to regurgitate the saliva my vocal chords needed for screaming. A few seconds passed. The owner of the rifle was hesitating. Kill me then or later? Shit, just when I was getting the best sex I'd ever had I might be shot dead. *Memo: Never leave the gun in the car, stupid!*

Sweat poured between my boobs and down my back. My hands were itching to do something, but what? I gulped again. A voice yanked the air.

"Can't you read?"

If I'd have known a prayer to recite, I would have. A few leaves spiralled onto my shoulder. Instinctively, I flicked them off. The cold metal pressed harder.

"Put up your hands."

I did.

"Turn around."

I did.

His voice had the calm gravelly tones of Clint Eastwood but it was Hippie Harry, not Dirty Harry, waving a rifle at me. I could see that he was much thinner than when I'd shot his dog, and his voice had dropped an octave, along with his chin. Under his floppy green and brown check shirt I noted he was wearing several layers. He glared at me. No way was I going to do anything to make his day. He aimed the gun at my chest.

"Who the hell are you?"

I squeaked like Minnie Mouse.

"I've come to talk to you."

"About what?"

How much to reveal at this precarious moment?

"The Aquarius Festival."

He and the rifle relaxed somewhat.

"Not a bloody journalist."

"Sort of."

"What sort of an answer is that?"

I moved my arms down a few centimetres. They were tingling. He gestured for the arms to go back up. They did. The rifle stayed where it was.

"You with the cops?"

Did he think past crimes had caught up with him? Did he expect a cop to be so stupid as to get caught so easy? Must mean he had a past to worry about. I blurted out the answer, waving my hands about with such indignation I almost knocked the gun out of his hand.

"Shit, no. Me, a cop? Never."

The absolute truth. His wrinkled face clouded over.

"Methinks the lady protests too much."

Shit, an educated hippie. I'd recognised the line from the one and only Shakespeare play I'd read at school.

"No. Honest."

His face drooped into the weary expression of somebody tired of treading water, the urge to swim vanishing with the hope. He waved for my arms to go back up. With some effort they did.

"You could have got your head blown off just then."

The corner of his mouth curled upwards, his was the unwitting smile of a baby.

"So what do you want?'

"As I said. To talk."

"You one of them investigative journalists?"

I nodded. Only half a lie. He strode over to the Wagon and peered inside. Luckily the Beretta was in the glove compartment. He came back and told me to lower my arms. Which I did. Gratefully.

"You'd better come inside."

He pushed me ahead with the rifle in my back.

"And no funny business."

Funny business? Me? He had the weapon. We headed a couple of hundred metres further down the track. There'd been a layer of gravel thrown down. The season had been unusually wet. He led me through an open door into his shack, basically one large room. No dog jumped up to greet him. No dog barked out the back. Several of the floorboards were broken, tipped at a slight angle, not dangerous, just inconvenient. Three walls were unlined weatherboard, with the end wall corrugated iron. A single brass tap over an enamel sink, together with a few roughly built cupboards indicated the kitchen, while a shoddy hospital style bed, complete with brightly coloured crocheted blankets, stood against the end wall, heralding that area as the bedroom. No mod cons here, though electricity was on. I could hear a generator whirring outside. A few old tapestry armchairs, which even the Salvos would discard, hung about the place like unwanted orphans. The whole shack creaked with age and hasty construction, the windows barely covering the space they were intended to fit. This was a never-finished project. The heavy hardwood beams, holding up the roof, were the only sturdy thing visible. An old table supported loads of books and magazines. Flamboyant cushions and the rickety chairs painted in red and blue added some brightness to the otherwise dull furnishings. The shack had a Dickensian atmosphere, crowded in as it was by dense bush. The only indisputably cared for object in the room was an ornate writing desk carved of rose coloured timber. From its age and condition it must be worth a bit. He followed my gaze.

"Spanish. Eighteenth century."

My eyes opened wide in genuine joy at this piece of history.

"A gift. From a friend. Supposed to have belonged to some Prince or other."

I immediately thought of Giselle and her supposed ancestors. Harry motioned for me to sit on a small, straight backed chair. I sat on it, squeezing my buttocks so's not to slip off. Time to begin.

"You don't remember me, do you?"

He eyed me up and down, peering hard at my face. He needed specs. So did I. His calloused hands streaked through his greying hair as if the memory of me resided somewhere in the matted mess. At that odd moment I wondered how come he didn't smell, either good or bad. Just, nothing. He eventually spoke.

"Should I remember you?"

"Cocktail."

"Cocktail?"

"I shot him for you. I was up here with my dad's .22 and my best friend."

After carefully checking his damaged memory files he grinned cheekily.

"So that was you. You were little more than girls. Yes, I remember. Good God."

He leaned the rifle against a plank and stretched out his hand.

"Well, good to see you again. How ya doing?"

"Real good."

A half truth.

"Forgot your name. Sorry. The old brain cells."

"Holly. Holly Day."

He laughed.

"Ah, yes. Clever. Well Holly, you did me a good turn that day. Never forgot it."

He'd forgotten me though. I was pretty sexy in those days as well.

"Your dad still got the rifle?'

I nodded. Another lie. I'd had it for ages.

"What about the gun. The pistol?"

He knew about that? Nobody knew about that. I'd hidden it for years. I raised my eyebrows. He grinned.

"Sergeant Lachlin."

So he'd told him.

"He told me how you two once 'exchanged products."

A novel way of describing it but accurate enough. Lachlin had been an obnoxious bastard, even for a cop. So, he'd made Sergeant.

"Want some tea?"

I smiled my thanks. He began to prepare tea but kept his eye on the rifle. This man trusted nobody. I was with him on that.

"Him and me were sharing some Afghani Black, long time ago. Got to discussing women, as us men do. Your name came up and he mentioned what you'd exchanged for the gun."

So, I'd swapped a one night stand with a little shit for an old blackmarket Beretta. Did it have to become public? Back then I thought I might need it. Now I might again. Never registered it. Never told Dad even when he eventually handed over his rifle. I'd made sure Lucy never set eyes on it.

"It was bad of Lachlin to mention it."

Harry shrugged.

"He was a nasty bastard."

Best to play dumb on that story. Harry looked up.

"You got some journo job spying on people then?"

"It pays the bills. Mostly."

"That's what Lachlin used to say."

I bet he did. Bent cops were ten a penny back in the eighties. Had anything changed? Not according to Lucy. Harry handed over a mug of steaming hot tea. I stood up and took it.

"I don't do milk, me."

He sat down on the rickety chair that was too small for me.

"So who is it you're looking for?"

"The father of my best friend."

"What's he done?"

"Nothing, as far as I know. She doesn't know who he is."

"Few of us in that position."

There was a hint of regret in his voice.

"Sit down will you."

I did, carefully, in one of the armchairs.

"I've got a few of her mother's diaries. A certain MSS is mentioned a lot."

As if hit by a bullet he sat bolt upright, his lips drawn tight across his few remaining teeth.

"MSS?"

He swivelled himself round in his chair and stared out of the ill fitting window towards the encroaching bush. Once, back in the seventies, when hopes for a viable alternative lifestyle were strong, there would have been a large vege path between the shack and the bush he was gazing at. It had reverted to scrub.

"When are we talking about?"

"I have reason to believe an MSS was at the Aquarius Festival."

He squirmed. I continued.

"My friend was conceived there."

He turned round to face me.

"Lots were, I shouldn't wonder."

"So does a Martin SS mean anything to you?"

He turned to gaze out of the white casement window, probably retrieved from some tumbledown farm cottage. Not being sealed properly it must let in the rain. The region had some of the highest rainfall in New South Wales. He spoke to the scrub.

"There was a Martin somebody. Surname began with an S. Big man. Could be him. Tough. Sold drugs. Heard he got into politics. That'd be right. They're all out for themselves. Suit him down to the ground."

There was a streak of anger in his voice as he turned to gaze at me.

"Haven't seen him in years. Never had much to do with him. Prefer women, me."

His eyes roamed wistfully over my body. Had Lucy been standing in front of him he'd have had an apoplexy for sure. I needed more information.

"This Martin."

"Just give me a minute. Jogged my memory, you have. It's all you're interested in, finding the father?"

I had to lie.

"Uhuh."

He limped over to the desk and rolled up the lid. Inside it was packed with letters and notes, all neatly sorted into compartments.

In one section there was a pile of photographs. Compared to the rest of the shack the desk was an obsessively neat person's paradise. Shit, how much an hour would he charge to get my cottage looking like the inside of his desk. He pointed to his well ordered display.

"Have to keep memories neatly packaged. Then nobody can upset them."

A strange philosophy but hey, I'd never been a hippie.

"No matter what else they do to you, they can't take away your memories."

There was a profound mind hidden within this junk of a man. He rummaged through his vast collection, some restrained by paper clips, some held together by pink cotton solicitors' ribbon. He worked slow as a snail planning a long trip. He peered at each photo in turn, then handed one over.

"That's him. The big bastard in the middle."

I grasped the photo as casually as I could, only willpower preventing my hands from shaking with excitement. Harry pointed at the picture.

"Nineteen seventy-three."

There were three men in the shot, all with long hair held in place by woven headbands, all wearing coloured long shirts over baggy trousers. Pseudo Hippies at that point. Martin had his arms around two men who were much younger than him. Harry peered over my shoulder. I could smell his tobacco breath. A drug he hadn't given up.

"He was a poufter. Still is I expect, unless somebody's managed to kill him off. Don't know he ever slept with women but he could have. Never tell what he was up to most the time."

So, Martin Stanford-Smythe could be Lucy's father.

"Women and men, you reckon?"

"He was a control freak, I know that."

I stared hard at the picture, trying to imagine the other two men thirty eight years on. With Martin there could be no mistake, his age, his height, the set of his jaw, the steel blue eyes, the sneer, all pointing to the man who'd stopped me in the street, the man at my brothers wedding. My heart banged like a message drum.

"Did you ever notice a specific woman with him?"

"Could have. Like I said, he was a collector of the young and the vulnerable."

"Can I keep this photo?"

"Be my guest. I've only kept it all these years because him, the red headed one on the left, he's my brother, Jason. Was my brother Jason. Should have left him in Sydney."

"What happened?"

"He died of an overdose. He was only seventeen when that bastard got his claws into him. Ended up on crack. All sorts of stuff. I told him he was an idiot. I tried to warn him off it. I tried to warn him off that bastard. Never worked."

His anger dropped a couple of registers.

"He was too young, too stupid. Did some nasty things, mind."

"What did the police do? When he died."

"What they always do. Nothing. He was just another statistic."

I wondered how come the local cop, Lachlin, had done nothing. In such a small town he'd have known them all, been friendly with most of them, probably. Harry quietly closed the window, enclosing himself within his memories. I felt guilty for raising them. Tears had formed in his eyes but he sniffed hard and they didn't fall.

"He was no age at all."

Harry spoke to the floor.

"I gave up the drugs. Even weed. Made me a morose hermit. Why they call me Happy Harry down town. It's a joke. I'm a fucking joke."

He looked up. A sorrowful sight. I remembered his sorrow when I'd put down his dog. He'd been spaced out back then, bewilderment and hurt combined. He was hurting again. He'd been reminded of his lost brother, and his dog. Love takes many forms. I conjectured on where his brother could be buried. Out the back of the shack I guessed. I didn't like to ask. Shit, I was turning into a softie. *Memo: No emotional involvement, remember?* I'd got all I wanted for the moment. Brian had printed up some cards for me. I handed one over.

"Call me. Anytime. Landline or mobile. If you think of anything else. You do have a mobile?"

He nodded, took the card and read it out loud.

"Holly Day. Market Research. Etc, etc."

He roared with laughter allowing his tears to flow.

"Etc, etc. I like it!"

"Etc does cover a multitude of sins."

"Good on you. Nice to catch up. Must do it again."

I agreed we would. We shook hands and I thanked him for his help. As I made my way through the door it squeaked on its rusting hinges. Harry made for the rifle. He stood watching me as I walked out. A few metres down the track I turned. He was leaning against the door jamb, melting into his dark, ancient, spiritual surroundings. I felt fond of him already. Almost as an after thought he yelled out to me.

"You never said who your friend was."

I threw back the answer waiting to view his expression when it hit him.

"Lucy Knight. Her mother is Giselle Knight."

His eyes opened wide. His grip on the rifle tightened. He moved his feet further apart as if the ground was shifting beneath him. A classic Clint Eastwood stance. The voice though was dream-like.

"Giselle, the gypsy. Everybody knew her. She spread her love around, if you get my meaning."

I sure did. It meant any number of men could be Lucy's father, including

Hippie Harry himself. I walked on, waving my farewell over my shoulder, pleased with myself for managing to stuff one of his moth eaten beanies into my pocket while he wasn't looking. Bound to be hairs on it. DNA. Lucy could do worse than have Harry for a father. Okay, maybe he'd been, and still was, a no-hoper, but he was definitely kind. Sad even. But then, that could all be an act.

Once in the Valiant I did a U turn and headed back to the bitumen. At least Hippie Harry had once believed in something. So what if the hippie dream of eternal love, peace and harmony hadn't worked out, had anybody done any better? Shit, I was turning into a greenie. Better than being a pinkie like Auntie. Maybe.

ELEVEN

I hadn't thought too much about Mario since the wedding, and I didn't really expect to hear from him again, but he'd phoned asking about the diaries. Under the influence of drink and lust at the wedding reception I'd mentioned them to him. I expected him at eight a.m. I'd been up since six. I needed time to evolve from the half-drowned-cat look to that of a sexy babe. A time consuming worry. While putting on my sleek cornflower blue tights it occurred to me that he'd be requiring breakfast, before or after he'd had me. It was already seven forty-five. No time to shop. I checked the fridge. One rasher of bacon, two eggs, couple of slices of white bread, drabs of vegemite in a messy jar and two shrivelled up cherry tomatoes. For my lifestyle, quite a healthy choice.

The doorbell rang three minutes early. I skidded down the hall, gave my hair one last flick, practised fluttering my eyelashes and opened the door. Mario held a bunch of yellow chrysanthemums, unwrapped, clearly snitched from a neighbour's garden. Only lust prevented me from slamming the door in his face. He grinned like a guilty ten year old as he handed over the straggly bunch.

"Last minute decision."

In spite of the pathetic bouquet I beckoned him in. I pushed Mario into the kitchen, panting enthusiastically but instead of the rampant shagging I'd prepared myself for he gave my cheek a friendly peck. A peck? He pointed to the flowers.

"For the, the enjoyment at the reception."

That put a stop to the panting. A stolen bunch of flowers for the shag in the limo? I felt like kicking him in the groin. Best not damage the goods. I glared. He reassessed his comment.

"It was wonderful."

I melted, naturally.

"I do like the flowers."

Which I did but they hadn't stopped my libido dropping to ground level. I put the flowers in a vase. I turned with the forced glee of a newly-wed, hoping he'd elevate my desire to somewhere more appropriate.

"There's a choice of four things on the breakfast menu."

A slight lie. He spoke through clenched teeth.

"Sorry, I meant, I would come over breakfast time. I have already eaten."

My libido stayed where it was. I grimaced, picturing him scoffing down his morning spaghetti and meat balls, in a white tiled kitchen with garlic hanging on a rope from the ceiling. I'd seen a few Italian movies on SBS. He smiled, innocently.

"You see, I only eat a certain kind of fibre for breakfast."

I wasn't going to ask.

"You know, cereals."

"I know what cereals are!"

They're shredded cardboard tossed in a kilo of coloured sugar and furiously shaken by machines, that's what cereals are. He nodded towards the fridge.

"You go ahead."

The morning was not going to plan. I forced a smile.

"Coffee then?"

"Please."

I busied myself with the plunger while he sat staring at me. I hoped he wasn't seeing what I'd seen in the bathroom mirror an hour before. I gathered up a serious frame of mind.

"Did you know that there's criminal activity going on all around us?"

His face brightened.

"In this beautiful part of the country?"

He was taking the piss. The nerve. I was doing my best to come over like a real investigator and he thought it was funny. He loaded it on.

"You mean country towns have criminals?"

He broke into laughter. I'd taken the bait.

"It is not funny!"

"The way you told it, it is."

"Oh."

I felt both stupid and miffed. *Memo: Watch out for this guy's oddball sense of humour.* I handed over his black coffee, poured milk in mine and blatantly piled in four spoonfuls of sugar. My glare dared him to comment. He grinned. I did not stir the drink. I pointed to a kitchen chair. He sat. No thought of sex now.

"I'll fetch the first diary."

"Right."

I left him sipping his coffee. I'd already searched through several of the diaries and while there were lots of trivial details, including the references to MSS, hard evidence was scanty. I returned and plonked the diary on the table.

"I thought it'd be easier if I read it out loud."

"By all means."

He waited, patiently, lips parted in eager anticipation. It was like being back in Grade six. I settled on the stool, pushed the hair off my forehead, took a deep breath, flipped over the first page and began.

'May 1973. Day one.'

"Nothing before that day?"

If looks could kill I'd be out collecting for his funeral. He recoiled.

"Sorry."

"I should think so."

'Day one. Train up from Sydney. Packed. Mostly Uni students. The ripple of excitement is amazing. Everyone laughing and shouting and talking at top volume. It is a seriously fabulous feeling, like we're

comrades embarking on a peaceful revolution. Subjects discussed cover the full range; art, law, politics, religion, society, money, the environment and of course war, at which everyone groans. We sound like a bunch of lefties. We mostly are. We all agreed the world needed to be saved from itself. Lots had brought their own stash. Joints passed round. Everything for the common good, filling the train with a cute smell.'

That fitted the legend.

'Arriving at Nimbin was like being in a time warp. Talk about a one horse town. A few straggly shops, a pub and of course the church. Basically one longish street then paddocks and mountains. Amazing. Sad it's so far from the beach but the boys are going to build a sauna and there will be swimming in the creeks for sure. Some of us joined forces before the day was over. We settled down in tents and make-shift huts with some on the backs of Utes or inside Kombi vans. Not much privacy but the communal feeling is good. Liberating. I shared a tent with one boy and three girls. Late in the evening I met MSS.'

I paused to emphasise the reference to MSS. Mario made no remark but stared into the distance at my unwashed crockery. *Memo: Get into some sort of routine with the washing up.* I began again.

'MSS. Older than most of us. Has to be almost thirty. He just blew in, checked us all over and stayed about an hour. One girl said he was with the cops, or maybe the government. He had sinister eyes, cold as steel yet his smile was seductive as any cult leader. He told us he was happy to help anyone who wanted it. Us girls guessed what that meant but the boy thought he meant drugs. MSS showed interest when I said I was a painter. Creepy. We were all glad when he left. The three of us shared a joint and half a bottle of what I think was brandy. We soon forgot about MSS. HP arrived later. We'd met on the train. We huddled up together. A nice first day.'

"Another initial. HP."

"Do all women keep names so secret?"

"If they think somebody's likely to read their thoughts, yes."

Mario nodded thoughtfully.

"Good point."

What I couldn't understand was her keeping such an ambiguous diary at all. Mario, as if reading my thoughts, came up with a suggestion.

"Maybe she intended to write a book someday."

One answer. He pointed to the diary.

"Any more?"

"Heaps."

He settled back to listen.

Day Two. Woke to misty fog. Made my way to the tap outside the Hall. Used one of the toilet holes dug yesterday by a bunch of he-man types. Funny squatting over a hole, divided from the next squatter by a metre high strip of hessian. Fun though, chatting in between dribbles, grunts, plops and farts. Everyone laughed at the particularly loud ones. Kate, a big built girl, did her best to outdo the men, equal opportunity and all that. Later we went to the Rainbow Café, rented by the Student Union. Volunteers get one Nimbuck a day to be exchanged for a meal. A great collective idea. After sundown it grew cool and damp. A few musicians braved it onto the open stage. I danced until I was fit to drop. The Incredible String Band played. Spoke briefly to the organisers. They were expecting over eight thousand people to attend over the ten days. Law students excite us with their talk of freedom of speech and assembly. Hari Krishna's constant chanting gets me down but their food is good and cheap and they have their rights. A group of students put gumboots on sticks and marched around chanting, Harry Gumboots, Harry Gumboots. Not exactly the right thing to do yet we all laughed. Had sex with HP. Not bothered if it does or does not happen again.'

Mario leaned his chin on his hands. He seemed to be far away.

"You're not interested in this, are you?"

He lifted up his head.

"In my experience you have to read a lot of boring information before you come across a gem."

"There's the extra initial, HP. And she did have sex with him, so he is a potential candidate."

"True but it could also be a blind alley."

Was the man negative or what?

"Here, MSS again. *'MSS asked to see some of my work. He said he would buy whatever I paint. Odd. Why would he want to buy my work?'*

Mario pointed to the diary.

"Now that is a gem. It says a lot."

I couldn't think why it said a lot. Martin SS could just have fancied her. Having read it verbatim I decided to do the rest shorthand.

"I'll only pick out the gems from now on."

Picking a gem was good practice for any investigator, like following the nose. *Memo: Time for a check up of my bashed nose.* I turned each page and scanned for what I thought was interesting information, gem or no gem.

'Used sauna for the first time. Fabulous idea. Built of corrugated iron with a forty four gallon drum for the fire stuck in the wall and lots of rocks in the middle to pour water on and make steam.'

I was impressed.

"I might build me one of them."

"The Romans had them at least two thousand years ago."

Another black mark. He's more of a smart arse than I am. I kept going.

'Dark and crowded in the sauna. Sweaty naked bodies, all crushed together, all giggling. Felt a man slip inside me. It was HP, so I went along for the ride.'

More than once meant more chance of conception.

'Lay next to BT who noisily bonked a brown haired girl with big tits. Afternoon, collected magic mushrooms. Abundant Nature. Locals provide cows. Cows provide dung. Dung helps to provide mushrooms and so the world goes round.'

Mario stood up.

"All this sex and drugs we know about already, right?"

It was legendary and I had to admit there'd bound to be a fair bit written about it. There was also the mention of MSS and HP. And it was Giselle herself speaking.

"There's been reference to two sets of initials that might be useful."

"Possibly."

"Mario!"

"What day are we on?"

"I've skipped heaps but day four."

"Six more days of the festival then. And no certainty it was during the festival that your friend was conceived. It could have been days after. Or even before."

"Lucy seemed pretty sure it was during. And she was there, sort of."

Mario laughed and strolled into the kitchen to put on the jug. The coffee had gone cold.

"Four sugars."

I was getting just as excited about the Case as I was at having him around.

Almost. I kept reading.

'Morning. Painted a landscape in oils. I'd had some materials bought up from Lismore. Did another four. Next day, MSS bought them all. He asked if I painted on ceramics. Said I could. He asked who my favourite painters were. That man is so weird. He has to be on something stronger than I am. Still, I took the money.'

Mario bought in the coffee.

"So, Martin was pestering her to paint for him. He must have had something in mind."

"So it seems."

I flicked through the pages repeating blah, blah, blah, when there was nothing significant. I stopped at one paragraph.

"Listen to this."

'The local policeman mentioned to a group of us that he thought HP might be a government spy. I doubt it very much.'

Mario leaned over my shoulder and read the page.

"A government spy. Really?"

"The Student Union. They had to be communists, right? According to the far right nut cases. Nothing changes."

"Ah, yes, dear old ASIO. At the beck and call."

That sounded a bit strange coming from Mario but then he'd said he was a journalist and they know heaps of stuff about heaps of things.

"Do you really think ASIO was there?"

The idea of ASIO was exciting.

"Anything is possible and this HP could have been a mole."

"That's a definite gem then?"

"It very well could be."

He gave me a cuddle. I did my best to concentrate on Giselle's written thoughts.

'Cool band. Slept with a musician. Lead guitarist. Fantastic. I like him. Pity he's only passing through on his way up north. Never told me his name. I never asked.'

"A musician. A complete unknowable but it could be him."

Mario shrugged.

"One chance in a million."

"We are all one chance in a million, no matter what any religion promotes."

He grinned.

'Sunshine through mist. Fabulous. Saw the brightest morning star. Made me sing Lucy in the Sky with Diamonds all day. If I ever have a daughter I shall call her Lucy."

For me, that was a one hundred per cent gem. I recalled the number of times I'd heard Giselle singing or humming that tune.

"Go on, Holly."

"Sorry, daydreaming."

'Several times was offered LSD. Refused. Why buy speed when the mushrooms are free for the picking?'

She was clearly wanting the experience of drugs. But then wasn't everybody?

"Pity she didn't refuse everything, always."

Mario squeezed my shoulder.

"You feel sorry for her."

"She's my best friend's mother. I've always been fond of her, especially after my own mum died. Besides, nobody deserves an addiction like hers. And look at her now. Who knows what she's been through. She was, is, special."

Mario kissed me full on the lips. I grabbed him and kissed him back. Things were warming up. We dragged each other to the bedroom. My shirt was almost off and his pants were dangling at his feet when his mobile rang. Shit. I fell onto the bed, alone.

"Don't answer it!"

He did.

"Sorry."

Sorry! *Memo: He answers his phone even when sex is imminent. Another black mark.* He put away his mobile.

"My, er, informant. Something I'm working on. I have to go. It is truly important. Sorry."

That word again.

"Is it a gem? A diamond? Or a ruby lipped blonde?"

Mario sighed loudly and tucked his shirt in his pants.

"You are being stupid."

He was right, I was. He gently stroked my face, as if understanding my disappointment. Was he disappointed?

"This information will not wait. You and me, can."

Shit, what did he know? He made for the door. I made for a cold shower. When I got out I phoned Lucy. The news was neither good nor bad, the doctors being their usual non committal selves. I told her before she asked.

"Leech, still no positive news as to your father's identity."

"Sure. Keep trying. Have to go. Mum is going off for some tests."

"Okay. Bye."

"Bye."

Deep down did Lucy really want me to find her father? Or was she doing it only for her mother's sake? I returned to the diaries, refreshed and satisfied by the Mars Bar I'd eaten.

'Day Five. Been sick. Magic mushrooms? HP spent a few hours with me. No sex. A group visited and discussed the logging of old growth forests. Had sex with BT. Was too ill to say no.'

Another possible father.

'HP visited. Shared a joint. No sex. Later, the cop told me to keep away from him. Cannot believe there is anything bad about him. Day Six. Big day. Drug bust. Three men growing nine seedlings, fined eighty dollars each. Batch of police arrived. Twenty First division, police not army. Media thronged because the police made out it was heroin being used. It was not. Student lawyers worked for the accused. A pump gun was stolen from a cop. After threats it was returned, by a third person. Not me. This last action galvanised all the people here. A sort of bonding occurred. Love, peace and harmony in action. Beautiful to see. Except now the Alpha males are re grouping. MSS prominent as usual.'

So he was still there and still stirring things up.

'Day Seven: Spent time painting. MSS called and paid for several sketches. He asked if I was aware that some of the Masters had been proven forgeries. I was surprised and said so.'

A major clue to Martin SS's real agenda? My mind turned over the bits of the jigsaw that were beginning to form. It seemed unlikely that MSS was the father. No sex with him was ever mentioned. I flipped to the final day.

'The mass exodus. Many stayed on. Some hoping to set up special titles on blocks of land for sale. Some close in. Some far out. HP asked if I wanted to be part of a community called Rumbledown. Told him, no money. MSS offered to lend me three hundred dollars to buy in. I took the money. I bought in.'

She'd fallen straight into the trap. That's how it seemed to me. Life would never be the same for Nimbin. It would never be the same for Giselle. Or Lucy. Or me, for that matter.

TWELVE

Tantalising though they were, the diaries offered up nothing definite about Lucy's father. All I had to go on were the initials. It could well be someone not even mentioned, which would leave me up the creek without a paddle. I couldn't rule out Hippie Harry or Martin SS, even though Giselle hadn't mentioned sex with them.

Brian phoned. He'd spent the last week searching out information on Martin Stanford-Smythe. He was a right wing conservative, had won his seat for a second term and was popular with the voters. He'd had dozens of trips overseas, some official government business, some his own. Very convenient. He'd been associated with De Rossi Constructions for years and was an adviser when tenders for government contracts went in, including for Aged Care Facilities. He'd supposedly declared his business interests, although there were vague trails to off-shore tax havens. The import/export business run by Marina de Rossi, now Marina Knight, dealt in art works. It appeared to be legitimate. Information was piling up. The kind of people Giselle had been involved with were widening the scope of the Case, inspiring more and more questions. All a good investigator needed was to come up with the answers.

I'd spent all afternoon on an easy Case, searching out an idiot who'd been abusing somebody's fifteen year old daughter. I caught up with him, cool as ice, collecting her from her private school, ready to whisk her away to who knows where, to do who knows what, for who knows how long. I took photos of the two together, his hands all over her. The rest was easy. Show photos to him. Bit of verbal blackmail. I drag her into my car. She is handed over to daddy. Me happy with a nice fat fee. What they did with him and the girl was up to the father and the cops. Me, I'd put his tackle through a meat blender. He was old enough to be her grandfather and she needed a good talking to, at least.

After that escapade I bought chips and pizza, a bottle of red, a packet of smokes for the odd occasion I needed one and lots of Mars bars, needed all the time. Before watching my favourite TV show I intended to list all the initials and known men who possibly had, or definitely had, sex with Giselle. There was also the unnamed musician. Was there a reason Giselle had even mentioned him, apart from liking him? A clue or a drug fuelled lapse?

After showering I was ready to relax with the paperwork when I thought about my message bank. It was six p.m. Auntie Gert, her voice pitched high as a Chinese kite, told me she was dropping round dead on seven with some important news and I needed to supply tea. Shit, I'd already eaten. Anyhow, what important news could she possibly have? That her second hip was on the way out? That another of her friends had died? Aspirin overdose? That dad had ripped into her for leaving her old dentures in his bathroom cabinet? Interesting stuff like that?

I checked the fridge. An apple, bits of bread and cheese and in the freezer one out-of-date meat pie and a carton of vanilla ice cream. It would have to be take-away. Luckily, Auntie loves Chinese food even though she hates the language, the high tones playing havoc with her hearing aid and deciphering R's from L's was just not on her agenda. I phoned the shop and ordered a large Special rice and a large Chicken Chow Mein. Best not to give old people too much choice else they'd come to expect it. I swept the rubbish off the table into a plastic bag, threw over a tablecloth I hadn't used since last Xmas, placed on it two napkins to match, cutlery, chopsticks and two crystal wine glasses from Italy, via Big W. I dashed to the takeaway and was back by six-fifty, hot and bothered, yet curious. I scraped all the food into two casserole dishes and put them in the oven to keep warm. There was a knock just as I closed the oven door. She was on time, behaving like a proper guest. Curiouser and curiouser.

She waltzed in wearing her pink cardie over a pink blouse with her pink polyester pants dangling over her pink sandals. A woollen crochet hat of three shades of pink was balanced on her head with a pink ribbon bow dangling from it. An eighty year old Shirley Temple. She made my heart sing. She followed me through to the kitchen and back again as I placed the dishes and bowls on the table. I directed her to sit. She sat. She grinned like an ape. At least she had her teeth in.

"Guess what?"

I played it cool.

"You're getting married again."

She schreeched with laughter.

"I might miss sex, my dear, but no way do I want a man 24/7, thank you very much."

An attitude we'd had in common for a while, but then Mario had arrived on the scene. She went on.

"Last Thursday Arthur Maloney asked me out on a date. I told him even his son was too old for me. Not enough spark left. He didn't even laugh."

This was exciting news? I placed a hefty portion of food on each plate. Auntie picked up one chopstick. She'd learnt how to spear a piece then push it into her mouth with some grace. Bad arthritis in her fingers. She gazed up at me. A large chunk of chicken was poised a millimetre from her bright pink lips.

"I got news might be good for a brilliant Private Eye."

She tells everybody down the Centre that as a private investigator I kill at least one crook a week. A good dash of fiction never hurt any old person.

"So, what is this news?"

She hesitated while she swallowed her food, hardly chewing, I noted.

"It could be just what you're looking for."

"You've found out who is Lucy's father!"

She screwed up her face like a newborn.

"No, of course not. But it might have a bearing on it."

"What might?"

I shoved a large batch of rice and chow mein into my mouth and sat staring at her while I chewed. She stabbed and shovelled a pale yellow curl of bamboo shoot into her mouth. This time she chewed, very slowly, pale glutinous sauce dribbling down her chin. Shit, she could be so infuriating. I sighed as loud as I could with a full mouth. She'd completed her swallowing.

"Anyway I don't know what all the fuss is about. Her father's bound to be a junkie. The place was full of them back then. Still is. Ask anybody."

I was tired and full of food and was far from being cool as a cucumber.

"Come on, Auntie. Out with it. Please."

She soaked up the dribble with her napkin, which of course meant I'd have to wash it. She settled back in her chair.

"There's a scam going on round here. Being going on for years."

It was probably the cheap roofing scam. Cash up front. Well known. I kept eating while side glancing at her. She eyed me with disdain. She was sulking at my lack of enthusiasm. I knew she wouldn't be able to keep it to herself much longer. She put on her indignant tone.

"Old people are getting their valuables stolen. Well some are. And most don't get paid what their goods are worth when they have to sell them."

So what was new? Second hand furniture dealers are up there with second hand car dealers when it came to daylight robbery.

"You should follow it up. You're a brilliant PI"

It was hard to squirm out of a compliment like that. I sighed loudly.

"Has this anything to do with my main Case?"

"You recall Patsy Dougherty?"

I lied.

"Vaguely."

"Her husband was one of those Ambassadors to somewhere. Overseas trips. Business deals all over the world. Lived in style. Posh house. Posh cars. Posh prostitutes."

Auntie drifted off as she chewed on the remnant stuck to her plastic teeth.

"And?"

"He died. He left her very well off. A masssive house. Lennox way. On the hill. It's all housing estates now. Disgusting."

"And?"

"She had lots of antiques and paintings. So when she had to go into one of those Homes, ones like you and your dad promised I'd never go into, well she had to sell most of it."

"And?"

She sat back and stared into space for a good five minutes. Old people seem do this a lot. Is there something out there only they can see? Some days I'd have happily handed her over to any Home that would take her. She stirred.

"She was sure to get good money for the house but then one day this trio came round to see her. Interested in buying her furniture and stuff. They said they worked for the people who owned the Old People's Home she was buying into."

My heart flipped.

"Was it a De Rossi Constructions Home?'

"I think that was the name. Anyway, she let them talk her into buying all her house full, as a job lot. All that money and no brains. Sad."

The scam sounded familiar.

"The thing was, she had a Picasso."

I laughed.

"Everybody has a Picasso."

Auntie flicked me an angry look.

"Not a print, you dumb-dumb. A real one."

"A real, genuine, Picasso?"

"Yes. He painted her great aunt in the nineteen twenties. Or was it the nineteen thirties? She was naked, so obviously a slut. Like that other woman I read about in the Woman's Weekly. Leigh Miller. Picasso painted her. She must have been a slut too. Anyway, Picasso gave the picture to Patsy's great aunt in exchange for her body. He signed it. The picture, not her body."

Auntie laughed at her own little joke.

"How do you know all this?"

"It was passed down to Patsy."

I could feel the dollar signs gathering involuntarily in my eyes.

"It must be worth heaps."

"That's just it. She knew it was. She was stupid, but not that stupid. So she said they could have the rest of the stuff for the agreed price but not the Picasso. They tried to make out it was only a print. "

"They would."

Auntie drifted off again. I slammed my hand on the table.

"And?"

She sat bolt upright.

"It went missing."

"Missing?"

"The Picasso. It was all part of the scam. They must have cased the joint and took off with it first chance."

"And it was never recovered?"

She shook her head, the pink ribbon fluttering.

"They came back later and told her they'd auctioned it off and had a copy painted for her. Which they gave her. That was the story."

"And the money?"

"No idea about that. She's a bit doo-lally nowadays."

"What about the police?"

"She wouldn't call the police. Not her. There'd been a bit of bother with her husband way back."

"Are you taking the piss?"

"That's discrimination, that is. Just because I'm old."

She grinned.

"I bet you are really, really interested?"

"How did you find all this out?"

Auntie Gert touched her nose with an arthritic finger stained with sixty odd years of tobacco.

"I just do. They had the cheek to go back and say her place at the Home had been sold to somebody else."

"It all sounds a bit iffy?"

"Exactly. The really important news is this. As they were walking out of her house, she heard them whispering but she made out the name of Giselle Knight. She wrote it down."

My heart leaped. A genuine gem. I leaned over the table. Auntie Gert grinned, a satisfied look on her face.

"That got you."

"How did they know about Giselle?"

"She never said."

"Who were these people?"

"She was a bit vague. Memory gone. But she said the man was very tall, well dressed, a Scots College type. With polished shoes. She recalled that."

Funny how her generation noticed polished shoes.

"And two old biddies were with him. To make her feel comfortable, I suppose."

Two old ladies. Too much of a coincidence.

"Sisters. Twins even. Dressed the same. Plump. Plain. Not as sexy as me."

I did my best not to laugh. This was unreal. The way they were being described, it sounded like Tweedledum and Tweedledee from the Op Shop. I wanted to crush Auntie to my chest. But that might have caused a heart attack so I refrained. I had enough on my plate without a hospital run. Another piece of the jigsaw.

"So why not call the police?"

"I told you. Calling the police is not something Patsy Dougherty would do. Her late husband was involved in some dodgy deals in his time. It might have opened up a can of worms."

"You think those people might have threatened to reveal stuff about her husband?"

"Could have done."

"But a Picasso?"

"Bound to have been insured."

"Maybe that's all it was, insurance fraud and she was part of it."

"I don't think so, my dear."

"So all this was never officially reported?"

"And she had to find another Home. She's got a place few miles out of Sydney. Not a De Rossi one either. I've got the address."

"How?"

"I used to clean for her. Kept in touch. Once every few years."

"We could visit her. I'll pay the fares down."

"And back, I hope."

She placed her elbows on the table.

"It's been a while since I saw Patsy. She might be totally demented by now."

I'd take the risk. It was a connection I had to follow.

"I'll book for early next week. Ok?"

Auntie Gert stood up and made for her bag.

"Let me check."

Like she had somewhere else to go. She had.

"Doctors on Monday. Not that they do anything. Tuesday Aromatherapy. It doesn't work but I like the smells. Thursday, toe nails. Wednesday looks good."

"Wednesday it is then."

"I'll need to pack panty pads. The bladder's playing up again."

"I'll pay for the extra twenty kilo baggage."

"I'll take the extra thick ones then."

I shook my head at her honesty and humour. Is that what her wisdom was? Honesty and humour?

"Anything else?"

"You trying to get rid of me?"

I was hanging out for my usual dose of Mars Bars and *Midsomer Murders*. I had to lie.

"I am a bit busy. With the Case."

Auntie Gert eyed me knowingly.

"You got that Italian coming round?"

If only.

"No."

"You got any icecream?"

"Icecream?"

"The meal was very nice, Holly. I like icecream for afters. Doctor says it's no good for me. What does he know. I bet I outlive him."

She probably would. Out of spite. This was a chance to please her with something that was white instead of pink.

"I have vanilla ice cream. Especially bought for you."

Her eyes lit up. She licked her lips expectantly. I knew we'd be watching tele together soon. The sight of her innocent pleasure was worth the lie.

THIRTEEN

Auntie Gert's timetable left me a few days free, so I was off to see Hippie Harry again. He knew more than he was letting on. I wanted to ask if Martin SS was the only one to buy Giselle's art work and if it was him who supplied her with drugs. Or was it the man she moved up north with? If so, who was he? Mario wanted to come with me. I wasn't keen. Pleasure is one thing, work another. A journo out for a scoop is bound to be a liability, but he'd asked me on the point of our having sex. Cunning. Lust made me quickly agree.

As her mother's condition was stable, Lucy was driving down from Noosa to meet up with me at Nimbin. She'd chattered on the phone like an excited preschooler so I guessed she was happy to escape the drama of a mother in hospital. When asking the locals if they knew anyone who'd been at the Festival, I didn't get much joy. Didn't expect to. Small towns are notorious for keeping small town secrets. Serious questions from strangers are generally answered ambiguously.

I sat with Mario at the Mirage Café, our table close to the pavement, a good vantage point to view the goings on at the top end of town. We'd both settled for tea and muffins. A couple of customers acknowledged me with a token nod. Mario was viewed with more suspicion, having refused all offers of weed with an arrogant flick of his hand, as if swatting mossies. I'd at least refused with a pensive sigh. The young were offered buds. Made me feel old. *Memo: Start saving for cosmetic surgery.*

We sipped our tea. I cast a gaze over the other customers.

There'd be a boat load of stories tucked inside their heads. I'd already sensed a philosophical divide between the early hippies and the second influx from the late eighties onwards, the latter being considered more no-hopers than true believers. Hard drugs abounded, although cannabis was still top of the list for locals and visitors alike. Commercial hemp growing was touted by the serious environmentalists of the region, which struck terror into the minds of right wing conservatives, god botherers and the ignorant. A good story line, I'd have thought.

"Mario, why not write about the clash of drug cultures in Australia, the old and the new?"

He gave me a withering look, then calmly checked his watch.

"What time is your friend to arrive?"

Shit, he'd lived on the Northern Rivers for years and still hadn't learned to slow down.

"Time is more laid back up here. Eleven could mean noon. Sometimes anything up to two p.m."

I enjoyed laying it on thick. He coughed pointedly at a man ferociously enjoying the sensation of a spliff the size of Texas. I decided to go through one of the later diaries while waiting for Lucy. I flipped open the book. Though most eyes were turned away, ears would be primed in our direction.

We both spoke quiet as we could.

"There's a few interesting things I didn't tell you about yet."

"Like what?"

I pointed to a paragraph.

"Here's one."

I turned the book round for Mario to read. He drew back.

"I see what you mean. A nursery rhyme is odd in this context."

"Odd? It's weird."

It had to be another code. No harm in reading the lines out loud.

"This little piggy went to market."

A few heads did a smart quarter turn. Not wanting to give anything away I put on a pathetic whine.

"Are country children really taught this colonial rubbish?"

Chuckles applauded my sentiment. Mario beamed pleasure at my cunning. Either that or his tackle was caught in his boxers. There were other references, some the same line, others different lines.

"This little piggy stayed home. Hmm."

Mario stared down at the page, doing his best to make sense of the initials and the nursery rhyme.

"It is clearly a kind of…what we think it is, but in reference to what? That's the hard part."

"Exactly. But."

I mouthed my response, trusting nobody in the café could read my lips from where they sat.

"Could it be, you know, piggies equals cops?"

Mario seemed unconvinced about this interpretation.

"Is there a similar subject being commented upon whenever these lines are used?"

"Not that I can sort out."

A lie. I'd already worked out that each time Giselle sold a work of art, one of the nursery lines would be written, along with a number. That could be the price. It was pure assumption but I wanted to keep it myself. Mario stood up, extricating himself with ease from the broad planked bench. He picked up our cups.

"I'll fetch more tea."

Pondering on a connection between little piggies and art, I almost jumped out of my skin when Lucy slammed herself down opposite me. Instinct made me snap shut the book.

"Leech. Hi."

I could smell her anger.

"I've been stuck behind one of those fucking tourist Kombies. Bright colours, dim fucking inmates. All the way up. Until they wheeled off to snap pickies of the Rock, or to share a bong, or take a pee, or whatever it is they do at such heights. Have you any fucking idea what doing under forty k's an hour does to a person like me?"

I had a very good idea. It was sitting in front of me. I touched her hand gently.

"Good to have you back, Leech."

She settled her tiny bum on the bench and leant over to me, letting the contents of her burgundy lace bra topple right to the edge of her black singlet. Eyes goggled from every direction. A guitarist began to strum what sounded like an Italian love song. It could have been from *Lethal Weapon* for all I knew.

"Things are going real well for mum. For once the fucking doctors told me the truth."

I hated to think how she'd got the truth out of them. Bagged them in the store room with a few karate chops?

"That's great."

Mario arrived with a tray. Lucy flicked her hand in his direction.

"Piss off, mate."

He almost toppled over with shock. Lucy stretched her small powerful body towards him, her hands pressing on the table to support her aggressive stance.

"This table is full, so fuck off!"

All eyes were on us. A stoush would vary another possibly boring day for the locals, but I was in no mood for it.

"Sit down, both of you!"

Lucy glared first at Mario then at me. She sat. Mario hovered close to me, the tray in mid air.

"This is Mario. Lucy, Mario. Mario, Lucy."

"What the fuck is he doing here?"

Sensing no fight was imminent the customers returned to their eating, yarning, strumming and smoking. Lucy's eyes smouldered.

"It was supposed to be you and me, Flab."

"I must have forgot to tell you."

Her eyes glazed over. Guilt trundled through my veins like a cattle train. I deserved the abattoir ending. I should have told him not to come. Am I addicted to him already? Lucy, seething, stupidly turned up the volume.

"Did I ask you to share MY case with HIM?"

Eyes and ears quickly returned their attention to us. Now it was my turn to be mad. I sizzled a glare at her. A Case could mean cops or Social Security, both unwanted visitors. Shit, I could have killed her then and there. I began the frustrating exercise of freeing my legs from the bench, hitting Mario in the groin as I did so. Served him right. I hissed a command.

"Let's get out of here."

I swung out towards the luke warm sunshine. Lucy, jacket flung over her shoulder, flounced out onto the pavement. Turning at the entrance she shouted to the onlookers.

"Why don't you all fuck off back to the planet you were on before I arrived!"

Mario was slowly making his way out, shrugging at everybody with an apologetic look. The silent consensus seemed writ large, 'women and their emotions, huh!' I pounded down the street.

Lucy caught up with me. She slung her jacket to the ground. She would have sensed me steaming anger. Her voice was low.

"I opened my big mouth, hey?"

"You sure did."

I strode on, panting heavily. Lucy trotted beside me.

"Where we going?"

"Just follow me."

"Where to?"

"The ends of the earth?"

If the earth had been flat I'd have dumped her right over the edge. We walked on fast. The Wagon was parked somewhere behind the shops. One main street. A few shops. Easy. Nothing wrong with my memory. *Memo: Is thirty eight too young to start HRT?* I read it was good for the brain.

I took the second turn to the right and there it was, my beautiful burgundy slice of heaven. As I unlocked the Valiant Lucy moved in close.

"Sorry about my big mouth."

"It'll be all round town by now."

It was an unreasonable comment. I'd already made my presence felt by asking so many questions but it was the way she'd put it. Her puppy eyes beamed apologies at me. I relented.

"Okay. We'll forget it."

Taking this as complete forgiveness, Lucy resumed her usual behaviour. She whispered cheekily in my ear.

"Does his hairy chest turn you on?"

I was getting so close to killing her.

"Get in! We'll pick your car up later."

She flip-flopped to the passenger side. Mario had caught up and settled himself in the back. I didn't care if he'd heard about him being hairy. I started the engine.

"We have work to do."

Lucy and Mario spoke in unison.

"Work? Where?"

"Harry's place. Hippie or Happy. I need to ask him more questions."

Lucy was unravelling her iPod.

"He some kind of clown?"

In normal society's terms I guess he is a clown. To me, though, he was a regular nice guy. I jerked the Valiant into first and roughly straightened up the vehicle. Lucy toppled forward. Made me feel better.

"Belt up!"

I reversed and backed out between a pink early model Kombi and a dark green Bedford van straight out of the dinosaur era. I pushed on into the main street and headed for Harry's place. With Mario quiet as a lamb and Lucy plugged into her crap music I had time to think. How best to question Harry? Who were the people in all the other photographs he had in his desk? Had he had sex with Giselle? At least I had his DNA to check. *Memo: Phone Brian if he's found a suitable place to send the DNA samples for analysis.*

Reaching the track to Harry's place I chugged nice and slow

over the rutted road. I was within a few hundred metres of where the barbed wire gate had been when I noticed something was wrong. I slammed on the brakes. We all lurched forward, Lucy screeching like a cat on heat.

"What the fuck!"

Mario, by now aware that something was wrong, pressed his finger to his lips. Lucy unravelled herself from the iPod. We all stared ahead. The broad white backside of an ambulance rested next to a cop car. The cops had cordoned off the place. Lots of instructions were being shouted. They couldn't have heard us coming. At high speed the Wagon roared like a tank, in first gear it purred like a nose trimmer. I shoved into reverse and gently edged back out. This was neither the time nor the place to be trapped into answering questions. Lucy noted the backwards movement.

"Are we lost?"

"Cops everywhere."

She bristled.

"Fuck."

Mario emphasised the point.

"And an ambulance is here."

"Somebody sick?"

It could only be Harry. I hoped it was a mild stroke or a broken leg or something he'd soon recover from. Had he managed to call for help on his mobile? Shit, my contact numbers could be in it. And he had my business card, somewhere. I turned left instead of right at the bottom of the track and parked in the shade of a eucalypt.

"We'll wait until they're gone."

Mario suddenly leaned over to me.

"I'll go and check it out."

"But the cops?"

"I can tell them I'm with the local paper, after a headline."

Lucy was in favour.

"That's a fucking brilliant idea."

"No it's not. That'll alert them to people knowing stuff."

"I will say the paper had a tip off. I could mention your brother."

"Don't you dare! I don't want him dragged into this. Not yet."

I looked in the mirror and noted Mario was smiling, ruefully. That was weird. He tapped me on the shoulder.

"I can maybe find out something important."

"Or you could just blow my cover."

"Not if I'm on my own."

"So, you want the Wagon."

Mario nodded.

"And what if they take the number and trace it to me?"

Mario sighed loudly as he opened the door.

"Do you really think you are the only one with brains. I shall park it out of sight. And give a false name, of course."

"Of course."

I wavered between miffed and respect.

"Oh, go on then. Don't be long. We get out here, Leech."

Mario drove off, crunching the gears like an L plater. I cringed. That was my gear box he was wrecking. He chugged up the track then veered out of sight. Me and Lucy went back to our hiding place. Lucy plugged herself in again and I squatted on a thick low branch. I found myself worrying for him. That was bad. Sure he was a spunk but great sex is not conducive to a long term relationship. Everybody knows that. *Memo: Concentrate on the Case not his body.*

He was back quicker than expected. He clambered out of the driving seat and sat down beside me. He put his arm around my shoulder. Bad sign. My breath somehow snagged in my throat. He spoke quietly.

"It is not good news."

My heart sank. His comforting arm had given the game away.

"It's that bad?"

Mario gazed ahead of him. He was trying to get the words out. I thought I'd help.

"He is going to be alright?"

He shook his head, slowly.

"Forensics are here. A body has been recovered. They would not tell me any more."

I gulped.

"Harry is dead?"

Mario nodded.

"How?"

"I'm sorry. I really am."

His voice was gentle. I looked over at Lucy, jigging to her crap music. If Harry was her father, her father was now dead. I pulled the plug out of her ear.

"Harry, the guy from the shack, he's dead."

"Fucking hell. What of ?"

The response was shot out by Mario.

"We don't yet know."

"So, I never got to meet him."

That was all Harry meant to her. Someone she never got to meet. I couldn't blame her. All Lucy wanted was for me to find the kind, decent, preferably famous man who'd fathered her. Mario's voice was calm.

"We can wait here until they've all gone. Or we can leave. Whatever you wish."

My wish was that Harry wasn't dead but I felt obligated to check things out.

"We should take a look round."

"Are you certain you want to?"

He looked at me with what would be described as love in the romance mags. Probably pity. A common error. I marched over to my trusty vehicle.

"We'll wait here."

We clambered back into the Wagon. I voiced my thoughts.

"Harry told me he was off drugs, so it can't be an OD."

"That's if he did stay off them."

"I guess."

It was only weeks since I'd met up with Harry again. Was it the abuse of chemicals that had eventually got to him? Liver gave way? Kidneys? Heart? With the cops and forensics at the scene there had to be more to it. I didn't want to dwell on what it might be.

The cops stayed for a further ten minutes after the ambulance wound its way down the track and out onto the bitumen. Once they'd gone we trekked on foot to the shack. They could have left a lowly cop to guard the place. Even so, Mario strode ahead. As a journalist no way should he ever be attached to the armed forces, he'd get everybody shot. Lucy wobbled on heels more appropriate to a night club than a bush track. I stepped out in trainers so used to sliding over rough terrain they'd win a gold medal at the Olympics if there was such an event. We kept to the grass so's not to leave easily visible footprints. I'd forced Lucy to leave her iPod behind, so she'd hear me if I gave the command to run like hell. As we approached the deserted shack there was only one thought on my mind. What was I going to find?

FOURTEEN

We stooped low, like soldiers on maneouvres scanning the horizon. Ten metres from the shack we halted. I took out my gun, hoping I didn't have to use it. I was a Beretta virgin. Not many women could admit to that. Mario stuttered an expletive when he saw the weapon, his thick eyebrows shooting upwards.

"A gun?"

I shrugged and whispered.

"It's a semi automatic. Like me."

I was somehow certain somebody had killed Harry; they could try with us. If I killed anybody I'd plead either self defence or insanity. I gestured for Mario and Lucy to hold back. Tiptoeing to the gently swinging door my heart used up blood like an express train using diesel. I gave the room a quick reckie. Shit, the state of the place. I beckoned to Mario and Lucy.

Replacing the gun in my bag I gazed about me. Mario and Lucy stumbled in, eyes gawking. The shack had been well and truly trashed. Momentarily struck dumb, we shuffled around, eyes swivelling from one corner to the next. Lucy was the first to break the silence.

'What the fuck happened?"

She'd covered her mouth with the tail end of her scarf.

"And if I ever smell this bad, shoot me."

A few persistent flies buzzed around searching for their prey. Mario heaved a sigh. Every drawer, cupboard, box, shelf and piece of furniture had been overturned, their contents strewn haphazardly across the floor. What had once been Harry's food supply was now littered in lumps and powdery collections. Crockery and bottles had been smashed to smithereens. The remains of a cereal breakfast were scattered across the table which tilted to one side, its legs kicked from under it. Mario voiced all our shared opinions.

"Why go to this trouble?"

"Maybe he wouldn't give them what they wanted?"

Or had Harry simply gone into a crazy rage and given himself a heart attack? No, it had to be another kind of crazy had done this. Lucy had it sussed out.

"Whatever they were after they fucking well killed him for it."

Mario snapped back.

"We do not know that for sure."

"They fucking took him away dead!"

"That is certain, yes. Cause as yet unknown."

"So what were they fucking after? Drugs?"

I took hold of Lucy's arm.

"That's what I need to find out."

"So, start investigating."

She shuffled off, kicking up dirt and paper, restless, kid-like. What puzzled me was whether Harry had even attempted to defend himself. He'd kept his rifle close when I was with him.

"He clearly didn't shoot at the intruder. No blood splattered all over."

Mario replied in his usual calm manner.

"Blood can be cleaned up easy, if it is fresh and you know how. On the other hand if he knew them, trusted them, he would be caught off guard."

My thought exactly. Plus, if there'd been more than one attacker he'd have stood no chance. I handed out plastic bags and gloves.

"Let's look for evidence."

Lucy guffawed.

"They wouldn't be that fucking stupid. Leaving evidence?"

I wagged my finger at her.

"People make mistakes. Even the cops."

"Do they fucking ever. Usually send the innocent ones to prison and set the guilty free."

Mario was shaking his head. I needed something to help explain the tragedy.

"There could be some tiny piece escaped notice. Right?"

Lucy kicked a can across the room. I let fire. Words, not bullets.

"Leech, have some respect! That belonged to a man who's not long died!"

She turned and glared at me.

"Whoever did this never had no respect for him, hey?"

She was right. We began to look for whatever presented itself. I perched the rickety chair I'd sat on against the wall. Strange feeling. I shivered. The tapestry armchair was on its back. I inserted my hand inside the ripped upholstered edge. Nothing. The rolltop desk had been reduced to kindling. All the contents were missing. All possible evidence destroyed. It was a job done with violent intent. Probably in front of Harry's bewildered eyes. That thought made me urgently want to find his killer. I understood it was a case for the cops, but if I could help in any way then maybe I'd be able to live with myself. It could have been my questioning of him that had led to his demise? *Memo: Remember, no emotional involvement?*

I raked out the scarred remains of what had once been inside the vintage Rayburn stove. I drew out the ash tray. A miniscule scrap of a photo that had survived the burning caught my eye. It was of a young girl, a tousle of hair, half a nose and a cheek, with the hint of soft childish lips close to the scorched edge. It could have been Lucy as a four year old. I placed it in my pocket. Lucy moved about aimlessly.

"Why don't you go outside, Leech and keep watch?"

She brightened up.

"If I see anybody do I kick his head in or tear off his balls?"

"Either is fine."

She'd do it too, as long as they didn't get to shoot her first. I had my head under the sink doing my best to unscrew the rusted pipe when I heard Mario gurgle. I cursed myself for leaving the gun in the bag. I withdrew my head, expecting him to be on the receiving end of a Gluck. Mario was alone, staring up at the ceiling, his mouth wide open, his fists clenched, his knuckles pure white. I followed his gaze. A twenty centimetre piece of frayed rope dangled from one of the rafters. The ends had been roughly hacked off. They must have cut Harry down. Mario's voice was barely audible.

"He must have hanged himself."

I was having none of that.

"Or somebody strung him up."

We both sank to the floor and pondered on the image of Hippie Harry swinging. I felt only anger. Mario sobbed. Shit, journos, no guts whatsoever. I put my arms around him and gave him a hug. There was a slight snap of a twig outside. We both shot to our feet. I called out softly.

"Lucy?"

I eased myself over to my bag and got out the gun. Pressing ourselves behind the door we waited. Lucy popped her head round the door and whispered.

"Yes?"

I pointed with the gun up to the rope. Her eyes widened.

"They fucking hanged him."

Mario had stemmed the tears but a choke remained in his voice.

"He could have done it himself."

The idea of Harry committing suicide didn't gel with me.

"No way!"

"How do any of us know what makes a person choose in the end?"

Lucy marched over to him and flashed him the look she gave to boyfriends when they said they were leaving her.

"What are you, some sort of fucking social worker?"

Mario brushed shaking hands through his hair. His lips were so tight I thought they'd snap. Shit, what was it with him? I touched his arm.

"You alright?"

"I am fine."

With that he pulled back his shoulders, pushed out his chest and faked a grin. He turned and left the shack. Lucy followed. Time to go. I took a last look round the place and joined my friends. We sauntered down the track, my feet plodding to the slowing beat of my heart. Sadness was at last enveloping me as I tried to accept the fact that Hippie Harry really was dead. The drive home was going to be quiet.

Cruising through Nimbin I wondered if the news had got round. How many people cared? How many would come forward with evidence, with gossip, or downright lies? Somebody always knows something. Who would say anything.

At length, my brain recuperated fully from its numbed state, I began to think rationally. Why had the portion of rope been left? It was evidence. Fingerprints. Okay, so forensics should have wiped it, taken a sample even. Which is what we should have done. Cut the whole thing down in fact. Had Hippie Harry been killed because he knew too much? Because I'd questioned him about Giselle? Had I stirred up old turf wars? Could it be suicide? Guilt scratched through my veins like barbed wire. I'd liked the man. He'd trusted me. That only made it worse. What had I done to him? Was it because he'd had sex with Giselle?

"What reason would they have to kill him?"

Lucy spoke with downright certainty.

"He was a hippie. A fucking junkie for years, you bet. He'd know dealers, big time crims, growers, distributors, even where the money was laundered."

Mario nodded.

"Possibly."

"He'd have all that knowledge tucked away in what was left of his brain. Which fucking cops were bent, which gang owned which plantation. Come to think of it why haven't they killed my boss? He knows the lot of them."

Mario answered quicker than I could.

"While Paul Diston is their lawyer he remains useful to them."

A light went on in Lucy's mind.

"I'm not fucking useful to any crims. They might kill me!"

Mario laughed.

"It's not fucking funny! I'm his assistant. I'm getting to know names and stuff. I could be in danger."

She had a point. I suspected we could all be in danger, the closer to the truth any of us got. So far, I was a million miles from anything like the truth.

"Better find another job, Leech."

She looked at me as if I was crazy.

"Where else am I going to get a job where I get paid so much for doing so little?"

There was no answer to that. I thought of the fragment of photo in my pocket. It did look like a young Lucy. I was excited about checking it out more thoroughly. Mario had found a couple of receipts from the Health Food store in town. One for ten kilos of bread flour. Nobody buys that much flour if they're intent on killing themselves. And the other receipt was for a thirty dollar top up on his mobile. His mobile. Shit. I'd left messages. I'd be traceable. I could be next on their hit list. I mentioned this fact. Lucy was scathing.

"And you the fucking clever one."

"Leech, all this started out as a search for your father. I had no idea this other stuff was going to turn up."

She lapsed into a few moments of silence then threw the next line out in short clips.

"Anyhow. That old man. Harry. The clown. He couldn't be my father. A no hoper. A junkie. So we can count him out."

Perhaps. My main concern was how to get my hands on Harry's mobile. I expected it was too late. The cops would have snaffled it straight away if the killer had missed it.

The rest of the journey we spent in normal rubbish talk. Like how useful it was to have crows and magpies clearing up the road kill, and taking bets on where the first perfumed wattle flowers had blossomed. We even debated seriously whether a wallaby we'd glimpsed hopping away was in fact a small kangaroo. Anything to take away thoughts of Harry.

I was chuffed to have a sample of his DNA. I'd decided not to confide to Pete what I'd discovered. It was a precaution. Now he was married to a De Rossi I had no clue if he was or was not involved in their business dealings. If they made him Managing Director of some subsidiary or another then I'd be sure he'd sold out. Innocent until proved guilty, that was the law. He is my brother. I love him. But how to get the mobile?

"So what do I do next?"

Mario answered as if he'd been thinking about it too.

"It is a good idea to let whoever is involved to make the first move."

Great. Their first move might be my final move. To the cemetery.

Soon as we got home I flopped onto the sofa with a large glass of red. Mario turned on the TV. The three of us cuddled up on the sofa, me between Mario and Lucy, just in case. The news came on. It was the Barbie Doll presenter, complete with blonde hair and American teeth. She ploughed through the car accidents, political blunders, the latest Sydney shootings, the war reports, brief celebrity scandals, football scores, the weather and then it came.

'Breaking news. A man in his late sixties has been discovered dead in his home near the Northern Rivers town of Nimbin. A police spokesperson said the man's death was not being treated as suspicious.'

As one, we shot up off the sofa. Lucy's mouth was wide open. Mario frowned. I spoke our thoughts.

"Not suspicious? Who are they kidding?"

Mario switched over to the National News. Harry wasn't mentioned, though we could have missed it. There was an angry tremble in my voice.

"They have to be joking. It's so obvious."

Lucy began marching around the room.

"It's going to be another fucking cover up!"

Considering she hadn't met Harry I was surprised at her vehemence but then she knew first hand how so called justice worked. Mario's response was, as usual, rational.

"They cannot state it was suicide, or anything else, until they have contacted relatives."

"Mario, suicide? That is bullshit."

Lucy agreed.

"Of course they killed him. You saw the fucking rope. Reckon he could have fixed that up himself and dropped from it?"

Mario was unflustered.

"It happens."

He was definitely out of order.

"No way would he kill himself, Mario. He agreed to meet up with me. Sure he was scared of somebody. Even warned me against the weirdos."

"The evidence so far would not stand up in court."

Lucy yelled at him.

"Listen, smartarse, if Flab says the man wasn't the type to kill himself, then he wasn't. Right!"

Mario shook his head.

"Why would anyone want to cover up the death of an old Hippie?"

Lucy pressed home her reasoning.

"Because he knew too much, that's why. About drug deals. About bent cops. About criminal activity. About why Humpty

Dumpty fell of the fucking wall! How the fuck should I know but they've sure got rid of him for some reason. You saw the rope."

Mario's face went ashen. Why?

"We have to find out what really happened."

"Too fucking right."

I glanced at the fury in my best friend's eyes. Was she at last pondering on the possibility that Harry might have been her father? That would make his murder a more personal insult. She stopped pacing the floor and turned.

"Maybe that old hippie knew my father...Nah. Fucking stupid idea."

I feigned ignorance of any connection. Telling lies got easier the more I did it. I announced my decision.

"I'm going back up there, now.

Mario hesitated.

"We went through anything that could resemble evidence, Holly."

"I know that."

Lucy sat down.

"Yeh. Nothing can bring him back."

"Leech, we are talking murder!"

"Sure but what good?"

I put on my jacket, grabbed my bag with its usual weapons and fetched a couple of torches from the laundry.

"You two wankers stay here and watch for any news updates."

I slammed the door behind me. I wasn't keen on driving up there by myself but I would do it. I could be brave even when I was shit scared. It just took a lot of whistling. I'd started to back out the Valiant when the pair came chasing after me clambering into their jackets. All the doors of the Wagon were open. No central locking in my little beauty. *Memo: Lock all car doors when away from it. Second Memo: Check the cost of bomb detectors.* Okay, so I was being paranoid. Investigators have to be. I let the Valiant go as fast as it wanted. No traffic this time of night.

We smelt the smoke long before we could see it. The fire had almost died down, pressed into the ground by the damp air that descended each night. Easing my way along the track with only side lights was eerie. Like being in a movie. A Clint Eastwood movie played in slow motion.

The smoke from the smouldering remains of the shack spiralled up in a thin column, only to disappear among the tree tops. Ahead of us, where once the shack had been, miniscule flames flickered among the debris. I stopped twenty metres short of the jagged remnants of the door that now swung limp, its squeaking hinges clinging with two screws to the jambs. We sat and stared, unable to believe the final devastation. Lucy unplugged herself from the iPod. She made her usual bleeding obvious remark.

"The bastards have torched the place."

The three of us stepped out of the Wagon and trod with care towards the rubble that had once been Harry's home. The fire had been well planned. Barely a branch of the surrounding trees had been scorched. Water from the tank had been sprayed around, water still dripping in parts. Dirt was raked around the shack to prevent the fire spreading. Tyre tracks had been removed. No footprints existed. This had been done by a Pro. Mario breathed deeply, ready for action now the battle was over. I was keener than ever to win the war.

"Let's check the rope first."

Most of the rafters were charred and still glowing, their thickness halved by the tremendous heat that must have roared through. We each of us stared up to where the rope had been. Not a skerrick left. Whether burned away or taken down was hard to say. There was only one thing left to do.

"Check for anything that might reveal fingerprints."

It was a pointless order, considering the state of the place. The job was too good for anyone to have been careless, but I needed to make some effort. I was picturing Harry, first when I'd put down his dog. Then as I was getting to know him again and finally, as a body swinging from a rope. I gulped down my despair and watched the man I was reluctantly falling in love with begin to search the area.

"It would take a good knowledge of fuels to reach the heat in such a short time."

"Exactly."

I had no concept of what I was agreeing with.

Lucy was wandering about, her iPod now back in her pocket, releasing her brain to contemplate.

"Why did nobody come when the fire raged?"

Good question. It would have spelt danger to the whole forest, the whole community. Nobody being there when the cops and ambulance were around was also strange. Disasters usually draw big crowds, even in isolated places. One year people drove two hundred and fifty kilometres from the coast up to the Northern Tablelands just to see snow in April. Was everybody in this area threatened not by fires but by secrets?

I wandered around kicking over the simmering ashes, not caring if my hundred and fifty dollar trainers got ruined. It was lucky I'd got the scrap of photo when I did. All that was left of the desk was a pile of glinting ash. The Rayburn sizzled with cast iron defiance. The bent and blistered tin roof had caved in, the pale light of the three quarter moon beaming through it, sinister. This was a David Bradbury location. Yet it was no film set. It was all too real. All too hellish. Lucy suddenly headed for the doorway, her voice producing a choking sound. It reminded me of how her mother had sounded that night, years back, when she'd said her brief goodbyes and went up north. I linked arms with my best friend.

"Come on. We've done all we can."

She flung herself from me and raced out of the door, her flat shoes allowing her to move fast over the scorched ground. I strode back to the Valiant hoping I never had to tell Lucy that Harry had been her father. I took a last look round, witnessing the death of an era. I was reminded of when mum died. Shit, every day I missed her.

As if struck by lightening Mario suddenly raced round the back of the ruins, close to where Harry's dog, Cocktail, had once roamed. At some point I'd thought the shed might have been used for growing cannabis or producing chemicals of some sort. Whatever, the first spark would equate immediate destruction. Me and Lucy stared lethargically after him. He rejoined us as I clipped shut the door. He'd found nothing useful. Fire had raged through the sheds. I turned the Wagon round and began the journey back. Sadness filled the air. Lucy gazed out of the back window.

"One minute people are there, the next they're fucking gone."

The story of her life. Mario sighed.

"That is the way life is."

What was it with him? Cold and hot. Soft and tough. Funny and sad. Changeable as the weather. I reckoned Harry would never have changed. He was a constant. Was he a constant in Giselle's life for those few years? Had he kept in touch? More questions. Another day. Another night.

FIFTEEN

I'd spent a few days finding some stupid bloke who'd borrowed some cash from some other stupid bloke who was in some stupid sort of trouble himself and so needed cash in a hurry. Blah, blah, blah. I'd found the first bloke hiding out in an old farm shed on the way to Grafton. I drove down to the address and took some photos, passing them on to the client. Job done. Payment received. It was great getting work but I couldn't stop thinking about Harry and how he'd been left spinning in the wind.

I was not in a good mood. I wandered around the room feeding on a warmed piece of Pizza that had, under the pink flouro down the Deli, looked better than it was tasting. I needed a caffeine hit. I needed to find out about Harry's DNA sample. *Memo: Call Brian.* Shit, the Case was turning out to be real messy.

It was getting late. I couldn't eat any more food, not even chocolate bars but I could watch TV. First, caffeine. While waiting for the coffee to plunge itself into addictive mode I listened to my message bank. First was Auntie Gert asking when we were visiting Patsy Doherty. *Memo: Book the flight!* Second was from some bloke I'd dobbed into his Insurance Company. The language made even me blush. The third was barely audible, all crackly. I had my finger on the delete button when curiosity overtook me. I played it back several times, volume on tops. The first word I made out was 'coming'. Ho, ho, a pervert. The second word sounded like another innuendo? Cock? Tale? No, cocktail. Couldn't be THE cocktail. Could it? Harry's dog? I replayed the message over and over, straining my ears and my brain, trying to decipher it. At last I got another word. 'Pox', or was it 'box', followed by 'run'. Got to box run? By the run? Coming to the pox run? A few more seconds of indistinct noises then the line went dead. I revved up my intrigued brain. Only me, Harry and Lucy knew about my connection with his dog. And maybe Lachlin? Then, like the dull blow of an axe on Ironbark, it dawned on me. The speaker was Harry. I'd been listening to a dead man talking. Before he was dead. I hoped. The thought made my stomach heave. Poor Harry. I couldn't bring myself to play it back for a while. I had three words to work on. A clue but to what? Cocktail, run, box or pox. Had to be box. What box? Where? Then the run. Run to the box? Where to run? What box? And what had Cocktail got to do with it? Shit, my brain was being bombarded with illogical images. I was gulping down the last of the sweetened coffee when it clicked. Harry was trying to tell me about Cocktail and the dog run which had been fixed up between the shack and the bush. There must be a box hidden somewhere.

I shivered as I thought of Harry making the call to me, with his killer, or killers, stealing up on him when he'd phoned, and I hadn't answered. I could have helped him, perhaps. Why not call the cops? Had he seen the game was up and was doing his best to warn me, rather than try to save himself? What or who was he warning me about? Martin SS? Giselle? The two old ladies? A clue to who Lucy's father was? Was that his final gift to her? I felt worse than before. I snaffled three Mars Bars out of the fridge and tossed them in the bin. I had to make a sacrifice, no matter how facile.

I shifted my butt and clambered into my all weather gear, gumboots and Japari jacket. I wondered whether to call Mario but he'd likely be tucked up between smooth silk sheets with his cool blonde. Stuff him. Besides, what the hell did I need him for. A certain tingling in a certain area told me what I needed him for but that could wait. Packing the hardware in my bag, I checked that the baseball bat was on the front seat of the Valiant and jumped in.

It was close to nine by the time I turned the key and edged out into the traffic-less, pot holed streets on the edge of town, dark, except for the lazy light cast by the moon slipping through the stretched out clouds. The weather was cold, wet and miserable. So was I. The lonely howl of a distant dog pierced my ears, the call of the wild. I pulled up my collar, wound up the window tight, put on my sunnies for atmospheric effect and began to whistle. The whistling of *'whenever I feel afraid'* reminded me of my dad, which reminded me of mum, which reminded me of The Beatles. When they were at the top of the hit parade mum was well and truly alive. She'd be proud of me, I knew that. I pushed out my breasts and hugged in my chin and continued whistling, all the way up the mountain road. I thought how good it would be if Harry was waiting for me by his door, rifle slung low, a flick of his head inviting me inside for a milk-less cup of tea. But he was dead. Nothing could change that fact. He was being buried on his property in three days time. I was going, hang the possible danger. Shadowy animals scuttled across the road. Whether they were small wallabies or large rats was hard to tell. As long as they didn't make a clunk under my tyres I didn't care what dreams were being chased. The trusty Valiant drew me closer to the shack, and to what I hoped would be a useful discovery.

The lemon moon peeked down, turning every patch of bush into a dark imaginary creature. The forest seemed alive, trees walling me in, shadows ready to attack, creatures scuttling across the path. I thudded the Wagon to a halt, told myself off for being a scaredy cat, gathered up my torch and weapons of mass destruction then stepped out. I cast the wide ranging beam of the torch well ahead of me. It was a new addition to my pack of tools and lit up a large circle of the ground, now damp and soggy from the mist. The fire had been more or less quenched, a few threads of smoke left to swirl their way upwards. I trod with stealth towards what would have been Cocktail's old run. I kept the light from the torch burning in front of me. I moved quick as I could to where I expected Harry's message to lead me. The kennel was small but the run had five metre long cement block walls on either side of a patch of dirt, now overgrown with weeds. Running from one end to the other, fixed to star picket stakes, was a strip of thick wire. His collar fixed to it, Cocktail would have spent hours pattering up and down while his master attended to his own life. I figured that if there was a box it would be hidden either in the remains of the kennel or in a gap in the wall. Patches of debris squashed underfoot as I made my way forward. I remembered Cocktail whimpering as his death approached. Animals sense their ending, whether from a bullet or a stun gun. Do humans? Shit, I never wanted to find out.

Clambering over the concrete wall I ducked under the wire. All that remained of the kennel was a lopsided bit of rusted corrugated iron roof and a few planks of hardwood. I poked inside with a piece of wood. A snake could be bedded down for the night. Nothing slithered out or stirred within. No box was inside, only a slushy pile of dirt and animal crap. Now to start on the wall. I worked my way along, prying my gloved fingers into anything resembling a hole, shining the torch into any likely hiding place. I was almost three quarters along when I saw it. The torch light glinted on a metal box almost covered by damp decaying leaves, unaffected by the fire. I reached for it and began to pull it out. It got wedged. I tugged. Then I heard the noise of a branch snapping underfoot. Somebody was out there. Sweat poured between my boobs. I flicked the torch in the direction of the noise. The figure of a man was outlined against the shadowy trees, only a metre or so away from me. I froze in disbelief. My hand moved to the bag for my gun. Too late. With lightning speed the man tackled me to the ground. My bag flew off. My torch dropped somewhere close to my feet. He rolled me around in the dirt. Shit, he was making a mess of my jacket. I fought like a tiger. I growled a lot. Where was Lucy when I needed her? After a good dousing in ash and dirt the assailant heaved me to my feet. This was a big mistake for him. With all the force I could muster I jabbed my elbow into his solar plexus. He groaned. His hands loosened sufficiently for me to feel for my bag. I found it. I flipped out the gun and pointed it at him. He was bent over, moaning like a teenager with toothache. He turned to run. I raised the gun to shoulder height.

"Stop or I'll shoot!"

My body felt like half of it had been torn off and I was saying I'd shoot him? Some chance. I stayed where I was. He stayed where he was. I grew confident.

"Arms up."

He raised his arms. He was trembling like a low density earthquake. Maybe he'd been hoping to scavenge any drugs that survived the fire. Was he alone?

"Where's your mates?

His voice was squeaky.

"I'm on my own."

I shone the torch full on his face. It was him, the nose basher. Him again. I couldn't believe it. My nose quivered in recollection.

"It's you!'

Silence.

"What are you doing here?"

He said nothing.

"I can use this weapon, you know."

He remained shaking.

"Please. Don't shoot!"

He didn't sound like the maniac who'd attacked me. He must have been on steroids that night.

"Give me a good reason not to."

"I'm doing what I've been told to."

"Who told you to do what?"

He shuffled his feet as if trying to warm them up.

"Can't say. Else they'll kill me."

I waved the gun closer to his face, at the same time surveying the surroundings. I'd not noticed any other movement out there in the dark but I figured with my gun trained on him nobody else would leap out at me. Shit, I was getting far too rational.

"So it's them kill you, or me kill you?"

"Honest. They will."

"Tell me who they are."

"I can't do that."

His face drooped with fear. I aimed the gun between his eyes. The moon had poked its way through a gap in the clouds to check out was going on. I put on my best Clint Eastwood impersonation. I'd seen every movie he'd been in.

"Make my day, punk!"

"You what?"

Sad to meet somebody who'd never heard the legendary phrase. Under other circumstances I'd have thumped him but I needed to know more.

"Are you alone?"

"Apart from you?"

Here was me thinking he was thick as only one plank.

"Come on, they wouldn't send a fuckwit like you out on your own to burn down that, that house."

It hit the mark.

"I never torched it, honest."

"So what are you here for?"

"To find...to look for, something."

It was then I caught on. I shone the light right in his eyes. He blinked like a feral cat caught in the beam.

"Harry's mobile?"

He remained silent.

"So did you find it?"

He shook his head, shifting from foot to foot, eager to run but scared to.

"Can I put my hands down?"

"When I say so, right."

It had to be one of the drug gangs he worked for.

"You a junkie?"

He shook his head vigorously. Too vigorously.

"WAS a junkie?"

He nodded.

"You did something you shouldn't have?"

He shook his head, less vigorously this time.

"Saw something you shouldn't have?"

He stared straight at me, then slowly nodded.

"How come they haven't strung you up as well?"

He screwed up his face like a baby about to cry. Shit, not another one. No way was I letting him off the hook yet.

"Plenty of places round here to bury a scumbag like you."

The young man shrugged. I was thinking drug deals. Big deals. Maybe even murder. Was it Harry he'd seen strung up? Did he know why? Why hadn't they got rid of him? He was a witness. He was a nobody. Runts weren't usually left to run free. Not in the cop shows I'd seen.

"You protected by somebody?"

He said nothing.

"Somebody's son?"

Silence.

"Somebody's nephew?"

The slight movement in his face gave him away.

"Not Sergeant Lachlin?"

It was a wild guess, but the way he licked his lips told me I'd hit the bullseye.

"So where is he?"

"He was sent to Sydney."

"For being a naughty boy?"

A grin spread across his face, the closest he'd come to revealing the truth about anything. He didn't seem to be the average hoodlum.

"How come you got involved in crime?"

I was sure he was a tiny cog in the wheel of something big.

"You can put your arms down."

He did. They hung loose beside his defeated body.

"What would you rather be doing?"

His whole body was transformed into a bright sparkling bundle of interest.

"Doing up old cars, like your Safari."

So, he'd seen the Valiant. A lover of classic cars. A soul mate at last. If I'd have fancied him I'd have shagged him there and then.

"How about you and me work together?"

"On the Valiant?"

Shit, it isn't in that bad a shape. Well, it is but what an insult insinuating it is.

"No, on this business with Hippie Harry."

"Happy Harry."

"You know what they did to him, don't you?"

His eyes pleaded to be let off answering.

"You were there?"

"I swear I didn't know what they were going to….."

His voice trailed off as he realised what deep shit he'd dropped himself into. Good as a confession. I lowered my voice to just above seduction level.

"You could be a sort of double agent."

"A what?"

"You keep me informed. About what they're up to."

It took a few seconds for the concept to sink in.

"Nah. They'll bury me alive. They do that to people who…"

So, I'd been right about people being buried in concrete foundations. He closed his eyes. Was he praying? Was he remembering what he'd been made to watch? How many killings had he witnessed? Now his Uncle Lachlin was not around, was he safe? I relaxed my stance, lowering the gun a little. I could still pepper his knee caps if he, or anybody else, tried anything.

"What's your name?"

There was no reluctance. He didn't try to be clever, which was good. People get careless of what they say and do in front of people like him.

"Jimmie Claymore."

Weird name. Probably false.

"Right, Jimmie. I want you to forget you've seen me and we never had this conversation, right?"

"You mean pretend you never spoke to me?"

I sighed, silently.

"That's right. As far as anyone else is concerned we never met. Up here or anywhere else. Get it?"

"Right."

"And I promise not to ask about the nose job."

He flashed me a smile of apology. He looked very young. I figured he wouldn't last long under interrogation. That was his bad luck as well as mine.

"So what will you tell them when you get back?"

"That I came up here and found nothing. And saw no one."

"Good boy."

I was taking a big risk but had few options. I needed to get rid of him so I could take home the box. I waved my gun for him to move off. He grinned, childishly.

"Is that thing really loaded."

Why do they always have to ask.

"You want to find out?'

That wiped the grin off his face. I pointed the gun at his knees and moved my finger to the trigger position. He covered his knees with his hands, as if that would stop a bullet.

"Where's your car?"

He pointed in its direction.

"Best get going. One thing."

I'd moved the gun to his chest.

"Yeh?"

"I want you to get something from your uncle. For testing. You know, saliva, semen, blood, hair, the fresher the better."

He looked at me as if I was a weirdo. Clearly the connection with DNA hadn't sunk in.

"I need his DNA. For testing."

"What do I get in return?"

"Your life, Jimmie. Your life."

He thought this a fair exchange.

"Right."

"And make sure you drive off real easy."

I sounded like Clint Eastwood again. I followed him to his Monaro. A beauty of a car. Racing yellow. Two door model. In perfect condition. I guessed Jimmie had spent half his young life restoring it. Nothing would restore his brain to full capacity. Had he damaged himself with hard drugs. I thought I'd give him a decent send off.

"You've done up your own car real good."

His pleasure shone like a two year old given a favourite toy for Xmas. He stared at the gun still pointed at him.

"Would his spunk be okay. He's a real wanker!"

He chuckled at his little joke. I did my best to smile.

"Whatever."

I waved him off as he moved his car in perfect motion back down the track and retraced my steps back to the dog pen. If anybody else had been with him they'd have captured me by now. Or killed me. I found the box and pulled it out. It was small but heavy. Metal. It was locked with a padlock. No key. No problem.

Driving back I sang *Lucy in the Sky with Diamonds* all the way. No need to whistle. I'd survived. Mind, Jimmie was hardly a vicious criminal. My watch said midnight. The moon tinted the hilltops silvery yellow. In town the roads were quiet as death. One huge truck, shuttling goods to supermarkets, shunted its way slowly along the highway before I turned off. I imagined some of the homeless stirring on their blankets under the bridge as I drove over it, drug addicts and winos sleeping off their daily dread of what they'd need to survive another day. Survival of the fittest must have begun the moment the first human eyes popped open.

Once home I took a jemmy and a hammer to the box. It opened easy. It contained the best treasure possible, Harry's mobile and my card. No link to me. I tipped out the rest of the contents. A photograph of two men and a young girl. Lucy? One of the men was Jason, Hippie Harry's brother. The name Jonathon Squires was scribbled beneath the other man. A key was the only other thing. I carefully placed them all in a brown envelope and put it under my pillow. I checked my weapons and put the Beretta on the bedside table. Jimmie was a loose cannon. Not loose enough to cause trouble, I hoped. I took off my boots and snuggled under the doona. I decided not to eat any chocolate bars. No sacrifice at all compared to the price Harry had paid to help me out.

SIXTEEN

I'd just finished a crispy bacon sandwich when I heard a scuffling noise at the front door. I hid Harry's box in the dishwasher and grabbed the pepper spray out of my bag. I was just about to make the trek down the hall when I heard Lucy screeching at full throttle.

"Where's the fucking key!"

Shit, I'd forgotten to put it back under the rock. Again.

"Hang on!"

"Flab, what the hell are you up to?"

When roused her voice would turn back a king tide. I did my impression of jogging. I could smell Lucy fuming outside the door. Soon as I'd opened it she shot past me and plopped herself down on the sofa, somehow finding herself a place amid the mass of papers.

"What's happened? Is it Giselle?"

"She's back in Intensive."

At least she wasn't in the morgue.

"That's not good."

"They said she was getting better."

This newly converted concerned daughter was scary. She stood up, hands on the slim hips I'd envied since my teens.

"You can come up with me."

The tone was on par with a Royal command. I'd reserved flights for me and Auntie, plus there was the funeral. I didn't particularly want Lucy at either event. Had to choose. My best friend or the Case? Could I face denying Auntie her trip? No way. I conjured up a credible excuse.

"I've got this lead I need to follow up and I need to check some DNA samples. Sorry."

The lies rolled happily off my forked tongue. I could go into politics easy. Lucy glared at me through narrow strips of disrespect fringed by black kohl and mascara. Anger spilled out of her.

"You don't give a stuff about her, do you?"

I was miffed to say the least.

"Of course I do! Me, investigating down here, I'll do more good."

Reluctantly, she mulled over this piece of logic, her fingers jingling her gold hoop earrings. Suddenly she sounded calm and reasonable. Lucy calm and reasonable? Shit, another miracle.

"Can't any of it wait?"

"Leech, if your mum is a lot worse and she's going to…"

I didn't have to finish the sentence.

"Okay! You're right. As fucking usual. Fine. Spend time on the Case. That's what I asked you to do."

She stared out of the windows. I heard the magpies carousing. Lucy turned back to me.

"She can't die, Flab. Not now."

I pulled her to me and we hugged like we'd done a hundred times before. Generally it was over some stupid male. Now was my chance.

"If you have time there's that stuff you can do for me up at Noosa. Remember, I asked?"

She gritted her teeth.

"I'll find time. Can't be with her 24/7."

"I'd like a sample of Giselle's DNA."

"Fuck, why? It's my father that's missing."

"For comparison."

The chances of Giselle not being her birth mother were a trillion to one.

Though, it's on record that babies have got mixed up. And that was in hospitals, not mountain side huts.

"You can brush her hair, bring back a few hairs. That's normal. Wear gloves though."

"Oh, right. Brush my mother's hair wearing gloves. Real normal that is."

I almost laughed as I pictured her doing it.

"Wear white cotton ones."

She stared at me for a full minute.

"You, Flab, can be such an arse hole."

She was right. I could be. An important feature for an Investigator.

"And a swab from you. Now."

A car accident. A fatal mugging. Anything could happen. Better getting it alive than when she was in a mortuary. She sat, resigned, shaking her head.

"Why do I put up with you?"

I'd often asked myself the same thing about her. She sat patiently while I wiped the inside of her cheeks. She went quiet. Too quiet. Was she thinking about her possible father? If Giselle died would she still want to know who he was? Mario suddenly slipped into my thoughts.

"How about Mario coming up with you. If he's free."

"Why the fuck would I want him with me?"

"I'd feel better if you weren't alone. Especially snooping."

"Snooping?"

Her eyes lit up.

"There's some evidence I'm after. Mario can help. But you'll be in charge."

That pleased her ego. I smiled.

"I'll give him a call."

I dialled. He answered. He sounded tired. I couldn't help but gloat.

"Had a tough night with the blonde babe?"

He spoke loud.

"That is not funny."

I changed from sarcastic to seductive.

"So, what are you doing today?"

"That depends on what is on offer."

I was drooling in my knickers. He was expecting to be invited round for a shag. I had to disappoint us both.

"Lucy has to go see her mum. Urgent. Up at Noosa. I'm real busy the next few days. I was wondering if you could go with her."

Silence followed. Lucy dashed over and yelled into the mobile.

"If my mother is going to die I need to go, and now. Holly is busy, so are you coming with me or what?"

Who could resist such an offer? Mario stuttered his acceptance. When I told him to leave within the hour he spluttered even more. If the blonde babe was there I hoped she'd got her dildo. Mario waited.

"There's a few things to do. You and Lucy."

His groans were like the death throes of a martyr.

"It might mean staying a couple of days."

His annoyance was controlled.

"I do have a life you know."

Pay-back time.

"That is not funny."

I clicked off and turned to Lucy.

"You may have to take a few risks."

"A bit of break and enter, is it?"

"Mario can keep watch."

"He'll be fucking useless."

"Two heads are better than one?"

"Don't fucking remind me."

I didn't want to go there.

"So. While we wait for Mario, you can make coffee and I'll make a list of what you have to do."

"Right. I suppose."

She shuffled her way into the kitchen and I began to write. I needed them to snitch at least two white boxes from the Gallery, assuming the art works hadn't been moved on. One that was labelled 'This little piggy goes to market' and one 'This little piggy stays home.' I also wanted DNA samples of the gallery owner, so bits of his anything really. I hated to think of him being the father but it was possible. He might not have been such a sleazebag back in nineteen seventy-three.

Mario arrived as commanded. Sensing the danger of my lustful thoughts Lucy immediately dragged him back to his car. I quickly handed over the instructions. The kiss was brief bliss. The pair drove off, beaming their goodbyes.

I phoned Auntie Gert to remind her of the flight time and remarked, pointedly, that in Sydney, only whores and bag ladies wore pink everything. She sniggered, which meant she'd wear pink everything. Shit, I had to admire the woman's audacity.

The flight down was uneventful, except when Auntie Gert, a perfect parade of pink, outran an elderly man to the toilets, ensuring he wet his pants in full view of everybody. We arrived at the Home with Auntie accusing the taxi driver of being a crook for charging too much.

Patsy Dougherty was ending her days shacked up in a classy Old People's Home, renamed by the politically correct as an Aged Care Facility. Anything to conceal the truth. The modern brick and tile buildings were surrounded by well mown lawns, shrubs the size of trees and trees the size of a mountain, with strategically placed security fences hidden behind rows of robinias. It was entrenched in a few hectares, awaiting more government money for expansion, so even if an inmate managed to escape beyond the flash fencing there'd be nowhere easy for them to shuffle off to. A good builder, like a good market researcher, gave their clients exactly what they wanted. At the imposing wrought iron gate we were given a serious verbal grilling. Even USA Homeland Security would have been satisfied. Auntie pertly offered herself up for a body search but the young man politely declined. *Memo: Chivalry is not entirely dead.* It took a fair time to convince security I was not intent on setting all the inmates free. If only.

At last, we were ushered into a foyer of white walls, black leather chairs, grey floor tiles, a circular red rug and two small glass topped tables. The kind of décor totally unrepresentative of the old people living there. Relatives and visitors were fed the image of modernity and so, by implication, well cared for residents. The usual bullshit. For a brief moment I felt pleased me and dad had promised not to put Auntie Gert in such a place.

We followed directions to Patsy Dougherty's room. Men and women shuffled along on walking frames, with the more helpless ones being pushed in wheelchairs by young things with fixed smiles. Inmates had the desperate air of prisoners on death row, which was exactly what they were. Several oldies stared back at us, eyes dead with unknowing. *Memo: Check out the best country to get Nembutal.* Auntie was clearly disturbed by the scene.

"They'd all be far better off sitting on a sunny verandah, smoking cannabis or chewing on hash cookies and drinking gin and tonic. Then they'd at least enjoy their last few years."

I was with her on that. At least Hippie Harry wouldn't have to suffer the indignity of living in such a space.

SEVENTEEN

To discover as much as I could about the missing Picasso I needed Patsy Dougherty to have retained at least a portion of her memory. Otherwise a wasted trip. The door to number eight was shut tight. I knocked hard. From inside a grunt invited us in. The room, large as a double motel room, was a mixture of beige and white, the sole window opening out onto a courtyard across which stood a brick wall. The user friendly shower and toilet had sparkling white tiles, floor to ceiling. The wardrobe with its double mirror doors meant that no way could Patsy avoid viewing her decrepit self each time she needed to pass it. Décor probably designed by a fit, totally up himself, thirty year old.

The old lady was slumped in a winged arm chair, her eyes pinned to a television set. She was dressed in a Laura Ashley frock of pale yellow and white, over which she wore a pale beige cardigan. She wore tan stockings and black court shoes. Her hair was coiffured into a bun and her makeup, though light, was perfect. Auntie told me she'd grown up on the North Shore and had been a socialite. Then she and her husband retired up to the coast, cut off from her old friends. I saw her as a whisky on the rocks person, possibly with a few white powder parties up her sleeve.

No doubt being used to interruptions from staff she hadn't bothered to look up as we entered. A huge photograph, of a man dressed in World War Two uniform, on which hung many medals, dominated the wall above the TV. Auntie had bought a bag of goodies as a surprise gift. She moved in beside the old woman and offered it up. Patsy snapped at the bag, feeling the contents with her purple blotched arthritic fingers. Auntie Gert grew bolder.

"Now, how are you keeping, Mrs Dougherty? I'd be bringing you a few of your favourites. The McVities biscuits, imported from England of course. And humbugs. You were always saying how the world was full of humbugs."

A high pitched laugh broke from Auntie Gert. I was totally bewitched by her sudden Irish accent. Silence from Patsy, who opened the bag on her lap a fraction at a time, with Auntie hovering close by like a favourite grandchild. Her glee faded when the old lady spoke.

"Do I know you?'

The voice was imperious. Auntie's jaw dropped.

"It's Gertrude Wilson. Gertie. I used to be doing some housekeeping for you in that beautiful home of yours, on top of the hill at Lennox. You could see the ocean from there. Beautiful it was."

Auntie Gert sighed with envy. So did I. Patsy carefully opened the bag, tore out a biscuit from the packet and carefully inspected it, as if she were a CWA competition judge.

"I employed a cleaner. Was that you?"

Reluctantly Auntie agreed that she was. There was no let up from Patsy.

"You were not very good, as I recall."

Auntie bristled. Her hands shook. Undaunted by the insult she continued her conversation.

"And I did the occasional meal for you. When the cook was off sick. A problem with the drink, as I recall."

"Ah, yes. The disastrous dinner parties."

"None were mine, I hope."

"Oh, yes indeed, they were yours. And you did not have the drink as an excuse."

I sensed Auntie Gert was fast reaching the end of her Irish tether and was struggling not to hit the pompous old bitch.

"I always paid my staff so very well."

This was too much for Auntie. She was ever keen to keep the red flag flying.

"Oh, you think so, do you? Well let me tell you, Mrs-oh-mighty-Dougherty, you paid the award wage, no more, no less. And I was worth every penny of it!"

Shit, this was not going right. I didn't want Patsy off side. Auntie breathed deep and then forced a loud laugh, her false teeth doing their best not to fly out.

"Did you like my little joke now?"

"No, I did not."

The eyes were once more averted to the TV screen. To my surprise Auntie swanned over and switched off the set. Patsy stared angrily at the woman who'd committed the crime.

"What do you think you are doing?"

"You and me have things to talk about."

The old woman fidgeted in her chair. She drew herself up as close to a dignified posture as her weak body could sustain. I glimpsed the woman she once had been.

"About what?"

"About that husband of yours for a start."

Both pairs of eyes turned to the photo on the wall. I kept my eyes on the two women. Auntie kept her voice low and persuasive.

"He was a very handsome man, was he not?"

Patsy's eyes misted over.

"He was extremely handsome. And such a charmer."

"A Captain, he was?"

"He should have been a General. Gerald was never overly ambitious."

Auntie Gert winked at me. The old woman relaxed back in her chair.

"Is it my birthday? Is this some kind of silly surprise? Is that why you are dressed up as a fluffy pink rabbit?"

Auntie gritted her dentures and pulled her pink cardi tighter round her chest.

"I was wanting to bring you a few gifts, that was all."

I stared out of the window, unsure if I'd ever get a word in. The sun hovered on top of the tiled roof opposite. I turned back. The two women were holding hands, Patsy as surprised as I was. Auntie squeezed the dry, wrinkled hands in her own dry, wrinkled hands and spoke gently.

"Tell me about the Picasso. The one you inherited from your great aunt whatshername."

"Great Aunt Matilda."

"Yes, her."

"It was sold. At Sothebys."

Auntie and I glanced quickly at each other.

"So, you took it to them and they gave you a cheque, did they?"

"Dear me, no. Business is not done that way. A very kind gentleman said it would be better if he took the painting to Sothebys to sell. The money was paid directly into my bank account."

"Are you sure about that?"

"He was such a nice man."

"Does this man have a name?"

"Rather handsome. Square cut. Scots College type. My dear husband went there you know. All the best families did."

"I don't suppose you have a copy, do you?"

"Of the man?"

"Of the Picasso."

"There was some talk of a copy."

My ears shot up.

"But what would I want with a copy."

The old woman flicked her hand in the direction of nowhere.

"I believe there is one somewhere."

Somewhere? A thrill ran through me. Then, as if suddenly hit on the head, Patsy slumped in her chair, her chin sunk on her chest, tears falling from her eyes. Auntie patted her hand.

"There, there."

I was ready to push the red button. Auntie shook her head. She put her arm around the old lady's shoulders and began to quietly sing. Shit, my eighty year old auntie had a decent voice. Must be all that practise down at the Community Health Centre. It was a Vera Lyn classic. World War Two stuff.

"We'll meet again, don't know where, don't know when but I know we'll meet again some sunny day."

Patsy lifted herself out of a dream and joined in.

"Keep shining through...."

Abruptly, the singing halted. Tears, released by long held memories, rolled down their cheeks. I blew my nose real loud. Auntie sighed.

"Those were the days."

"We loved each other so much. Gerald and I."

"Of course you did."

"The sapphire for my engagement ring was extraordinary, you know. The size, the cut, the colour. Mined in Ceylon, of course."

No point telling her it was now called Sri Lanka. The left hand was stretched out and gazed at, as if the sapphire sat next to the plain gold band she still wore.

"He loved me so very much, you see."

He'd probably had scores of mistresses. His sort always did. In the movies at any rate. He'd more than likely given them good jewelry as well as a good shag. Auntie Gert kept her mind on the job.

"And where is it now, the ring? I was wondering if I might see it."

Patsy shifted her bottom back and forth, her hands twisting in her lap.

"It is in my bank vault. It is safe there. I trust no one, you know. And that includes you."

"Fine, Mrs Dougherty, fine. Maybe one day you can show me."

If she had cleaned for the woman Auntie would have seen the ring on numerous occasions. It was my guess the sapphire ended up not in Patsy's bank vault but in someone else's, then passed on for cutting, and sold. I almost felt sorry for the arrogant old woman.

"Now, that copy of the Picasso. Where were you saying it was?"

"Oh. In the wardrobe. I think?"

I was over there like a shot, rifling through her clothes and shoes and boxes of this and that. I had no idea of the size of the painting. I must have made some noise. Patsy peered at me.

"Who is she?"

"My brother's daughter. She gets bored with old ladies like us."

I noted Auntie's Irish brogue was slipping. Patsy seemed not to have noticed.

"The young are so inconsiderate. So unlike the two elderly ladies who visited. It seems a long time since they came. I forget sometimes, you know"

I gasped.

"Two elderly ladies?"

"Yes. So very gracious. They had taken a great deal of trouble to find where I lived. Such kindness is rare. They came to comfort my grieving heart."

Auntie stifled a guffaw and glanced at me as I was sorting through the wardrobe. Then I saw the package. A fine merino shawl wrapped around what could be the Picasso. I pulled it out and rapidly pushed the shawl aside. The picture was roughly sixty centimetres by thirty. I stared at it, letting my fingers play with the edges of the frame.

"I can hardly believe I'm holding a Picasso."

Patsy glared at my overt enthusiasm.

"Stupid woman. It is a copy. Not a genuine Picasso at all. I rather dislike it. It is rather crude."

Auntie Gert took the picture from me and walked it back to her old boss.

"Are you sure this is a copy, Mrs Dougherty?"

"Of course I am sure. I did not want it made but the two kind ladies insisted."

Shit. A gem.

"I have explained to everyone here that it is a copy. I do not want it but I do not want anyone else to have it. No one can be trusted, you know. Even in an exclusive residential such as this."

The old lady seemed almost as lucid as Auntie, who gracefully sat down beside her.

"Could we take the painting away to have another art expert look it over?"

Patsy appeared about to have an apoplexy. She stuttered. She coughed. She pointed at Auntie.

"I shall call the police. Or someone of equal importance."

The picture was pushed at me as Auntie took the old woman's hands in hers.

"Don't be upsetting yourself, Mrs Dougherty. We shall wrap it up and put it back in your wardrobe."

The response was swift.

"I should think so! The absolute impudence."

I quickly put the Picasso back where I found it. It was idiotic. It could be the genuine article. The Picasso, fake or real, was secreted back into the robe but while Auntie kept her distracted I'd taken several photos of it.

"So, Mrs Dougherty, were the two old ladies sisters, do you think?"

"Twins, perhaps. Sisters at any rate."

Tweedledum and Tweedledee kept turning up, or at least it sounded like them. Did they take the sapphire as well as the genuine Picasso, or was that theft left to Martin SS? Were the old ladies part of a plan to soften up the victims? Could Patsy give evidence? Who would listen to a demented old woman. I guessed she was no threat to anybody.

The painting was of a young woman, naked, apart from a piece of muslin draped over her vital bits. Henson could have learned a thing or two about sensuality. Patsy's great aunt must have been at least twenty at the time, petite, small breasts, big eyes, slim hips, long legs, pouting lips, the usual sort men like to stare at. Picasso not only stared but painted her and, presumably, shagged her. Who knew in what order. Patsy was still on the same track.

"Most of the staff are very young, you know, and consequently are extremely untrustworthy."

Seeing it was time to leave, Auntie Gert leaned over to kiss Patsy on the cheek. She jerked her head away. Auntie stepped back.

"Shall we come again?"

The firm answer flew across the sterile room.

"Certainly not."

Patsy turned to face us, haughty as ever.

"It is not because I do not appreciate your visit. It is the memories such visits bring. Friends, staff, all so long ago. Much happier times."

The final words caught in her throat. Shit, she was human after all. Her eyes glazed over as she stared up at the photo of her husband. Auntie Gert walked softly round to the television set and switched it back on. Patsy took no time at all to escape back into the lives of the never ending soap opera stars, her own life over, bar the wailing.

"Off you go then."

A thin, twisted hand fluttered our dismissal. We had got what we came for. An important piece of a very incomplete jigsaw. We shouted our goodbyes, both trusting neither of us would end up in an Old People's Home. Once outside Auntie was jubilant.

"Did you notice how clever my interrogation was?"

"What was with the Irish accent?"

"All part of the adventure, Holly. It'll make a great story down the Community Health Centre."

I frowned my displeasure.

"I won't mention names."

On the flight home I thought of Hippie Harry and how if he'd lived longer he might have spent his last years sitting on a verandah, smoking dope and dreaming dreams.

Once home I scanned the Picasso photos into the computer and sent them off to Brian. He'd do an online search for catalogues around the world, checking which gallery thought they had the original. A picture of what the scams were all about was beginning to take some kind of shape.

I sat down to watch the last bit of *Midsomer Murders*. Predictable but enjoyable. I nodded off before the first dead body was discovered.

EIGHTEEN

It was pouring cats and dogs the day of the funeral, low grey clouds clinging to mountain tops like musty old army blankets. Gum boots, waterproofs and beanies were de rigeur, even for the Celebrant. Hippie Harry was laid to rest in his discarded vegie patch to the haunting accompaniment of a mellow flute, the gentle flick of a tambourine and the muffled beat of a drum. Respects were paid. No cause of death was mentioned. Elergies were brief and repetitive: how Harry was a decent, kind man who'd be missed. Clearly not by everybody.

It was midday. A pale sun broke through the drizzle, adding a placebo warmth to the hour. A couple of cops, complete with waterproof jackets, caps and holstered guns, stood discreetly on the edge of the crowd, their eyes swooping continuously over the forty odd attendees. I'd been wondering about the police presence but there they were, a silent force.

I began taking photos as soon as everyone crammed themselves into the large tent to devour the nutritious organic food. No Pizza, no Mars Bars. I was told food and drink for the Wake was supplied by members of the Community, of which Harry had been a part. The hash cookies went first. Drinks were, for the most part, non alcoholic. Nobody wanted to get paralytic with the cops there. A dog barked some way off, alerting everyone to the fact that the rain had stopped.

I wandered off to check on the dog. It was a Kelpie cross, tied to the same wire Cocktail had once endured. It raced boisterously up and down, unaware of the sad event taking place. Walking back

I saw the green Kombie being parked some way down the track. Tweedledee and Tweedledum carefully plopped themselves out of the van, their identical black walking shoes soon steeped in mud. They discarded their raincoats to reveal their matching grey skirts and jumpers. Scarves were not quite identical but close enough. I was intrigued that they'd shown up.

Weaving their way towards the tent they trod with great care over the damp dirt ridges. I followed, staying out of sight. Wading into the tent they confronted a man I'd not previously noticed. I crept closer. He was around sixty, wore a suit smart enough for a traditional church funeral and had teeth that flashed each time he opened his mouth, which was frequently. He held a glass of orange juice. My camera began working overtime. The three spoke earnestly, too quiet for me to hear. I moved in behind them. Tweedledum's voice was formal.

"We are sorry to have missed the ceremony."

The man's eyebrows shot up.

"He won't be missing you old biddies, will he?"

Proof of their connection to Harry. I blazed with anticipation of what else might come. The three separated themselves from the main crowd. I took up a better position and stood, camera clicking. Tweedledum volunteered her opinion.

"Harry was essentially a good man. He should never have become involved."

The man gripped her arm so tight it made me wince. His voice hissed.

"Listen you stupid old biddies, you just watch yourselves. Right?"

The threat was very clear. The women stayed firm.

"Harry should not have been made to pay."

The sister confirmed the opinion.

"He was a good man."

The man replied tersely.

"He was no longer to be trusted."

I zoomed in on his face, clicked, then spent a few seconds reviewing the shots. My heart flipped. The face was familiar. Another piece of the jigsaw? I must get a sample of his DNA. I was just putting away my camera when two young boys barged into me. I stumbled, arms flailing, lips mouthing profanities. All eyes turned on me. The last thing I needed. The man, seeing the camera, made a grab for it. Quick off the mark Tweedledum and Tweedledee pushed him aside. I clung firmly to the camera and my bag. I was surprised to note that Tweedeldum had snatched the man's glass from him. She pocketed it. The man, aware of this, made a move towards her just as a cop strolled over. He backed off. She winked at me. What was going on? The cop lingered until I was back on my feet then strode off. I brushed myself down, my dignity intact. The man narrowed his eyes, clenched his fists and marched off. People sidled back to their previous conversations. The two old ladies beamed at me then edged me in between them. I could be squashed to death. Was this how nutcases kidnapped, then killed, their victims? Their manner was matter of fact.

"So you did attend, my dear. Harry would be most pleased."

What could I do but nod?

"We are most pleased also."

I felt like Alice in some weird Wonderland. Yet the scenario was no figment of anybody's drug induced imagination, it was for real. I placed my hand on my bag and spoke with all the strength of purpose I could.

"I met Harry years ago. I liked him. Felt I ought to say farewell."

It sounded plausible. Tweedledum took my hand.

"We both regarded Harry with great affection."

They remained on either side of me, real close. I was wary and yet committed to seeing it through. I might learn something useful from them. Why they took the glass, for example. I played my cool card.

"So were you and Harry friends?"

Tweedledum sighed heavily.

"He was always part of the plan, my dear. As were we."

Tweedledee nodded agreement.

"Very business like, the plan."

The pair moved me forward between them. I'd need a battering ram to dispose of them. Or a gun. We were well away from the crowd. Then suddenly they stopped and almost leapt out in in front of me, leaving me free to escape. Oddly I chose to stay, curiosity overtaking fear. I stood firm. They stood firm. For a while my mind, frazzled by conjecture, wavered between fight and flight. They stared hard at me.

"We need to talk to you, my dear."

"And we have absolutely no wish to hurt you. So you can relax."

Relax? Who was she kidding?

The dog barked. A bad omen. A bad omen? What am I? Some crazy chick who suddenly believed in omens? I clicked my brain into rational mode.

"Well, we can meet up some time."

Tweedledum smiled again.

"We were rather hoping it could be now."

"We wish to unburden ourselves."

"To confess."

To confess? To what? Killing me? Killing other people? How many people? I knew I should have studied psychology and learnt how to handle weirdos. I pushed my knees together to prevent them trembling. They remained unperturbed.

"I am Faith and this is my sister, Edith. Twins. And of course we know who you are."

I hadn't a clue how they'd known me in the first place but at least they'd confirmed their status. Tweedledee surveyed the distant funeral scene.

"We have come to a decision."

"We have had enough. Of what we have unwittingly become a part of."

"We shall talk to you inside the van. That will be safer."

Safer? Who for? I made to move.

"Please agree to come with us, Holly. We shall not force you but we feel it right that you hear what we have to say."

I parked my brain out of wild imaginings and into neutral. I was an investigator after all. My job was to investigate, rationally. Plus I had weapons to use, if necessary. I shrugged and walked back with them to the Kombie. They walked arm in arm. First time I'd seen them properly touching. My head buzzed. My hands began to sweat. Had my mango juice been spiked? The Kombi door was slid open and we stepped inside. I was guided into a seat. The pair sat opposite me, hands limp in laps, eyes on me. Settled comfortably, the two old ladies began.

"It all began as a little adventure for us. A little pocket money to help with our income. And at first we saw nothing wrong in what was required of us."

Tweedledee nodded wistfully and continued the story.

"Sometimes valuables come into charity shops. Relatives of the deceased totally ignorant of what they had donated. We contacted a dealer. He was encouraged by what we found."

I bet he was. Tweedledum continued.

"It was a few years before things started to become more than a little profitable. Then we were told to assist people to move into various Aged Care Facilities, up and down the coast."

"The De Rossi's?"

Both women nodded simultaneously.

"We had to sell belongings they could not take with them. Their new accommodation being somewhat smaller."

Tweedledee nodded.

"Down sizing, they call it. Rather a terrible name."

I silently agreed.

"It was famous painters, quality jewellery, anything of real value that we were to look for. We had to recommend to the owners such possessions be valued and …a man…would come and collect them."

My cue.

"A man?"

"An expert, or so we were told."

Tweedledee interjected.

"By this time we were being threatened to keep quiet about what was going on. We were trapped, a part of it, you see. Part of the plan."

Her sister tapped her thigh nervously.

"The guilt soon set in but we were, as Edith says, trapped. We did not always let the dealer know what we had discovered. So, some people kept their valuables. We hoped the dealer would not check. He sometimes did. Sometimes we got away with it."

Tweedledee sniggered like a school girl.

"You remember the plastic bag, dear? The one containing forty thousand dollars."

I'd have fallen off the seat if there'd been room.

"Mrs Alice Peel, deceased. Poor thing had lived like a pauper for forty years and all that money hidden in her pantry."

Naturally, I was expecting them to say they'd kept it. Shit, I would have. I think. *Memo: Take stock of my integrity.*

"We donated it to the Salvation army. Not our own church. Too many people know us there."

"Gossip mongers, churchgoers."

Both women smiled in remembrance of what must have been happier days spent at their allotted church.

"Precious gems were to be placed on ceramic eggs, a la Faberge. We had both travelled to Paris, when we were rather young and rather innocent."

Sighs preceded the brief silence this recollection prompted.

"Giselle Knight was very good at that kind of thing. Although her forgeries were also excellent. As good as any by Jack Weston."

The name meant nothing to me.

"Imagine, a forger, is now collectable. For his forgeries. Sad state of the world."

Another heavy sigh escaped from the heaving chests opposite. So Giselle was a forger of paintings as well as an artistic creator of the ceramic eggs encrusted with precious stones. Heavy stuff. Another piece of the jigsaw slotted neatly into place.

"Galleries abroad are rather fond of her eggs. They fetch high prices with or without precious gems in them. Relative to their value of course. Excellent workmanship, you see."

"They are exotic. Oriental, I think."

"No, dear. It was an East European influence. The Hapsburgs? Or was it the Romanovs?"

Edith shrugged as if it didn't matter. It didn't. While two and two were adding up, it still didn't quite make four.

"How were the eggs sold, the precious and non precious?"

"Oh, rather a clever plan. For a start there was a code."

"Yes, a code."

I knew it. The pair fingered the gold crosses hanging from thick gold chains around their grey turkey necks. There was regret in their stroking.

"We must also make you aware that we took no part in the drug deals. As soon as we learned of this aspect we refused to do anything in that line."

"Did Giselle Knight know about the drugs?"

"Of course but what choice did she have? She was enslaved by her own habit."

Tweedledee carried on.

"By making and selling hundreds of eggs with only worthless gems on them the really valuable ones were able to slip through any security net. What lengths they went to, to secure passage, is unknown to us but bribery, threats, murder even, would not surprise us."

"So, the code?"

The two women conversed via mental telepathy.

"It is rather a simple process. 'This little piggy went to market.'"

As if reminded of their childhood the pair clapped their hands with joy and began to chant, '*This little piggy went to market, this little piggy stayed home and this little piggy went wee wee wee all the long way home.*'

The pair seemed to be intoxicated with relief at unburdening themselves.

"The eggs are the piggies, you see. Those that go to market are the valuable ones which are sold to the highest bidder. Those that stay home are worth somewhat less, sold mainly for their artistic value. Though still extremely high prices from collectors, especially overseas. The ones that go wee wee wee are sold to whoever will buy them, definitely not precious."

So that's what the nursery rhyme meant in Giselle's diaries. Her accounting system. Shit, how come I couldn't work that out?

"And the forgeries?"

"One copy to the open market, sold to whoever believed it to be an original, usually an overseas gallery. Even the best experts have been fooled over the centuries. Further copies could be sold to private collectors, as an original. The original often went straight into the bank vault of a person who had ordered it, so to speak. At some point it would be sold for a profit to another collector who had even more cash to spare. It is a big global business, my dear."

Tweedledee stared hard at her sister.

"Sometimes a copy was kept by the owner."

I thought of Patsy.

"Did Giselle realise how big the operation was?"

"We think she had no idea."

"And Harry?"

"Ah, poor man. He had the misfortune to dearly love a terrible brother and a woman with a drug habit."

"So Harry was involved."

The two women conversed in silence again before speaking.

"He was simply a man in the wrong place at the wrong time. A man caught in criminal activities not of his own making."

"He knew of wicked things yet never did a wicked thing in his entire life. He was extremely fond of Giselle."

Eureka! And I had his DNA to prove it.

"Not in a nasty way."

Okay, not Eureka. By nasty, she clearly meant sex.

"They were like brother and sister, you see. It broke his heart when she was taken away."

"Why was she taken away?"

"It was far easier to hide her and what she was doing. So many more people and houses and of course countless private yachts and aeroplanes for transportation. A criminals paradise, you might say. Since the nineteen seventies at least. "

The media consistently had field days on the subject.

"And Patsy Dougherty's Picasso?"

"Ah, dear Patsy. We liked her. For her we enacted Plan B."

"Plan B?"

The two women smiled at a memory only they were meant to be privy to. I waited. No more offerings on the subject.

"And her sapphire?"

"Straight to Hong Kong. Most likely crafted into an ostentatious piece of jewellery displayed like a trophy by some extremely untalented celebrity."

It was all falling into place, sort of. Edith turned to look at her sister, now lost in thought.

"At least we ensured Giselle's financial security."

Faith stirred.

"We are very proud of that. One day, years ago, we opened a bag delivered by the usual courier. Her minder was away. It contained almost half a million American dollars."

"In cash?"

I could hear myself spluttering in awe.

"Criminals love counting money, my dear."

Faith smiled.

"We persuaded her to buy the house with the cash. No legal

difficulty at all, with her connections. She maintained the money was from a grateful admirer of her work. In a way that was true."

"Her name on the Title Deed. The title deed in a safety deposit box."

Harry's key? That's what it must be for, a safety deposit box.

"Which bank?"

"We cannot tell you that. It would put you in as much danger as us."

True but I needed to know. Their faces clouded over.

"We know rather too much for our own safety, you see."

Shit, two old ladies possibly buried in concrete foundations? Not right. Their hands crept across their lap and met up mid way, revealing both affection and trepidation. Had I walked into a trap? Maybe kidnapping me was part of a deal, their freedom for mine. I should have dashed out but I couldn't help myself. I had to keep asking questions.

"What happened to the minder?"

"He came back. Beat up Giselle then dissapeared. Maybe to South

America. Maybe he was put in a bag and dropped into a river, or into a block of concrete."

It went from bad to worse. One last effort.

"So, give me names. The big boss."

The women gazed at their joined hands before they reached over and clasped mine. Unadulterated fear flickered across their faces. This had to be a trap. I stood up and began to open my bag. Was somebody expecting to make their day by killing me? Better if they made mine. I took out the gun and pointed it at them. They huddled close. Shit, how could I even think of shooting two old ladies.

"Oh, my dear, we have already decided we must die."

That threw me. I lowered the Beretta.

"What?"

Faith whispered the final confession, a sob in her voice.

"We have two bottles of that…you know the special liquid… to …you know…You understand?"

I did understand. Mexico must be doing a roaring trade.

"So why not give me names?"

"We have made other plans, my dear. We are going to put things right before we…depart this world."

Faith moved over to sit beside me. She put her arm around my shoulder just as the door to the van was angrily shot back. I looked up and immediately wet myself.

NINETEEN

Martin SS stepped in. My gun was pointing downwards. His gun, the latest model Gluck, was trained on me.

"Drop the gun, you stupid bitch."

I dropped it. One day I'd get him for calling me names. Bitch, bad enough, stupid, no way. I turned to the sisters expecting them to be laughing at the trick they'd pulled on me. They sat, quivering slightly. Martin waved the gun at them.

"As for you two old dears, it's all over for you."

Shit, he was going to kill them. In front of me? They'd had nothing to do with kidnapping me. I got in as quick as I could.

"We were just talking about Harry and his sex life. In the seventies. He was a right womaniser, apparently."

I rattled on swift as any stupid bitch would.

"Hard to believe it, with his looks, hey? Who'd fancy him? I certainly wouldn't. Course, too late now."

I soon ran out of words. Martin roared with laughter. Moving further into the Kombie he pushed the two ladies aside and grabbed me.

"There will be consequences."

Like as if we hadn't already noticed consequences. Faith spoke, double chin held high, big chest out, eyes blazing.

"She is an innocent in all of this. Let her go."

Martin's response was to slap her across the face. She hardly flinched, the heroine, even as blood dribbled from the cut on her lip. I made to move. The gun touched the side of my head. He spoke directly to me.

"I said we should have got rid of these two hags years ago. A liability, that's what they are. And they know what we do with liabilities."

He tugged at my arm, dragging me along. While he was busy playing the gangster role I glared meaningfully down at the Beretta. Were they ever going to take the hint and pick the thing up? My heart thumped as I was yanked closer to the exit.

"And, do take care driving down the mountain you two. Never know what might cause an accident. Dope heads in beat up Bedfords, alcoholics in Utes, burst tyres, faulty brakes, snipers. No end to the ways a person can get killed on that road."

Both sisters threw me a smile, then with a speed amazing for their age, they grabbed Martin's legs and toppled him over. I went for my gun. He was laid out on the floor but the Gluck stayed in his hand, pointing directly at me. My gun was aimed at his head. He laughed.

"That old thing? They went out with Al Capone."

He was probably right but I remained waving it at him, while feeling for the pepper spray with my other hand. He got up, whipped his gun at my head and pushed me out of the door before I could get my trigger finger to work. The Beretta flew onto the ground. Stupidly, he bent to pick it up. I kicked him hard up the backside. I'd seen Lucy do something similar to an ex boyfriend. Martin SS fell forward and rolled over like a true artist yet his gun never left his hand. Shit, it must be stuck with Araldite. Whatever, I looked down to see the weapon pointed directly at my knees. I quite liked my knees. Useful for walking. Would have been good for running if I'd been smart enough half an hour before. He smirked.

"A shattered knee cap. Not nice."

"No silencer, I note."

The cops were out of sight but not out of earshot. In public they'd have to be seen to be doing their duty. We both knew neither of us would shoot anybody. He scrambled to his feet. I wanted the old ladies to get clear.

"Let the ladies go."

He chuckled.

"Why not? I can fix them anytime."

Tweedledum and Tweedledee stepped gingerly out of the side door.

"Off you go. Go on. Shoo."

As they moved carefully past me Tweedledum whispered that I should keep the picture. Giselle's picture? Martin pushed her away angrily. The pair sidled down the side of their van and lifted themselves into the front seats. They gave me a dignified wave as they did a U turn in the mud. I waved back as if it was a friendly farewell instead of a final goodbye. One shouted:

"Be brave, my dear. Remember the painting. Use your brain."

Martin was at the height of his hubris. Therefore, careless. He turned towards the two women.

"Brain? Her?"

Just as he turned back to face me I sprayed the pepper into his eyes. He groaned as his left hand moved to cover the pain. The gun stayed fixed in his other hand. It had to be Araldite? Through the fuzz that must be before his eyes he waved the gun around.

"Don't you fucking move!"

I moved alright. Fast as I could towards the Kombie, which strangely had turned round and was moving towards us. Shit, they were going to run him down. They couldn't kill him. I needed him as evidence. My heart raced faster than their Kombie was travelling. I waved for them to stop. They kept coming, tyres slipping and sliding in the mud. Martin was staggering about, rubbing his eyes.

The van grew closer. Martin held a crisp white hankie against his one eye, while peering at us out of the other. I was gasping for breath, having run my limit of a hundred metres. *Memo: Definitely got to get fit!* The gun was back in his pocket. He'd seen enough to realise the Kombie was making for him, the accelerator revving with revenge. He yelled.

"This is only the beginning. For all of you! Including that bitch Giselle. She survived once. We'll make sure the next time. You get me?"

I did. Momentarily I regretted not letting them run over him. He raced off as fast as his legs could take him. He'd soon reach the funeral tent and the cops, cops he could be friendly with. The Kombie sped a few more metres, sliding on the wet grass. They'd get bogged if they weren't careful. Martin, his eyes more sightful, paced the last hundred metres like a chook with its head cut off. I waved frantically at the women. The Kombie slowed as Martin disappeared towards safety. It was with sadness that I climbed in beside them. They weren't weird or wicked. Just naïve and old. Gone from hopeless to helpless.

They gave me a lift to where I'd parked the Valiant. I clambered out. They handed over the glass they'd snitched, amazingly in one piece. I stuffed it carefully into my bag. The man's saliva would be a great DNA sample. Tweedledum and Tweedledee drove off, gone from my life for good, if they did what they said they were going to do.

As soon as I reached the bitumen I drove like the wind, overtaking the Kombie winding its way with great care down the mountain road. Why such caution? Maybe they didn't want their bodies mutilated by a crash. We waved at each other, me dazzled by the excitement, they calm as the Queen waving to her subjects.

Once home I re loaded the pepper spray, checked the gun, safely secured the glass in plastic and supped on red wine while trying to connect the disparate pieces of information I'd collected. I was only shaking a bit and once I'd showered I could hardly tell the difference between normal and shit scared. A Mars Bar got rid of the final shakes. I'd found out a lot about art scams and forgeries and a bit about the involvement of drugs in that trade, yet nothing about Lucy's father. Unless Harry proved to be the father.

There were no messages from either Mario or Lucy. No news

was good news. I eventually lay down and drifted into a dream in which Harry was spinning rapidly in the wind and I was spinning right next to him. Weird thing was, I was free to whirl any way I liked, which I did, like a kid enjoying myself. Must have been one of those trick knots.

TWENTY

As anticipated, the morning news had a two minute grab about
the suicide of two elderly sisters. No names, but it had to be
Tweedledum and Tweedledee. They'd made the national news because
they'd apparently sent copies of various documents to the Minister for
Police, the Attorney General, a world famous barrister and an ABC TV
journalist. Clever. Paper-shredders the world over would be working
overtime. So would the people-shredders. Evidence of any kind to be
disposed of. Tons of concrete awaited undesirables. Was I to be one of
them, even though I'd innocently stumbled across the crimes? If I lived
I'd certainly gain kudos by having helped bring criminals to justice.
Shit, I might even be on the front page of the tabloids.

What and how much to tell the cops was debatable. Everything
I knew? Nothing? Part of it? It seemed plausible that Lucy's father
could have been involved in criminal activities, or at least aware
of them. Hard to say, having no real clue to his identity. I had to
continue to sift fact from fiction. I'd sniffed the scent of success. It
smelt good, even though it put me in danger.

I was uploading photographs from camera to computer when
Mario phoned. Feeling slightly vulnerable, which was a great
excuse, I asked if I could stay at his place for a few days. After a
pause big enough to drive a truck through he questioned whether
it had anything to do with the death of the two old ladies. I fluffed
up my voice and whined like a frightened puppy.

"I just feel a bit uneasy."

"Did you call Pete?"

I quickly gave myself away.

"Are you some sort of idiot? The police might be a part of it!"

What was I saying about my cop brother? Then I reminded myself that not only did my brother now belong to the De Rossi family, so did Mario.

"Oh, forget it!"

I slammed down the phone. It rang immediately. For two whole seconds I ignored it.

"Holly?"

I yelled louder this time.

"Mario. Listen up. Somehow I'm involved in fraud, drugs, forgeries and murder. In case you are the least bit interested I could be on somebody's hit list!"

I slammed down the phone for the second time. My heart was thumping. Why hadn't I mistrusted him before? I was blinded by his body, that's why. I was also being paranoid. Yet, the people who'd killed Hippie Harry clearly meant business. Why had Mario been so upset when it was clear Harry had been hanged? Guilt? Complicity? Shit, better to stay close to him. I called him back.

"Are you going to put me up, or what?"

His answer was calm.

"Of course. I can sleep on the sofa. If you wish."

"No need."

My voice quavered itself down a notch or two.

"Thanks."

"I look forward to it."

I converted to the rational investigator I wanted to be.

"Did you manage to do the gallery job?"

"As instructed, boss. Will a few blobs of blood do?"

"Shit, you didn't kill him!"

He chuckled.

"Of course not. It was on a piece of gauze left in the bin. Cut himself shaving no doubt."

"And the eggs?"

"Packed and ready for you to inspect."

"You did check the contents?"

Now it was Mario's turn to be annoyed.

"What do you take me for?"

I took him for his body but right then I needed his brain.

"Good. How is Giselle doing?"

"Out of Intensive."

Seemed she was not going to die just yet, which took the pressure off me to discover the missing man, the one she'd created Lucy with.

"And Lucy?"

He laughed that husky laugh of his. I itched with lust.

"Bored as a caged tiger. I have to say her break and enter techniques are extremely refined."

"She learnt when she was young."

Mario chuckled some more. Was he taking the piss?

"Two thugs accosted us as we were delving in the garbage bins. Lucy dealt with them very efficiently."

He was enjoying himself.

"She would."

I imagined Lucy joyfully kicking in the heads of the so called thugs. Mario, fascinated by her expertise, would have stood by.

"I had to protect the precious eggs, of course."

"Of course."

I was thinking of him holding on to me. Lust is a powerful challenge to serious conversation. He filled the silence.

"Do not go out until I arrive to pick you up. Right?"

"Right."

"Be careful, Holly."

Be careful? Did he know something I didn't? I put down the phone shaking from a mixture of longing and fear. With my weapons close to hand I went back to the photos. I was interested in the man the sisters had apologised to. Why him? Why so deferential? Would his name appear in the sister's documents? I zoomed in on the face. I stared hard, then wham, it hit me. The resemblance was amazing. He and Harry, they had to be related. And the hair, it had a red tinge. Jason's hair was red. But he was dead. Harry had said so. So was it a cousin? I peered at it again. I hadn't seen the wood for the trees. Shit, I hadn't even seen the trees.

Had Harry lied to me about his brother dying from an overdose? How had he really died? Had Harry been lied to? Who identified him? Was it Jimmie? He'd be little more than a kid back then. Is that how he'd been dragged in? So many pieces to fit together. I sensed everything was connected. I poured myself another glass and chomped on a Mars Bar, leaving my mind to lose itself in the maze of possibilities.

The banging on the door made me jump. Too soon for Mario. I grabbed the pepper spray and moved down the hall. The front door was being hammered on. Such impatience, I could have been sitting on the loo! I peeped through the peep hole. On the doorstep a young man waited, a package in his hand.

"Who is it?

A monotone voice replied.

"A package for Holly Day."

Another peep. The package, no more than 20cms square, could easily hold a bomb, or it could be a pair of pink flannelette jammies sent sarcastically by Lucy. Best not take any chances. I opened the door as far as the chain allowed.

"Please leave it by the front gate."

The voice came back with those annoying words.

"Sorry ma'm, company regulations. Must be signed for."

Keeping the pepper spray ready, I put my hand through the gap to sign. The young man, totally unfazed, pushed the computer pad towards me. I scribbled an illegible signature and withdrew my hand. He withdrew the pad. He hesitated, waiting to see if I'd changed my mind.

"By the gate."

He shrugged, gave the grin of somebody who meets all sorts of weirdos, and pranced back down the path, turning to grin once more as he placed the package by the gate. At least he didn't yell, "Have a nice day." Lucky for him, else I might just have shot him and made my day. After he'd gone I opened the door fully and stared at the brown packet. Should I wait for Mario? Should I call Pete? Or the bomb squad? But then if they were going to kill me, why not send somebody over to simply squeeze the trigger? They could have shot me, knifed me, run me over, strung me up, added me to concrete mix, had me for breakfast in any number of ways. Even had the Wagon fixed so I'd kill myself. *Memo: Get a mechanical check done on the Valiant.* I decided to take a closer look.

I swivelled down the path and squinted at the package. On the back Jimmie had scrawled his name. That was taking a chance. I leaned down to pick it up then recalled how I'd thought he'd give in easy if he was tortured. Who wouldn't. He'd do anything, including sending an incendory device through the post to me. I hovered above the innocent looking thing. At least if I was blown to pieces Mario could pick them up, rush me to hospital and have me joined back together again. I sometimes felt like Humpty Dumpty. Fat and stupid. Not often, mind. Still, I stayed a coward and left the package where it was. I had plenty of other stuff to occupy my mind; ceramic eggs, precious stones, forgeries, which worldwide galleries thought they had the Picasso original, photographs, as well as information Brian had emailed concerning Martin SS and his business associates. I needed real evidence before I contacted Pete or any other cop and most important, I wanted to ensure I got my fifteen minutes of fame.

I packed my black satin nightie, along with eight pairs of lace knickers, plus the usual Tshirts and track pants. It was going to mean lots of good sex over the next few days. That thought cheered me up no end until I passed the mirror and noted the ratshit state of my hair. I took a long hot shower, threw loads of perfume over myself and while waiting for my hero to arrive worked my way through all the information I'd collated.

TWENTY ONE

After the initial thrill of being with Mario it was depressing how after only four days we were both on edge. Whistling didn't help. The sex was great but tempers quavered beneath the affection. Little things irritated us both, like him not putting down the toilet seat, me putting down both seat and lid, him leaving the edge of the toilet paper all neat and square, me leaving it all jagged, him wanting steak rare, me wanting it burnt to a crisp. Tensions. Defensive insults. Shit, it was like we were already married. I had to get out of there. How to tell this to a man I lusted after.

It was Wednesday. He'd just come out of the shower, all hot, flushed and well prepared for the next round. Afterwards, I tried to compose a fanciful story about the need to leave. Instead, I talked about the package left by the gate. The one Mario had picked up for me. In it Jimmie had sent a few hairs from Sergeant Lachlin's comb. To give him his due, even in his post coital haze, Mario showed some interest.

"This is the package you thought was a bomb?"

He was trying to be funny.

"I simply left it for a while. Just in case."

He grinned and raised his eyebrows.

"Lachlin could be the father, I guess."

"It's possible. But hopefully not."

"Why not?"

"It's grotesque."

"Is it?"

"Believe me, yes."

He'd never know about me and Lachlin.

"I will have to take your word for it."

"Good."

"Why?"

"He was most likely bent anyhow."

"Possibly."

"Are there many bent cops in the Force?"

"How would I know?"

On and on it went like a game of ping pong, back and forth until I got up, showered, dressed in my daggy clothes and determined to go back to my comforting cottage. Anyway, I wanted to check Jimmie's photos against some of the others. I waltzed into the kitchen, hugged Mario and casually mentioned I needed a break. At my cottage. He was adamant.

"Too dangerous."

"Anywhere will be dangerous."

"How about you go to Noosa for a while."

I was furious, him telling me what to do.

"They could kill me up there just as easy."

"There is someone up there on assignment. He could look out for you."

"I don't need looking out for!"

"So what are you doing here, with me?"

"For the sex?"

This threw him. He settled his gaze on me. I refused to relent.

"It's Giselle who needs guarding."

"She already has a police guard."

I didn't recall telling him that. I must have. I suppose. He'd won. I was miffed. Next morning I drove home, sexually satisfied, morbidly depressed at only sticking it out for such a short time. I was also suffering from chocolate withdrawal. I drove round the block several times before parking out front. Everything looked okay but I couldn't be certain. Maybe I was being stupid. Noosa meant getting away. I trod carefully down the path, checking for trip wires or newly disturbed earth. I'd seen movies where land mines were inconspicuously buried. Or bombs. Bombs? Mines? I was thinking crazy stuff. I laughed quietly as I zig zagged down the path, pretending I was a soldier in the jungles of Vietnam, the ones I'd seen in the movies anyhow. Soon as I was inside, picked up the mail, repacked the weapons, cameras, diaries, the memory stick of photographs, a pack of Mars Bars and suitable clothes I secured the cottage doors and windows and began the long drive up to Noosa.

Lucy was well pleased to see me. First we went to the beach, quiet day, few kids, parents working, tourists shopping or eating, pensioners sitting on benches gazing out at their memories, bodies surfing on naked waves. Just an average warm Aussie beach day. As I breathed in the salty air my heart rate slowed to its slowest in weeks. Listening to the waves slushing onto sand, while gulls scheeched their discord, I pondered on all things missing.

I sat on my towel and watched Lucy dashing about in the ocean like a dolphin on Prozac. Shit, I loved her. The sister I never had. She waved for me to join her. I waded in as far as my belly button and halted. She pranced over to me.

"Come on, they're fucking prissy waves."

Scared of the sea since a kid, I'd never moved out far. The ocean was for me a dangerous enemy. I envied and admired surfers and swimmers with their arms windmilling enthusiastically while all I could manage was a flip and a flop, usually on my back. After fifteen minutes of flailing about I waded back out and flopped onto my towel. I turned my head towards the surf lifesafer, a suntanned spunk who clearly worked out for hours at the gym. Another lifesaver, older yet with a cute bum, searched the horizon from his brightly coloured canvas tower. A shark-spotting plane circled overhead. Suddenly I could no longer see Lucy. I stood up and scanned the sea. What was she up to? I called out to the lifesaver and pointed out to where I'd last seen her. His eyes followed my finger, calmly unaware of my fears. I ran over, my heart having palptations, my body sweating. Lucy couldn't drown. No way.

"My friend, she was out there a minute ago, now I can't see her."

There was an unusual choke in my voice. He eyed me with scepticism, no doubt used to quivering tourists.

"I'm serious. She's out there. She could be drowning. Do something!"

I felt like slapping his poker face but held off. I needed his skills. His eyes swooped the ocean in front of us. He called on his mobile and was soon joined by his mate. They seemed to be in no hurry. I was fuming. After a brief conflab they paddled out on their boards in a direction only they could calculate as being correct. After a moment of scouting they heaved a body out of the water. I stood on tiptoe, straining my eyes against the glittering sunlight to make out if it was her. The body was unceremoniously rolled onto the beach. I bent over to make sure it was Lucy. It was.

"Is she breathing?"

The two men worked on her for only a few seconds before she spluttered, sat up, shook herself and laughed. Anger welled in my chest. I wanted to throw her back in.

"You did that on purpose!"

She beamed up at the younger of the two men.

"Thank you so much for saving my life."

Both men, aware at being fooled yet not angry at the luscious shape before them, grinned like twelve year olds. I was furious.

"You were not drowning at all, were you?"

She eyed me with mock surprise.

"Of course I was."

The older lifesaver tousled her hair but spoke sternly.

"Best not try that again. One day it could be for real."

She looked up at the men under her spell and smiled sweetly, her lithe body inviting anything they might want to offer. I growled my disgust, flipped back my wet hair, deliberately shook my flab and sat down. The older man went back to his scanning of the ocean while the younger one lingered. No doubt he'd be shagging Lucy as soon as his tour of duty was over. I was furious. I was envious. I lay down. My mobile rang. I answered. A vaguely familiar voice whispered with an urgency that made me listen real good. It was Jimmie telling me I had to get to the hospital, quick.

"Is it Giselle?"

His voice raced on. I was to head for the basement.

"The basement?"

He rang off. I stared at the mobile trying to make sense of it. There was no sense. I had to do what he said. I scrambled to my feet. I began dressing. I shouted.

"Leech!"

She ignored me. Shrugging myself free of sand I yelled again.

"Leech, there's trouble!"

I was slipping my feet into sand filled shoes, ready to go. Lucy turned half heartedly to face me, her hands firmly around the lifesaver.

"It's your mother!"

That put an end to her delving into his body. She sprinted over.

"What's happened?"

I was cramming my towel, hat and sun lotion into my bag. She grabbed her sarong and wrapped it round herself, then snatched up her things. How much to tell her?

"Somebody phoned. We have to get to the hospital."

She didn't need to know about Jimmie.

"We have to hurry."

Hurry we did, her outrunning me back to the Valiant. I drove as fast as the enforceable speed allowed. Lucy sat quiet, thinking the worst, not questioning me until we reached the hospital.

"Mum is alright?"

I hated to think how bad she might be. If Jimmie had dared to make contact with me it meant trouble, big trouble.

"Just do as I say, right?"

Bewildered, all Lucy could do was nod and stick close to me. As we hurried down the corridor we left a trail of sand at every step. Hospital staff must be used to it. I walked to the information desk and asked where Giselle Knight was. The nurse fingered the keyboard slowly. I grew nervous. The name came through.

"Giselle Knight was released half an hour ago."

"Released?"

I felt Lucy's body tremble.

"She can't be fucking released. She's been in Intensive for weeks!"

My mind was racing. How come she'd been released? The nurse seemed very calm about the whole thing.

"It says here that her brother came to collect her."

Lucy snorted loudly.

"She doesn't have a fucking brother!"

Alarm bells clanged in my head. The lethargy of the nurse continued.

"We could call Security, I suppose."

This was too much for Lucy. She punched the top of the counter, knocking over a vase of flowers. I dragged her away doing my best to jam the dropped flowers back into the vase. Water trickled down the counter and onto the blue patterened carpet.

"Yes, you do that. And call the police."

Next move, the basement. I grabbed Lucy.

"Where the fuck are we going?"

"To the basement."

Something had suddenly dawned on Lucy. Her voice was low pitched.

"That's where they put people when they're …dead."

Shit, I hoped Giselle wasn't in the mortuary.

"Follow me and keep quiet."

"Quiet?"

"That's all I can tell you at the moment."

"She isn't really…Is she?"

"Just do as I say and that includes keeping quiet. Right?"

She had no choice. I punched the button for the lift. Lucy stuck to me like a leech, her strong body pressing against me for comfort.

"Did somebody take her?"

"We'll find her, right?"

Dead or alive, I had no idea which.

"She was supposed to have a cop guarding her."

"Even a cop has to piss occasionally."

A smile almost broke out across her face. I smiled back.

"She'll be fine."

Could be the truth.

"But why in the fucking basement?"

"Makes sense, if someone has taken her. If someone discovers she wasn't supposed to be discharged. Security would search in the Wards and the grounds. The basement would be the last place they'd look. Cops called in. Doors guarded. Roads blocked. Far better to hide her down here until all the furore has disappeared, then quietly walk her out as if she was a genuinely discharged patient."

It was all pure guess work.

"Fuck, that's pretty smart. They won't get way with it, will they?"

Lucy's childlike assessment reminded me of her vulnerability. I was the only one allowed to see that side of her personality. I checked the time. Seven minutes since we'd arrived. Thirty since I'd got the phone call. Anything could have happened. The lift door opened. We stepped out at basement level, me keeping Lucy close. I whispered instructions.

"Wait. And keep quiet."

For no rational reason, I turned right. We crept along a corridor lined with cream paint and rust coloured tiles. Lucy trotted quiet as a lap dog beside me. Reaching a corner I jolted with shock when Jimmie jumped out at us from behind a trolley loaded with crisp white bed linen. Instinctively Lucy went for him. He was jabbed hard in the face before I had a chance to stop it. He teetered backwards. He stroked his jaw and looked at me but nodded to Lucy.

"Who's the crazy?"

Lucy made a move. I tugged her back.

"This is Lucy. Giselle's daughter."

He stared hard at her, still comforting his painful jaw.

"Lucky for you it's not broken."

Lucy postured.

"Yeh?"

He postured back.

"Yeh!"

Luckily the interchange had been in hushed tones.

"This is Jimmie. He's been helping me. So what's going on?"

Jimmie pointed to a set of double doors down the corridor.

"I saw him take her. They're in there."

"Mum is in there?"

"Yes."

I felt for my gun.

"Only one man?"

"As far as I could see."

I felt for the knife. No point using a gun. Not without a silencer. Soon be discovered. Maybe even the pepper spray as the first option. I held it in my hand as we crept to the door. Lucy caught my eye.

"Can I have the blade?"

"No. Sorry."

Best not let Lucy loose with a knife at this stage. If it's only one man against the three of us, no worries. Unless he also had a gun and was prepared to use it. A possibility. The basement was a long way down and what with the air conditioners humming sound would be deadened. I replaced the knife with the Beretta.

We trod carefully and halted a couple of metres from the double doors. In the centre of one was a porthole window. Jimmie held up his hand for us to wait then pressed forward on tip toe. He peeped through the glass. Lucy chaffed at the bit. I began to wonder if Jimmie had changed sides. Not working for me at all. We could be walking into a trap. I had to risk it. And, I did have the gun. Jimmie turned back to us and explained the situation.

"He's got a needle"

Lucy's body shook beside me.

"Let's fucking get her out of there."

"We will. Promise."

I was surprised by Jimmie's composure. He'd seemed so childishly dumb before. Was it an act he'd kept up for his own safety? Jimmie squeezed one of the doors open a fraction and peered around it. He held up his hand, paused for a moment, then let it fall as if starting a race.

"Now!"

Like greyhounds chasing the stuffed rabbit we flung open the door and raced in. The man, ready to forcibly inject Giselle, was so shit scared when he saw the gun that he dropped the needle and made as if to run, then realised he had nowhere to go. He glared at Jimmie.

"You, you bastard. You're a dead man, do you hear me!"

Giselle, mouth gagged, ankles and wrists bound with rope to a wheelchair stared wide eyed. She mumbled something. I ran to her side. Lucy and Jimmie pounced on the man, kicking the needle to the corner of the room. I attended to Giselle, all the time keeping my eye on what they were doing to her attacker. It was not nice. They'd thumped him to the ground in seconds and were pounding away at his head and body. The kidneys were a persistent target. I ought to stop them. Lucy grunted with rage. The man groaned with pain and anger. Jimmie just grunted with callous enjoyment at each kick he delivered. While comforting Giselle I could only gaze at the flurry of hands, arms, feet and legs. The man attempted to drag himself away. Lucy grabbed his legs and dragged him back to the centre of the five metre by four metre room. He swore loudly. This bought forth more torrents of angry kicks. Shit, they'd kill him. Giselle, now free of tape tried to stand.

"Lucy, darling. Please stop."

I gently pushed Giselle back into the chair.

"Stay there, Giselle."

I wanted this man alive. He was evidence. He could lead me to the top people. Maybe.

"Don't kill him!"

Jimmie paused as he gave the man a few more contemptuous kicks. We'd saved Giselle's life, now I had to save her potential assassin's life.

"Leave him! We have to get out of here. "

I turned to watch as Lucy and Jimmie hovered above the motionless man.

"You might have killed him."

Jimmie, like a pro, leaned down and felt his pulse.

"He's got a good pulse."

"No thanks to you pair of maniacs."

Lucy jabbed my elbow.

"He was fucking going to kill my mother!"

"Well, she's safe now."

"Yes, I am safe now, darling."

Giselle was close to tears. Lucy wiped her bloodstained hands on the stack of hospital bed linen.

"The fucker doesn't deserve to live."

Giselle could only shake her head in disbelief. Whatever she'd been through, violence still clearly sickened her. I quickly wheeled her back to the lift. Once the three of us were on ground level my brain returned to a rational state. What now? Lucy stated the obvious.

"How we going to get her to the car without being seen?"

Tricky. Cops might already be swarming over the place. We had to make a move though, before anybody found the man. I had a brilliant idea.

"We'll take her back to the Ward."

"Are you fucking crazy?"

"We take her back. She gets into bed, a picture of innocence. Soon as the man is discovered the cops deliberate. Giselle is back in her bed. No connection made. We sneak away unseen. Simple."

Jimmie pondered on the idea.

"You're right about taking her back. I'll make up some story. You two stay out of sight. They won't remember me."

"What if they talk to you, Giselle?"

Slumped in her wheelchair, she mimed that her lips were zipped. Shit, she had guts. Jimmie took the handles of the wheelchair.

"They'd think she was hallucinating anyhow."

It was vaguely plausible.

"I'll meet up with you two later."

Lucy still wasn't so sure.

"It's crazy but we'll do it."

I thought of a possible flaw.

"What about the cop who was supposed to be guarding her?"

Was he in on it? Lucy's anger had yet to subside.

"I'll rip his fucking balls off."

"Best not."

Jimmie grinned cheekily.

"He was most likely tricked into leaving her alone."

With that probable truth, Jimmie wheeled Giselle back to the Ward. There'd been a shift change. New nurses were in charge. Me and Lucy hid behind a part open door a few metres away so we could see and hear what went on. Jimmie spun a great story. How he was a poor young artist who'd admired Giselle Knight since he was at art school. How he'd always wanted to talk with her. How he'd heard she was in hospital and had taken her for a coffee and hoped he hadn't caused too much trouble. Apparently not. The nurse casually punched commands into the computer.

"It says here she released herself. Her brother came to collect her."

Under her breath Lucy whispered.

"She doesn't have a fucking brother!"

Jimmie kept up his act.

"Sorry. That was me again. I pretended to be her brother. But she's now back, safe and sound."

He was good as me at telling whoppers.

"Nobody need know, hey? Could you wheel her back to her bed, please?"

His charm reminded me of Mario on a good day. The nurse's eyes roamed over Jimmie's body. She fancied him alright. Her fingers clicked over the computer keyboard.

"Very well. Just this once."

Blowing the nurse a kiss Jimmie handed Giselle over. She'd stayed appropriately bewildered. Jimmie joined us. I was impressed.

"Shit, you should audition for NIDA."

"I might just do that, after all this is over."

Back at the motel we wondered how long before they'd discover the injured man in the basement. He might be capable of getting out of there under his own steam but it seemed unlikely. He'd been given a right going over. If he managed to get to Emergency there'd be awkward questions for him to answer. I'd taken a few scrapings from under Giselle's finger nails. Sufficient for a DNA sample. They were in a plastic bag, settled next to the gun I'd thankfully not used. There were three beds in the motel room and Jimmie was invited to stay while he decided on his next move. The criminals who'd been behind Giselle's capture would be after Jimmie for sure.

"Where will you go?"

"Bali? Fiji? New Zealand, if I absolutely have to. Who knows?"

Unexpectedly Lucy kissed him full on the lips.

"Thanks for what you did."

Jimmie grinned.

"You did as much as I did."

A couple of soul mates, I'd say. Which meant I'd feel obliged to leave them alone for an hour or so that night. I shook his hand.

"Thanks for the warning."

He turned his gaze to me.

"You spared my life once. Just returning the favour."

Did he really think I'd have used the gun that night up at Hippie Harry's place? Maybe I would have. Maybe not.

After making sure Jimmie kept in touch I returned home next morning. Driving back I remembered I'd not thanked him for the bomb-free package. I hoped the criminal wasn't too badly hurt even if he deserved it. The cops would likely put his injuries down to gang warfare no matter what he said. Nobody would question why it happened in a hospital basement. Nobody would care.

TWENTY TWO

With Jimmie in hiding, Lucy and Giselle sorted out and Auntie Gert off on some tour up north organised by the Community Health Centre, I felt I should return to Mario's. I'd give it one more go. He welcomed me back. The first lot of sex was great. The single bed was comfortable enough, once exhaustion finally set in. We slept for eleven hours straight, which freaked him out, so out of his normal routine.

I'd said nothing about the event at the hospital. Not a word on the tv or the radio news so I left it at that.

With some reluctance I'd got used to Mario's hairy body yet his obsessive neatness was beginning to irritate. I'd coped with it before but I'd come back from the Noosa hospital pretty tetchy. I was questioning whether I could live his lifestyle: everything stacked in neat piles, books arranged in descending order of size, clothes hung in sections according to colour, shirts and sweaters each on its own hanger, linen stored in coloured sets and socks fitted together in pairs. All a bit unreal. Even food in the pantry was stored according to use by dates. Everything was white and clean and modern, stainless steel and glass overloaded the place. 'Sterile' was the word that kept coming to mind. Trendy yet sterile. As for the kitchen, it might cause a masterchef to have wet dreams, but it intimidated the hell out of me. Who needed six gas rings to cook on anyhow? Or an oven large enough to bake a red kangaroo in. It was all doing my head in. I longed for my disorganised cottage. Even Auntie Gert's pink everything was taking on an unaccustomed lustre. I could hardly speak to Mario that morning. It had been a mistake staying at his place again. Yet, I did feel safe there.

Once he'd left for work I sat with a cup of coffee and chewed on a Mars Bar I'd kept hidden. The unit was a clone of the other seven in the complex, the result of some architect's hallucinations, I imagined. The only brilliant thing was the ocean view. Cup in hand I gazed through the window. Surfers rode waves with the fervour of climate change sceptics, pretending nothing would ever change. Apricot sand curved into a beach that bared its beauty to a blue bellied sky, while waiting only for the vacillations of the Pacific Ocean to swallow it up. Shit, a view worth dying for. Well, almost. The thought of dying reminded me of the DNA samples, which reminded me to get stuck into the diaries.

I began sorting through them. Still nothing to indicate who Lucy's father was.

No information on the route the forgeries took from Giselle's hands to the eventual buyers. A text from Brian explained how four overseas galleries were certain they owned the original Picasso. Interesting, though not surprising, considering it was previously not catalogued. I'd checked library books on Picasso. His massively varied styles and painting materials would make it much harder to authenticate an original. A forger's dream. The artistic eggs were more complicated. No gallery, from the largest government ones to small independent studios, admitted to buying ceramic eggs with precious gems on, or in them. Mind, would they admit it? The general concensus was that chips of semi- precious gems might be included, but if so the eggs would be labelled as such. Yes, and pigs might fly! Shit, the way genetic engineering was evolving, one day they might fly.

Forgeries had clearly been sent around the world, and maybe to order. I suspected Martin SS was in a good position for that organisational task. Giselle seemed to have been both a forger and creator of the eggs. Perhaps not the only one but the only one in my sights. The eggs had labels attached according to their status. All would pass from country to country unheeded by Customs, Excise, Taxes and any other regulations intended as impediments to the wealthy and the criminal classes. It's common knowledge anyhow that only one sea-going container in a thousand is ever checked properly. While loopholes are a feature of any regulation, there has to be a well greased network, which, as Tweedledee and Tweedledum had implied, goes way up the political and social ladder. Finding the people at the top, let alone bringing them to justice, was way beyond my skills, although I was keen to retrieve as much information as possible before handing it all over to the cops. Even that prospect bothered me. As a cop Pete should have sussed out what was going on in the family he was now a part of. Was he blinded by lust? And what of Mario? Part of the same family. Was he genuinely helping me with my investigations or keeping track of what and who I knew? Sad to contemplate, brother and lover, both doubts in my mind.

It was over a week since I'd escaped the clutches of Martin SS at the funeral and not one threatening phone call since. I could have been found easy. No men in black cars followed me around either, as far as I could tell. As for bugs, well, I'd need an expert to check that out. The question was, were they leaving me alone because of Mario, or because I was no threat to them at all. The latter didn't do wonders for my ego. Strolling along the beach each evening had been Mario's idea. Was he parading me for them? Was I right to trust him? Was I being paranoid? *Memo: Check medical descriptions of paranoid.* I had to stay strong and independent. I could definitely do without Mario. I could possibly do without Lucy.

On the second night Mario announced he had to visit his uncle, Bruno de Rossi. It could have been an excuse. Something about a family gathering. I immediately pictured Marlon Brando in *The Godfather.* I joked about it.

"Is there another body to be disposed of?"

"That is not funny."

"Not for the body anyhow."

I almost mentioned the incident at the hospital but thought it safer not to.

"Uncle is going to Italy for a week or so. On business."

Fleeing the country? I kept up my questions.

"Looking for inconspicuous burial sites is he?"

Shit, I hoped Jimmie was okay. I changed from sarcastic to silly, *The Godfather* still influencing my comments.

"You should marry me, then I'd be part of the family. Then I'd be safe."

I'd caught him off guard.

"Like, you know, The Family? The Godfather?"

He shrugged. Not encouraging.

"You will be fine. Stay here. I'll organise for my friend to keep an eye on you."

"So I am still in danger?"

"Better safe than sorry."

"Safe?"

"If you do as you are told."

Charm on, charm off. In spite of his flippancy he must have some idea of the danger. How much more did he know? More than I did? I didn't push the point any further.

After checking my weapons and making sure the Unit was locked like a fortress I let Mario drive off. I phoned Lucy straight away, to let her know I'd managed to stay two days at Mario's place. The trouble with mobile phones is there's no way of telling where the person at the other end is.

"Hi, Leech, how are things going?"

"Fucking brilliant."

"Giselle's good?"

"She's so good I came back home. Made sure that fucking cop stayed with her 24/7. Said I'd kick his head in if he didn't. He got the message."

I bet he did.

"And what about 'the basement man'?"

"I heard on the grapevine that a cleaner found him. Alive. Cops took him off. Gangland attack, so they told the media. Drug gangs."

I sighed with relief.

"At least we're in the clear so far."

"We know fucking nothing about it, right?"

One way of treating it.

"Right."

Lucy had sussed out my low mood.

"He's fucking left you, hey?"

"Who?"

"You know who! The fucking hairy monster."

"As a matter of fact he's gone to the Gold Coast. Back tonight."

"Oh, yeh?"

"Yes."

"So you don't want me coming over?"

"Well, yes. Please."

There was a masterful pause as if she was having to make up her mind.

"I could be there in forty minutes."

"Thanks. Do you know where Mario's place is?"

"I followed that blonde babe to his place a couple of times."

"What for?"

"I figured you might want me to keep tabs on her hours of duty."

The voice was so matter of fact it bought home to me our differences.

"My problem is not so much the blonde babe; it's…it's.."

Shit, how much should I tell her? She read my thoughts as best friends tend to.

"You've got some news?"

For once I didn't have to lie.

"Yes."

"You've found him?"

"Not exactly."

"Flab, you've fucking found him or you haven't."

"It's a bit difficult to explain."

I slipped effortlessly into the new hole I was digging for myself.
"Him and, well, you..it could be that…"
"What!"
I hesitated. She jumped in.
"He doesn't want to know me, does he?"
Wrong conclusion but a great escape route for me. A lie was definitely in order.
"That's it. Not sure if I can go any further with it."
The hole would get deeper but it was giving me time to think. Lucy's voice dropped to soft.
"Who is it? This man. What's he like? Would I know him?"
My mind was scrambling information so fast it made an omelette of the few facts I actually had. I considerd this mish-mash calmly. Lucy grew impatient.
"Flab, fucking answer!"
What to answer.
"We'll discuss it later, right?"
"How much later?"
"When you get here."
"Thanks a lot, Flab. No, no. Sorry. I know you're doing your best."
I was doing my best alright, to scramble out of the hole.
"See you in a while."
"Sure thing."
I replaced the phone in the charger. Back to work on the diaries. I'd kept attempting to fit jigsaw pieces into a cohesive whole. While I'd guessed where missing pieces might fit it was mostly assumption and not evidence. Once Giselle was fully recovered and hopefully dry for good, I could assess how much she was aware of. All these years did she really just do as she was told? She couldn't have been off her brain constantly. Sure she was a long time user but one able to continue with some normality as long as she was supplied regularly. That was her sentence. Had she even thought about what she was doing? It must be obvious to

anybody doing a forgery what they were up to. Did her addiction take away any reasoning ability she may once have had? She hadn't been killed before presumably because she was needed. Now, with the two old ladies sending what must be incriminating evidence to the high ups, the crims must realise the net was closing in. Hence the De Rossi trip overseas? Giselle had become a liability and so could be wiped out with impunity. She'd have information in her head, even if the brain was damaged. She'd implicate herself but there were always deals to be made. Lucy must realise that as fact. Giselle's mansion had been ransacked. I had the diaries. So I'd be a target. Why hadn't Lucy been attacked? Was she to be their Ace. Her life for Giselle's silence? After the unsuccessful attempt at the hosptital Lucy could be kidnapped and held to ransom. I had to warn her. Not that she'd take any notice. Giselle needed continued protection. Lucy needed protection. I needed protection and my hairy hero had gone off and left me. Did he have something in mind for me? Baffling.

After another shot of caffeine the decision was made. I'd take the plunge and contact my brother. He was part of the De Rossi family but I had to trust him. I had to trust Mario. Mario and Pete, it was all too neat somehow. I was beginning to feel hemmed in. I phoned Pete and got his message bank. I told him to phone me back, urgent. Because of what they'd done to Harry and what had happened at the hospital, whoever was involved would be desperate to cover their backs. They must know the Fraud Squad, the Drug Squad, Customs, maybe ICAC, even ASIO would eventually be on to them. By now the information from the two old ladies would be circulating around various government departments. The news would be spread far and wide. The crims would be in a hurry. So what move next? I thought of Jimmie and wondered where he'd ended up. As long as he hadn't ended up dead.

I made a chart of all the names I'd come across on the Case and of all the connections between them. Once I'd finished, all lines led to or from MartinSS. I stood back and stared at my handiwork. It looked like a nineteen sixties piece of crap art, the sort rich boys paid trillions for. Crap art and crap music were always fashionable at some point in history. I put on one of Mario's CDs. Lots of violins and trumpets. I sat at the table and sorted through the photographs and compared them. The connections were proving plentiful. Perversely Lucy was only interested in the one connection, the quickie between her mother and some bloke thirty nine years ago. Time and place. So much known, so much unknown. Lucy wanted an answer. So did I, but any theory I had was intercepted by another. It could take ages.

Lucy's fantasy of a father as being kind and decent and possibly rich and famous was unshakeable. No point trying to explain the odds. So, until I proved otherwise, the truth would have to wait. I just hoped he wasn't a fat, balding nobody with three kids, eight screaming grandkids and a working wife who hated him. His shagging Giselle way back in the seventies, would likely be erased from his memory. He'd probably never told his wife. Perhaps he had no idea about his child. Could be he wouldn't want to know. That was my feeling. Could be wrong. I hoped I was.

I checked the time. Lucy was late. I sent her a text. She texted back. She was on the way. Stopped off for a few goodies. How could I argue with that? I pondered on the couple of keys I'd gained. One I'd found in the tin at Harry's place and the one sent by Jimmie. What the keys would open was another mystery. One could be the safety deposit box. Brian was working on the type and the serial numbers. His skills at hacking might turn up something. Could be a key to Pick a Holiday or such.

I moved the photographs around like a pack of cards. No startling revelation. I gazed out of the window at the fabulous scene, the sea its usual bright blue, waves rolling in as thick as old oil in a chipmaker, while surfers waited patiently for their next big wave. I envied them the exhilaration.

The man at the funeral was a puzzle. He resembled Harry.

Could he be Lucy's father, whoever he was? So far the possibles, according to the diaries and my suppositions, were Martin SS, the unnamed musician, Giselle's minder, Harry, BT, JM, HP and of course Lachlin, plus the man from the gallery. Trouble was, I only had DNA samples for four of them. Only two surnames I was certain of. What was Harry's last name? Had his name even been planted at the head of the grave? I searched my memory. I pored over the photos. No last name anywhere. I checked again the photo of Jason, Harry's dead brother. There had to be further clues somewhere. No DNA matches had yet come up. I'd read up on DNA. Three thousand genes made up one strand of DNA. Some can be switched on and some off. How incredibly amazing is that? Yet it didn't help me one bit. The phone rang. It was Mario.

"You took your time, Holly. I was about to send my friend in to check on you."

I'd forgotten about my minder. I gazed out of the windows, one after the other. No one in sight. He was discreet. If he was actually there.

"I'm fine."

"Look, I am sorry about this but I need to stay overnight."

Alarm bells rang but I shut them up. My brain was overloaded already.

"Oh?"

"A dinner party."

More scenes from *The Godfather* unrolled in front of my eyes. I pressed Mario for more information but suddenly his talk changed to the price of stocks and shares. Unintelligible stuff. Then he quickly said he had to go. As long as he didn't go into concrete foundations. My tone stayed light.

"I'll see you in the morning then?"

His voice changed from unusually fast to high pitched.

"Yes, yes, Mother, I have to go now."

Mother? Me? Shit, he had to be in trouble. The phone went dead. My first instinct was to call the cops. Well, Pete; but then the phone went again. I grabbed it. The voice was slower and calmer, though still intense.

"Sorry, mother. I forgot to say that I love you and please rest. Like I told you. God will take care of you."

God? Shit, the trouble must be real big.

"Mario?"

"I am quite alright. Bye."

He clicked off again. He said God would take care of me. Was that an alias for the minder? What was going on up there? I locked and bolted everything, checked my weapons and settled back to gaze at the pristine white walls. I didn't know what to think. I didn't even know how to think. My mind had gone blank. I revived myself a little by thinking of my lovely garden with its native grasses, pointless peach tree, bird-friendly hibiscus and bottle brushes. I recalled the scent of the magnolia. I imagined the birds hanging perilously on thin stems as they sipped nectar. I thought of the magpies carousing. I was missing my garden and my cottage. This aroused my tetchiness to fever pitch. My hands itched to throw something.

I charged around the rooms, throwing clothes and linen all over the place. I mixed up the cushions. I changed over bedcovers and stacked Mambo Tshirts onto bookshelves and stacked books on the floor. I dashed into the kitchen and mixed up all the containers. I poured sugar into the salt pot and coffee in the tomato sauce. Flopping down on the floor I gazed at the mess and felt liberated. Childish joy rushed through me. At least the place looked lived in. I doubted I'd ever be living there full time. It wouldn't work out. I lay down on the sofa and waited for Lucy to arrive. I wasn't sorry at what I'd done. A bit of disorder, like the possession of a gun, is good for the soul.

TWENTY THREE

I was having a great dream when the ring of my mobile burst into my enjoyment. It was Brian. Shit, the sun was only just popping its head over the horizon, my head was thumping and my brain was nowhere near ready to cope with any news, good or bad. Me and Lucy had downed a lot of Vodka the night before. She took a taxi home some time after four a.m. She had some business to attend to. Apparently. I'd simply flopped into bed and now a couple of hours later, the phone. I felt like shit. I rolled my head off the pillow and braved a false welcome to reality.

"Hello Brian."

Brian's response was not what I wanted to hear.

"There was a man found half dead in the same hospital as Giselle Knight?"

I sniggered.

"Isn't everybody half dead in a hospital?"

"Holly! He was a criminal known to police. He died three hours after being taken into custody."

This made me sit up. I plonked my feet on the carpet. Surely Lucy and Jimmie hadn't caused his death. He was definitely alive when we left him. Had he been killed to shut him up, or as punishment for not getting rid of Giselle? Had the cops been in on the death? Brian continued his train of thought.

"Do you think it had anything to do with your Case?"

A flippant lie flipped itself to the front of my tongue.

"I haven't a clue, Brian. Might be worth my while to investigate though."

"Just checking."

"Thanks."

"I'll ring soon as I have more info."

"After sun up please."

He rang off. *Memo: Get to meet up with Brian again, face to face, soon. He's a good mate.* Nothing so far to connect us to the incident. I sank back into bed. I was just drifting off when I heard the main door being opened. Shit, had they come for me at last. I shook myself awake, grabbed my gun and tumbled out of bed. Creeping from bedroom to living room I raised the Beretta in readiness, only to be confronted with a very large, very awake Mario.

"Shit, I could have shot you!"

He gently eased the weapon out of my sweaty hand and swept me into his arms, just like in the movies. He was going to make my day. With me placed back on the bed he pulled off his clothes. We moved quickly to the state of frenzy we'd grown accustomed to. Not expecting him to turn up so soon I'd worn my comfy nightwear. It was removed with a speed I approved of. He pressed his cool hard body against mine and grinned.

"See, I fancy you even in your flannelette pyjamas."

One big step for womanhood! The real thing began in earnest and continued to the bursting fireworks finale, his hairy body not a problem any more. We lay side by side, crammed against each other, the outer bits of my flab hanging off my side of the bed. Waves literally crashed on the shoreline, just like in the movies. I imagined early morning people walking their dogs, and pondered on how many dogs had peed up the trunks of the Norfolk Pines scattered like sentinels along the eastern seaboard. Most of the urine must eventually drain into the sea. Weird thought.

I cuddled up to Mario, trying to think of him as a lover who didn't belong to a criminal family. He never talked about his uncle's vast business empire, not even the legitimate one. In a way I was miffed. I'd expected him to be a knight in shining armour, openly out to defend the helpless and the vulnerable from the fraudulant and the greedy. How much did he really know? Had I stupidly let him in on too much? Was I safe from being part of some concrete foundation? Was he? My excited brain wouldn't stop exploring the possibilities. I was wide awake.

"Mario?"

He mumbled a response.

"Hmmm?"

"How come you left your uncle's place so early this morning?"

He supported himself on his elbow and gazed at me sternly, his eyes weighing me up. Shit, was he preparing to strangle me? Or was this the time-for-me-to-leave stance? He pecked me on the forehead and lay back down. I shook him.

"Mario!"

His words were crisp.

"I came across some interesting contacts at my uncles."

This was more like it. I played silly.

"Fabulous females?"

He sat up smartly on the edge of the bed and rasped his response.

"There was a Picasso hanging in my Uncle's study."

"What?"

My heart beat faster in anticipation of the next piece of information.

"Patsy Dougherty's Picasso?"

"Sort of."

"The genuine one?"

He rocked with laughter then grew sober.

"It was a copy. Note the word, copy."

I had already noted it.

"So, your uncle told you it was a copy?"

"Precisely."

"So you think he has the genuine one hidden somewhere?"

He lay back down again. I rolled half onto him and stroked his chest, twisting the long silky black hairs into a mock plait.

"My uncle is obsessed with money. If he had the genuine article and could sell it for a good price, he would. He would keep the forgery. Or copy, as he calls it."

"Wow."

But then what did that news matter? Few people outside of trusted business colleagues and family would be invited into the hallowed regions of his house, and what would they dare to say about it?

"He lost interest in the picture once dinner was served. A rather odd collection of guests."

"Like who?"

"Mostly business people. A couple of important figures in the public service, one or two political advisors, even a politician himself."

"Martin Stanford-Smythe?"

"No, he was overseas. The discussion was mostly about stocks and shares. The usual conversation. The value of commodities was a boring highlight."

The talk of commodities could include the price of gems, drugs and valuable paintings.

"So they talked with you openly? As a man."

"As a man?"

"Not just as a family member."

"How do I separate the two?"

Good point and very telling. Was he compromised by his being related to a criminal? Naturally, my next thought was of Pete.

"Was my brother there?"

"Yes, Pete was there."

Shit.

"He is part of the family now."

"But would they talk business in front of a cop?"

"Depends on the cop."

"Are you saying my brother is bent?"

"Not at all. Some conversations can be carried on so that only the initiated understand the full meaning. A sort of code. Like the diaries."

"So that was it. Giselle had learned a business technique."

I bounced out of bed but he grabbed me.

"They did mention the nuisance of certain investigations."

I felt flattered.

"Me?"

"More ICAC, Tax department and the fraud squad."

"Oh."

I felt bypassed.

"That doesn't mean you are not in danger. Possibly."

Possibly was supposed to make me stop feeling shit scared? A part of the job I was gradually accepting. I dropped out a fact.

"I haven't found out what Harry's key fits, not for certain."

"A safety deposit box, I imagine. But where?"

"I'm working on it."

"Let me know when you find out."

Was he fishing? I had to take care. Just in case. He moved on.

"There was another man at dinner who looked remarkably like Harry. In the photo, the one you showed me."

Did I show him? Must have. I was having senile moments at my time of life? *Memo: Write notes every day.* In spite of my misgivings about trust I surprised myself by racing to the drawer where I'd kept my things. I felt my naked flab flapping and didn't mind. I pushed past the mess I'd made of Mario's stuff and pulled out the photos I'd held in a folder. As I turned back Mario's bewildered gaze took stock of the state of his room.

"Did someone break in?"

I sat on the bed .

"No. I did it."

"You did it?"

"Yes."

"Why?"

"I was…bored?"

"Oh. I must remember never to let you become bored."

He grinned cheekily. I was getting to like him. Not his lifestyle but him.

Having sorted out the photo Jimmie had sent me I flicked it under Mario's Roman nose.

"Is this him?"

It took him only a couple of seconds to assent.

"How did you get that?"

"I found it."

No lie.

"See, across the bottom, it says Jonathon Squires."

Which could be somebody else's lie, or red herring. But this was the same face as on the photo of Harry's brother and the little girl. No doubting its veracity. The name Jonathon Squires was scrawled across both photos. I had to concede that a name can be changed as easy as a tampon. Easier in fact. It had to be him though. Surely.

"What do you think?"

"It certainly looks like him. The man I met went by the name of Jonathon Squires."

"Was he known to everyone there?"

"Not sure."

I'd expected more.

"Did this man talk much with Pete?'

"Your brother mostly listened to what was being said."

Was that a good or a bad thing?

"So who did this Jonathon speak to. Mostly."

"My uncle, mostly."

"Not to you?"

"No, not to me."

"So you wouldn't have got a DNA sample from him?"

"Holly, you never asked me to supply you with one."

I lowered my eyes. I already had his DNA from the glass. Mario lifted up my face and peered at me. Disconcerting.

"Have you seen him somewhere before?"

"Er. No."

A little lie. To be safe. I was getting real good at digging myself holes. I'd got out of them so far. Just. No need to mention that I had a photo of Jonathon Squires some twenty years younger. I shrugged. He questioned.

"Is he a candidate, for being Lucy's father?"

"He would be about the right age."

I replaced the photo in the folder.

"Any man between fifteen and ninety at the time would have been the right age."

Mario stood up and tramped to the bathroom. I didn't follow. The alarm clock went off, which reminded me of how much I had to do. Brian should have more DNA results back. He might also have some news about the companies De Rossi was involved with, the legal registered ones. His search on Marina's company should also prove fruitful. I had a Case that day too. A short one, photographing a bloke trying it on with an Insurance Company, claiming he'd damaged his back down in the supermarket car park due to the state of the ground. Bad luck for the supermarket that the cameras had been smashed by vandals. Their lawyer, Paul Diston, suspected he was not injured at all, regardless of the medical reports he'd managed to acquire. A lousy job but I had to keep my name out there. I might not become famous. Cops would no doubt take all the kudos. I might just get a newspaper mention. Could be in the funeral notices if things went wrong.

Mario stepped out of the shower, fresh and shiny as a hairy tangerine. I'd been sitting on the balcony, wrapped in a huge fluffy towel, soaking up the warming sun as it rose higher, pink strips among the clouds. Mario spoke from just inside the room, towelling the last of the water from his body. He spoke firmly.

"I learnt something else last night. Sergeant Lachlin died. Heart attack."

Shit, people were dropping like flies. I wondered about the heart attack and drugs that could cause it.

"Anything suspicious?"

"Not from what was said."

I wasn't convinced.

"You think the Sergeant could have been killed?"

"He was an old man, Holly. People do die of natural causes, you know."

Not when they're around criminals they don't.

"But he was one of your uncle's contacts."

"They certainly knew of each other. Part of the network. Who cares?"

"His family might?"

Again I thought of Jimmie. Where had he got to? I let my worry sink to the pit of my grumbling stomach. The seagulls were preparing for their day of dive bombing of both fish and people. I had a few hours before I had to start work officially, so once Mario was gone I'd contact Brian and see what information about Lachlin he could come up with. I felt bad at what him and me had done together. Okay, so I was young and stupid. Reckless even. What if Lachlin turned out to be Lucy's father. How could I ever tell her? I went inside and voiced my thoughts in a falsely lighthearted way.

"If Lachlin was Lucy's father she wouldn't be pleased. Because he's a cop for a start."

Mario yelled from the bedroom.

"Not all cops are bad, you know."

A debatable point for later discussion. Mario came out, looking a million dollars. He continued from where he'd left off, conversation wise.

"If he turns out to be her father Lucy should be happy he is dead. He was a bastard. A disgrace to the force."

The words were issued with a surprisingly vicious tone.

"You did know him then?"

He paused a moment then responded, matter of fact.

"Of him."

"Of him?"

"Sort of."

I could tell he was trying to cover his tracks.

"His name came up at my uncle's so I figured his connection would not have been, how can I say, reputable. He could have been involved in certain, arrangements."

"You weren't so positive before."

His voice had calmed to its usual rational mode. He placed his hands on my shoulders and pulled me close to him. His strong arms enfolded me. Shit, it was great. At that moment I never wanted a Director to yell "Cut". There was a slight tremble of Mario's body.

"Listen, Holly. I need to tell you something."

That he loved me?

"My father was in the police force. Killed. Shot. On a drug raid. The investigations were cloudy. A suspected cover up. Lachlin was part of that team."

So much for love.

"I'm so sorry."

I meant it. Weird. What did his father mean to me? Nothing at all. What did my own father mean to me? Heaps, if only I'd admit it. *Memo: Get in touch with dad. Soon.* At least now I had an inkling why Mario's interest in the Case. He'd been investigating it, for an expose I assumed. Too late to question Lachlin but not too late for his DNA to be checked. If he was Lucy's father, another difficultly. Were there any kind, decent men around back then?

"So it was definitely a cover up?"

Mario let me go and brushed the question aside as he did up his last shirt button.

"I was a teenager at the time. How would I know."

He moved away and grinned.

"I have time for breakfast before I go."

My heart skipped a couple of beats. He grinned.

"Food!"

Would I ever get to know this man? Did I want to? Whatever

happened down the track, I'd be forever joyful for these few weeks with him. He'd made me more conventional than I ever intended to be but approaching forty maybe it was time. He bounded up to the kitchen, his bum bouncing sexily. I threw myself under the shower. I was drying myself when he called that breakfast was ready. Yet another bowl of heavily shaken sweetened cardboard fibre. The things I did for lust.

TWENTY FOUR

The day began with another husband and wife Case. Another dissolute man. Another wife needing proof that her husband had more cash and property than he was letting on. Sad stuff. Exciting though, sifting through his financial papers under the guise of being a financial advisor. Quite pleased I got away with it. I'd closely watched an episode of *The Hustle* while snuggled up to Mario the night before. I'd got a few ideas on being brash. The wife promised me a bonus when the settlement came through. Decision time. Spend it on the mortgage or a truck load of Mars Bars.

DNA samples had proved that Sergeant Lachlin, Martin SS, Hippie Harry, the gallery owner and Giselle's minder were not Lucy's father. Five down. I was running out of DNA. Giselle's diary provided no further clues. I'd found out a lot but the one vital thing missing was the owner of the successful sperm.

Research into proven forgeries of the major painters had been completed by Brian. Technology had played a massive part in their discovery. Some obviously still slipped through. Several famous galleries abroad were convinced they had the original Patsy Dougherty's Picasso in spite of the question being raised within the industry. None, it appeared, were about to announce any doubt in their own expertise. Con artists depended on professional egos and the subsequent silence. While Mario seemed certain his uncle's picture was a forgery, I was not completely convinced. Who'd be game enough to suggest he was keeping the genuine article in his study anyhow? Clever. It was all guesswork on my part. What wasn't was the style of Giselle's early work. Me and Lucy had seen piles of the paintings she'd done during the seventies and eighties. They were all that mixture of realism and surrealism. I'd hung the one from the Op shop above my bed. I really liked it. Lucy never cared for much of what her mother had produced. Some days that included herself.

I was still unsure if the import/export business run by Pete's wife, Marina, was legitimate. It didn't matter unless she was a part of the gang's forgery business. It would be a perfect outlet. If she wasn't into crime, then she and Pete at least must know what was going on. Surely. This set me to wondering whether my brother had been corrupted. I needed to find out. I could ask him directly. I phoned him. No answer. I left a message. He'd told me to never phone him at work again. If he was an innocent in a den of thieves then he could be in big trouble. I sure didn't want him ending up in a block of concrete, or floating down some flood prone river.

I pushed down the plunger and poured myself a cup of caffeine. I phoned Mario to see how he was doing. I hadn't a clue if he was still working on the Sergeant Lachlin story. Confidential, he always said. Fair enough, a journalist's sources and all that. There was no answer. I swore loudly into the message bank, using words he'd never actually heard me say before. I drained deep of the coffee and let my brain race on. The key from Harry's box was most certainly to a Safety Deposit Box and Brian was working on identifying the bank. He suggested Hong Kong banks were the best bet, being more notorious than Swiss banks when it came to money laundering. The only money I'd ever laundered was a ten dollar note left in my jeans pocket. It came out crisp and wrinkled, like me first thing in the morning. As for the key Jimmie sent, I was nowhere near working that one out. It could be to a suitcase, or a brief case, or one of those holdalls with a lock. Where could it have been left? In a bank, a solicitor's office, a house, a railway station, anywhere in the world. I desperately wanted to hear from Jimmie.

Usefully Brian had proof of trips made by Martin SS to Hong Kong. I figured it had to be him who was Bruno de Rossi's right hand man. This reminded me of possible dangers to us all. I called Lucy. Her voice was heavy with dope.

"Yeh?"

"It's me, Holly."

"Hey Flab, how ya doing?"

She giggled. I never liked to think of her slim, strong body being overtaken again by any kind of drug. Been there, done that. So had she.

"You shouldn't be doing what you're doing."

"Are you my fucking mother!"

I held my breath for a second.

"How is Giselle?"

"Sorry, Flab. The hospital phoned. She's doing great."

"Good to hear. What are you doing later?"

"Not fucking much."

"I've got another job for you. Once you've come back to earth."

"Who wants to come back to earth?"

I sighed loudly.

"Leech, do you want to help me or not?"

"Sure. What do you want me to do?"

"A job only you could do as well."

"Yeh?"

"Yes."

"Heavy stuff?"

"Sort of."

"Sort of?"

"It's Pete."

"You want me to rough up your brother?"

She sounded genuinely confused.

"Sort of."

"What's all this 'sort of'? You're making me dizzy."

I'd forgotten how crazy the level of conversation is with dope heads.

"Just come over soon as you're ready."

"Flab, what do you want me to do to your brother?"

"More with, than to."

There was a distinct silence. Her brain would be trying to unscramble simple information.

"Say that again."

"Just come over, will you. I'm at Mario's."

"Now?"

I imagined the equipment being quickly pushed out of sight, as if I was right outside her front door and not on the end of a phone line. She'd be trying to work out her next move. I gave it to her.

"Leech, I don't reckon you should drive. Cops. You know."

"Okay! I'll walk. It's only two fucking kilometres. Do it easy."

She would too. It would give her a chance to get some fresh air into her brain cells.

"Thanks. And Leech."

"Yeh?"

"Get rid of everything, including the friends. Right?"

I could almost hear her brain clicking over, wondering how I knew about the everything and the friends.

"Promise?"

"I fucking promise!"

"Good. We don't want the cops dropping in, do we?"

It was meant as a threat and taken as one.

"I'll expect you soon."

I phoned both Pete and Mario again. No answer by either. I decided I had time for another shower before Lucy arrived. I was drying my hair when I heard the knock. Wrapped in a towel I eased my way to the front door, pepper spray at the ready, in case it wasn't Lucy. I peered through the tiny gap I'd opened. It was the same man who'd delivered the last package. This time it was a smaller envelope. I opened the door as far as the chain went. He stepped back at seeing it was me but in a different place. Stretching out his arm he pushed the pad towards me.

"For Holly Day. Sign here, please."

I replaced the pepper in my pocket and signed. He grinned broadly.

"You want it left down by the security gate?"

"This package is fine, thankyou."

"So did the last one contain a bomb?"

I frowned. He laughed.

"Just asking."

He spoke with the rhythm of a West Indian, though his skin was white. He laughed again as I took the envelope and closed the door, gently. I'd just turned round when I heard an almighty howl. I flung open the door. Lucy and the young man were battling it out on the patio. A Rugby scrum couldn't have been more violent. She was sitting on his chest.

"Lucy!"

She stayed where she was. The man was gasping yet smiling.

"Lucy, he's just the courier!"

Momentarily she stopped and looked first at him, then at me.

"Let him go."

We were getting dangerous, more to ourselves than anybody else. The man, a bruise already forming on his cheek slowly got to his feet. Lucy put her hand on his arm, miming the word sorry. He shook her away and dramatically hobbled off. We peered over the rails and watched him climb carefully onto his motorbike and whizz off. Lucy turned to me.

"I thought it was a fucking intruder, come to get you."

"He could charge you with assault. Tut tut."

I wagged my finger at her then stepped inside, secretly pleased she'd been there for me. Lucy followed, head down.

"The fresh air must have done you good."

"So, I fucking got carried away."

"One of these days, you will be. By the cops."

She grinned.

"They wouldn't dare."

I had to agree.

"Thanks anyway."

We sat on the sofa. Lucy wore her usual array of black leather and red. She blended in well with the surroundings. Maybe it should be her and Mario together.

"So what is it with Pete?"

I was beginning to change my mind about my original plans for him. I'd thought of getting him on film in a compromising position with Lucy, so I could blackmail him later, for information, if necessary. Stupid idea. Shit, he was my brother. He couldn't be bent. Could he?

"Well?"

"Coffee?"

"What is it you want me to do?"

I had to come up with something. Maybe if I just got her to test him. If he took up an offer of sex with the delectable Lucy after only being married a few months then surely he'd be capable of other dreadful things. A bit far fetched but if any woman could tempt a man it was my best friend. It was a shit thing to do but life was getting dangerous for us all. Lucy nudged me in the ribs.

"Flab!"

"I want you to offer to shag my brother."

She sat bolt upright.

"You what?"

"Just tempt him. Test him. See if he takes up your offer."

Lucy was bewildered.

"Offer your brother sex?"

"Well, yes."

The more I talked about it the more I realised it was a shit idea.

"Well, sort of."

"He's only just been married."

"Exactly. I want to check if he really loves his wife."

"For fucking sake, why?"

Good question.

"What's he fucking done to deserve that from his own sister?"
The hardest question. Now I'd gone off the idea completely.
"You're right. Stupid idea. Sorry I asked."
Lucy moved to another chair. She sat down opposite me.
"This is all getting to you, hey?"
"Whatever you say."
"Was it going to be some sort of birthday surprise?"
I laughed out loud at the interpretation of my hair brained scheme to trap my brother. I grabbed at the life line.
"Like I said. Stupid."
"So I don't do it?"
"No, you don't do it."
She kicked off her boots and wriggled her toes in the air.
"That's a relief. I never did fancy your brother. He's a fucking cop for a start."

I was pleased I'd been made to see sense. Lucy lay back on the sofa, sighed deeply and closed her eyes. I stood up and paced. I was jittery contemplating what I might have set in train if I'd tested my brother. I wasn't sure I could trust anybody one hundred per cent, apart from Lucy. We both needed food and drink, lots of it. I put up the suggestion.

"Shall I go get some take-away?"
She murmured something which sounded like yes please. I left her, no doubt conjuring up some fabulous S and M for my cop brother. Walking down the hall I noted the unopened envelope on the hall table. I'd check it out when I got back. I drove down to the local Chinese and parked. I was just organising my weapons in the bag when my mobile rang. It was Mario. He sounded annoyed.

"You've gone out!"
"Just to the Take Away."
He was really anxious, which made me anxious. I should have pretended Lucy was with me.
"Please drive back immediately. I mean it."
"I'm fine!"

"Holly!"

I changed tack.

"How did the meeting go?"

"What meeting? Oh, that meeting."

Shit, what was he up to?

"I'll be back tomorrow. Not sure of the time."

"I won't go out again."

"Good. And go straight home. Now!"

He hung up. He cared about me. I cared about him. I'd hung out for someone good for thirty eight years. Was it love? I put away the mobile and clambered out to get the food. My feet touched the ground the same second I felt the bang to my head. I gasped with the hurt. Stars clustered before my eyes as I dropped. A pair of hands began dragging me towards a black car. Shit, the black car. I tried to scream but nothing came out. No Neighbourhood Watch coming to the rescue, again. I did my best to struggle free. I made gurgling sounds. Hopeless. I made a faint shout for help. A hand was clamped over my mouth. The car loomed ever closer. I felt for my bag. Dropped when I was tackled. My throat was dry. My heart was pounding. My head was sore. I was well and truly miffed at being caught so easy. Why hadn't I listened to Mario? I was being pulled along like a lump of meat. The man was joined by another man, their bulky shapes outlined against the flashing lights of the Chinese shop. One man opened the door as the other tried to get me into the back seat.

Suddenly a cross between a whirling dervish and Bruce Lee pounded into view. I heard the crack of bones as Lucy yanked away the man who'd been holding me and slammed him against the car. He dribbled to the pavement. The other man flipped himself round to me. I was slipping and slithering about. Lucy grabbed his legs and threw him to the ground like a champion caber-tossing Scot. She yelled at my stunned face.

"Quick, Flab. Get up!"

I got up. Stumbling from the prone position to the vertical

was no mean feat but I managed it. Both head and heart thumped to the same beat. Lucy was finishing off the second man, the first lying silent on the ground. I stared around for my bag. Found it. I got out the gun and pointed it at the main man who was dazed but still lethal. He scrambled to his feet and made for me. I raised the Beretta to shoulder height.

"I'll shoot! Self defence."

He stopped. I stared over at Lucy. Do I shoot? Not without knowing I'd put him out of action for sure. *Memo: Get some shooting practice in, legal or otherwise.* I'd dug myself the deepest hole yet. Lucy took charge. She grabbed my arm and together we raced to the Wagon. The man was hobbling after us, his hands holding his stomach. Lucy must have done some very nasty things to his innards. I was panting at a hundred miles an hour. Lucy breathed normal. She snapped open the door to my sturdy Valiant and pushed me into the driver's seat, then flipped herself into the back. I drove over the speed limit checking my mirror constantly.

"He's not following. Why?"

"He's helping the one incapable of walking?"

I turned to look at Lucy. She was grinning like a Cheshire Cat.

"You enjoyed that."

"I sure did."

"Guess you saved my life."

"It's not saved yet, Flab."

She sounded so grown up. What a friend. We both knew we had to get ourselves out of it. They'd have to be armed. I'd been an easy target. Lucy had caught them by surprise.

"Leech, your car. The number plate."

"I parked it round the corner. We can pick it up later."

A cop car raced in the opposite direction. Lucy smiled and put her hand on my shoulder.

"I phoned the cops. Told them there was a fight going on down at the Chinese.

I said something about drug gangs."

I could have kissed her.

"How did you know?"

She pointed her slim finger, with its perfectly manicured nails, against her nose.

"A little bird told me?"

"Mario?"

She smiled and stared out at the road racing beneath us.

"Think you'd best slow down. Don't want the fucking cops stopping us."

"Too right."

"Back to my cottage, I reckon."

"Nowhere is going to be fucking one hundred per cent safe, Flab, but your place is good as any right now."

"Right."

So much for the minder. It was my best friend who'd saved me from a fate worse than death. Possibly from death itself.

TWENTY FIVE

What had they been after? The diaries? Me? Why not bump me off earlier? People were killed for much less than being a smart arse nuisance. There was that woman who killed her husband because he slurped his soup with a tea spoon. Must have sounded like a barge full of pigs. I'd have shot him too.

Lucy slept like a baby in the spare room. It took the smell of frying bacon to force her head off the pillow. She managed to ask for two eggs.

"You never eat eggs."

"There's always a first time."

She stood up, wrapped a sheet round her size ten body, tip toed to the bathroom and closed the door. I sat down to eat my bacon sarnie. Soon as I'd finished I began preparing hers. With due pomp she arrived, smelling of my frangipangi shower gel. I placed the plate in front of her. She tucked in. I poured coffee and sat opposite her.

"You risked a lot for me, last night."

She swallowed hard.

"What's to risk. I'd called the fucking cops."

I frowned.

"Soon as you left I heard another car spin off. It was suspicious."

"The thing is Leech, what were they after? The diaries?"

Lucy shook her head.

"You ask too many fucking questions. You're too visible."

"People my size always are."

"Come back to my place. Too risky here."

"Mario should be back soon."

"Should. Not certain, is it?'

I still couldn't work out why they hadn't threatened Lucy. She hovered with her empty plate and cutlery over the kitchen sink, staring at the greasy pan. She shrugged.

"They can wait."

She tugged my arm.

"Get your bags packed. My place."

She shushed me down the hall to the bedroom. I stuffed things into my overnighter. A gleam of light suddenly hit the corner of my eye. I turned slowly. It was the sun glinting through a slit in the curtain, hitting the blue stone of the dog's eyes and reflecting back on me. It brought back memories of when me and Lucy stayed with Giselle up the mountains. I mused on whether her works would become more valuable if she gained notoriety. My twenty dollar painting could be worth as much as a thousand, given time and scandals. That would buy a lot of chocolate bars. Not that I'd sell it. Weird how the two old ladies told me to hang onto it. Sentimental reasons I supposed.

"Flab, hurry up!"

Another thing. Of all the people I'd connected to each other, three of them were dead. Who'd be next. I tossed my bag over my shoulder and walked into the kitchen. A knock on the front door made me yell out to Lucy to wait for me. I raced down the hall, grabbing my gun out of the bag. The visitor knocked again. I stood with the gun while Lucy peered out of the peephole.

"It's a fucking man with a letter."

Not another one. I looked on the table. The letter I'd never opened was missing. Shit, where had that gone? The man called out.

"Hello?"

He'd obviously heard our voices. I nodded to Lucy. She opened the door a few centimetres. He stepped back, a frightened look on his face.

"I've got a, a letter for a, a Hol..Holly Day."

"Who are you?"

"I have a, a letter."

The man moved back further, his arm outstretched with the letter in his hand.

I reached out for it.

"Pass it over."

He did.

"Sorry, its…it's a ..bit late. Got delayed. Sort of a bit late. Sorry."

Having stuttered the apology he dashed back down the path and whisked out of the gate like his pants were on fire. Maybe it was the incendory device this time. Lucy slammed shut the door.

"So?"

I smelled it.

"Doesn't smell like a bomb."

"You a fucking expert on bombs?"

I wished I was. I turned it over, carefully.

"Flab, read it later."

"It could be urgent. He was no ordinary courier. They make you sign for everything. Even your own death warrant."

Lucy burst out laughing.

"That is fucking good, you know that?"

I was already ripping open the envelope. It was from Jimmie. Lucy tapped her fingernails on the hall table. I leaned my body against the wall, opened up the page and read out loud.

Holly. Not much time. Things real bad. The painting from the Op shop, keep your eye on it. Time running out. A good mate will see this gets to you. Thanks for trusting me. They're coming for me. Must go. Sorry. Jimmie

His signature was little more than a scrawl. I let the note drop to the floor. A heavy weight pressed on my heart. My mouth dried. They were coming for him? Had they taken him? Was that how it was with Hippie Harry? Lucy picked up the paper, read it, then put her arm around my shoulder.

"He'll be fine."

I nodded. I sat on a chair. Lucy poured me a glass of brandy. I gulped it down.

She hovered over me, her legs astride, her hands on her hips. A stance I'd grown to both love and admire. She leaned over and whispered.

"He'd have escaped. He would."

"I hope so."

Fatal mistake, getting emotionally involved. Okay, so I was new to the game. I took back the note and checked the envelope. No date. It could have been sent days ago. I should have questioned the messenger. I couldn't bear to think what they might have done to Jimmie. I had to believe he'd escaped, even if it was to New Zealand. What did he mean about Giselle's painting? I'd already decided to keep it. It didn't make sense. Shit, I'd been making no sense for ages. I'd almost set my brother up so I could blackmail him. One minute I was mad about Mario, the next mad at him. One day I was sure I'd help to get a bunch of criminals put away. The next I was thinking I could shoot them all on my own, when clearly they could kill me any time they wanted. I was growing more paranoid by the hour. I had to learn to trust. I'd phone Pete and put Jimmie on the missing persons list. Maybe advise Mario too. He could make a story out of it. It might smoke out a few people who had the answers I was looking for. Funny how I'd never seen anything he'd written. Must be for the Nationals. I wondered if Mario had put the minder back on duty.

I decided to take with me all the information I'd collected so far. I could have missed something. I'd have to pry deeper into the diaries, re check the photos, try to make sense of the charts and graphs I'd made based around Martin SS. Several emails from Brian explained the connection Martin SS had to a Hong Kong Bank. Amsterdam seemed to be where the search with Harry's key might end. Brian was searching other avenues. Where had the letter missing from the hall table gone? Lucy was getting restless.

"Let's go."

We stopped outside Lucy's brick and tile two bedroom town house. One in a block of six. She got out, undid the garage door and slid the Red Barina she was driving into the garage. I sat, patient and watchful in my Valiant, the engine still running. Everybody who walked past I eyed with suspicion. Lucy went inside to make sure her place was safe. I picked up my bag and stepped out, noticing a mosaic topped table in the garden next door. Tiny blue pieces of glass glistened in the rays of the setting sun. That was it! The blue stones! I'd cracked it. Either that or I'd cracked, period. A kookaburra laughed from a box gum opposite. I got back in my Valiant, shouted that I had something to do and skidded a U turn in the road. I raced towards my cottage. It had to be the painting the mob were after. Was there incriminating evidence hidden in the frame? Even tiny letters inscribed in the painting, names and so on. The dog seemed oddly placed. The dog's eyes? Were they precious gems and not bits of glass? That had to be it. Or was I going completely crazy. All this went tearing through my brain as I whizzed across town and drew into my street.

A large black saloon was parked under a trailing tea-tree opposite my cottage. I slithered to a halt a few houses down. Holding tight onto my bag of weapons I crept up the street. It was just on dark. I held the blade close to my body while making sure I could grasp the Beretta if needed. All was still. Neighbourhood Watch still not on duty. I sidled up to the black car. No shadowy figures. I peered in. Nobody inside. First task completed. Second task was to let down two tyres, pavement side. It took some effort to stick the blade in, and even more to pull it out. There was a slight downward movement in the tyres. I hoped the car didn't belong to a visiting doctor.

Treading softly down my brick paved path I checked for internal lights. None but a torch beam shone from the back, from my bedroom. Shit, a pervert after my lacy knickers. My silent wisecracking had wisely replaced my urge to whistle. The sweat on my forehead trickled over my thirty eight year old wrinkles. Gently and slowly I pushed open the slightly ajar front door. Adjusting my eyes to the dimness, I snuck in and navigated my way down the hall. Passing the kitchen I paused and listened. Not a sound. I proceeded down to my bedroom. The door was open a quarter of the way. I stood outside of it, straining my ears to decipher the huffing and puffing that was going on. Shit, a stranger was having sex in my bedroom. Was he alone? Nothing for it but to check. I kicked the door wide open, yelled out an order to stop and pointed the gun at the bed. I heard a whispered 'fuck' as I switched on the light. A man, startled by my entry, dropped his torch and trampolined across my bed. In spite of the gun he courageously threw himself at me. Stupidly, he missed and thudded onto the carpet at my feet. Rolling onto his back, he stared first at the gun then at the painting which was hanging lopsided on the wall. It was the man from the gallery. I was as surprised as he was. He looked so pathetic.

"You a collector of nineteen seventies paintings then?"

He sat up, his paunch now wobbling over the top of his trousers. His eyes were glued to the Beretta.

"Don't ya get shooting that. Please."

Gone was the plum English accent. He was back to being a small-time-thief, with the appropriate Sydney accent. He was gasping like an asthmatic. I glanced up at the picture while keeping the gun on him.

"Is it worth a lot of money?"

He shrugged. I'd wound the wire round the hook half a dozen times, making it difficult to take off in a hurry and this man had been in a hurry. He whimpered like a baby. I wasn't sure of my next move.

"Is there cocaine stashed in the frame?"

He seemed genuinely shocked by the question.

"I was never into drugs. Too violent."

"So why this painting?

"It is something…sort of, special."

I motioned for him to get up. He scrambled to his feet and stood, rocking on his heels. I figured he'd not make a run for it, not with the gun pointing at him, not with his weight.

"What do you mean by special?"

He sighed loudly and inspected the condition of his stomach.

"I wanted something for myself. Real cash. A lot of it. I've been doing their jobs for too many years. It's my turn. I deserve it. Ya know what I mean? I meant no harm to you or nobody. Not into killing."

"Sit down."

He sat on the bed.

"Explain. Or I'll shoot you. Before I call the cops."

He grinned, a cocky grin. His mouth began running away with itself.

"I nearly got away with it, hey? Had my tickets all ready. South America. I got a lot of stuff in my head. The cops'll love me. But I'd rather you let me go and say nothing. You can keep the picture. Brings nothing but trouble. They'd never let me get away with it anyway. The bastards."

He chuckled nervously as I went through his pockets. I had no idea what to do with him. He might be a tiny cog, but they had their purpose. I should call Pete.

"So. Tell me about the painting."

"I need to get out of here. And fast. Before they catch up with me. Ya hear what I'm saying?"

I faltered.

"Tell me what I want to know and I'll think about it."

"You're a stupid girlie who gets people killed. Ya know that?"

That was below the belt. I raised the gun to his head. He'd grown reckless.

"They'll wipe you out in one blast."

"They haven't so far."

"They had your every move down pat. Ya mean nothing to them. None of us do."

He was getting on my nerves. He sniffed as I wavered. Then, with the sudden twitch of his head, his whole body stiffened and his eyes widened with terror. He was staring at something over my shoulder. Shit, I'd been caught out again. He must have had somebody with him. I made a half turn to check. A swift clip from a muscled arm flipped the gun out of my hand. It flew up in the air, landed on the carpet and spun under the bed. While my eyes followed the journey of the Beretta my ears registered the single shot. The gallery man gave a brief grunt as a bullet clipped him in the heart. He reeled backwards then the force of his weight shifted him forward. He fell like a sack of potatoes, blood spilling all over my thirty year old carpet. I swung out at the man.

"You bastard, you've killed him!"

The bastard whacked me with his free fist. I was getting used to pain. He shouted.

"Get the painting down."

"What?"

He pushed me against the bed.

"Get it. Now!"

I scrambled up and tramped over the bouncy mattress then clung to the picture as I did my best to undo the many strands of copper wire I'd used to prevent it dropping onto my sleeping head. At last the painting was free of the wall. The man grabbed it. I was so indignant I shouted at him.

"I paid twenty dollars for that!"

My assailant belted out a roar Pavarotti would have been proud of, pocketed his gun and preparing to make his escape pushed me down onto the bed. I flopped like a marlin just hooked, waiting to be finished off. Then I heard it, the familiar voice and the usual blustering rush onto the scene. I almost cried with relief when I saw Lucy. Caught unawares, the man was at the receiving end of her martial art tactics before he could open his mouth to swear. Her voice rasped the air.

"What you think you're doing, you fucking bastard."

My cavalry had arrived. The man did his best to face her, the painting tucked tight under his shooting arm. He swore. Lucy swung her leg in a wide arch and slammed it into the man's guts. He bent over in pain but not before somehow managing to clip Lucy on the head with the painting. She was briefly out of action.

"Flab! Move!"

I jumped up, pulled my gun out from under the bed and pointed it at him at the exact moment he shoved his gun into my face. He grinned hard, then with a heave of his massive body he dashed out and slammed the door behind him, taking the painting. Lucy, back in form, was about to make chase when she tripped over the dead body. She eyed it with disbelief.

"Flab, there's a fucking bleeding body in your bedroom."

I tested for a pulse. None. None was expected. It had been close range. I gulped hard.

"You saved my life again.

"It's getting to be a habit, hey?"

"Call the cops."

"What about an ambulance?"

"Too late for that."

"You got any brandy left?"

That was what I loved about Lucy. Nothing fazed her. Apart from men. Some men. Some men, sometimes. We walked into the kitchen. She dialled while I made coffee and searched out the brandy. We sat and waited for the sirens. My gun was already in a safe place.

"I'd grown fond of that painting."

"Mum can paint you another one. Once she's real better."

I didn't mention that there was supposedly something special about the one just stolen by the killer. Perhaps the dog's eyes were precious gems. Perhaps I'd never find out what was special about it. Perhaps it was all bluff. Or a big mistake. I ate three Mars Bars before the siren was heard. It was time to check with my best friend.

"Leech, you do realise what your mother was messed up in, don't you?"

"I know she'll do time. I'll help her out best I can. "

We waited patiently for the door to open and the cops to swarm in.

"Flab."

"Yes."

"So what's our story?"

"Two strangers broke into the cottage. They roughed me up, looking for, for anything of value. The painting? Then one of them tried to rape me and the other man, the one with the gun, shot him dead. Then ran off. You came round when I called you."

I'd not told such a ludicrous lie before.

"Just wanted to get the story straight."

We'd tucked our arms around each other just as Mario and Pete burst into the room, accompanied by several other cops. Pete and Mario together? Too much of a coincidence. Who'd been informing who? Pete swept through the room like he'd done it all before. Guess he had. Mario marched over to me, his manner brisk.

"Are you alright?"

"Fine. We both are. Now."

The body was being looked over by Pete. He gave his order.

"Get forensics. And cordon the whole area off."

Pete turned his attention to me.

"Sis, stay with Lucy. We'll get the minder back. He never should have left. Right, Mario?"

Mario avoided my gaze. All good things come to an end. I spoke direct to my brother.

"So, how come you both came here together?"

"We were both on duty."

I gazed from Pete to Mario.

"We'll explain later, sis. Let's get you two out of here."

Pete nodded towards the two constables who led us down the

hall. For Pete it was simply business as usual.

"And don't touch anything on your way out."

Mario, his voice hoarse and full of guilt, called out.

"I will be round to see you as soon as I can."

I couldn't quite manage to tell him not to bother. Lucy eyed up her cop at her side then grinned cheekily at me.

"At least you'll get new carpets out of this."

I began to whistle as we made our way outside. I wondered why the gallery man had given his life for the painting. As I got into the Valiant, with a sultry constable in the passenger seat, I hoped no one would find the gun. Stuffed inside my extra large flanellette jammies it would doubtless escape detection if the forensics person was a young male.

TWENTY SIX

I'd been back in my cottage a few days. The minder made sure he was visible occasionally to at least give me a sense of being protected. I'd had a few good nights sleep. The vibrant ringing of the landline fully woke me. I rolled over onto my back. The sun shone through the curtains. Only the sound of traffic whizzing north to south and vica versa was audible. The birds must have come and gone. It was way past my getting up time. My head ached. My throat felt like it was being scoured with a toilet brush. I stretched myself out of bed and stumbled to the kitchen phone.

"What is it?"

"It is me, Holly."

The voice was indignant. My favourite vision in pink conjured itself up before my eyes. The image made me squint. *Memo: Still to get eyes tested.*

"Yes, Auntie?"

"Guess what?"

Five minutes out of bed and a guessing game? I did my best.

"You're dead and you're talking to me from the other side?"

"Don't be silly."

"Okay, it's me that's dead and I'm talking to you from the other side."

I felt dead. I didn't even recognise the person staring back at me from the small mirror above the bench top.

"Holly, you haven't been ingesting what you shouldn't, have you?"

"Mars Bars and Wine?"

"No wonder you sound terrible."

"For a zombie, I feel just great."

"You are being silly again."

"Auntie, I am fine, honest."

Honest? Even as a zombie I could lie real good. Truth be told I'd ingested a bucket full of wine and chocolate the night before, which explained my current physical and mental state. Mario had called round and explained how he'd been working as an undercover cop, how he and Pete had been on the De Rossi Case for over a year, trying to catch the big fish as well as the tiddlers. They were slowly but surely gathering sufficient evidence to put them all behind bars when along I came, blundering my way in, upsetting the apple cart, forcing the hands of the criminals and every other cliché he could roll off his tongue. Made me feel a right idiot. After I'd arrived on the scene everything had, much to their chagrin, shot off in all directions, making it tougher for them. What it all boiled down to, in my mind at least, was that I'd got Hippie Harry strung up. Mario insisted it wasn't my fault. I was naïve. No excuse. I'd grown too big for my boots. Trying to prove myself a good investigator I'd gone off half cocked. I'd jumped in where angels fear to tread. I used a lot of clichés too. Then there was Jimmie. Had I got him killed too?

Mario said he'd leave me to get a good night's sleep. Ergo, no sex. I was supposed to feel better when I got up. I didn't. He'd left around midnight. It was then I'd seriously got into the wine and chocolate. Lucy had only got into the wine. She'd collapsed before me. She'd sprawled herself out on the sofa, a misshapen bundle of black and red. I assumed she was still there. I was not in the mood for talking.

"Holly, are you there?"

"Just about."

"I have some interesting news."

"More?"

"It's about Patsy's painting."

I had to sit down. I dragged myself to a chair.

"Yes?"

"Listen. You will never guess."

I probably never would. My eyes were shutting themselves.

"What?"

"Patsy Dougherty has left me her Picasso in her Will."

This got my attention. My eyes even tried opening. My ears were wide awake.

"She died?"

"A few weeks back, apparently."

I hardly dare ask.

"Natural causes?"

"Of course. And I never went to the funeral. I feel guilty."

"It's only a copy, Auntie."

"It may not be."

"Auntie."

"Pete is bringing it round to your place. He should be there in a while. Just to make sure."

"Let me get this straight. Patsy left you the painting in her Will and Pete is bringing it to show me?"

"That is correct. He had to fly down to Sydney for a meeting. Something to do with art fraud. So I asked him to pick it up from Patsy's solicitor."

"Why is he bringing it to me?"

"It could be evidence, you silly girl. You are the investigator. There's some conditions about me having it. Not sure what yet. Pete will explain."

My brain was getting truly overloaded.

"Conditions for her leaving you a copy of a Picasso?"

"So you get yourself sobered up before he arrives. Do you hear me?"

"You coming over too?"

"I have a seminar to attend down at the Community Health Centre. Wait til they hear I have a Picasso."

"It is a forgery, Auntie."

"I bet I get lots of visitors to my place once the word gets out."

No point in repeating myself.

"Whatever."

Her voice dropped. It sounded like she'd got half a dozen oysters stuck in her throat. I thought of Marlon Brando in *The Godfather*. I still preferred Clint Eastwood.

"Don't you see, Holly. Patsy pretended it was a copy to keep it safe from thieves. Now she's left it to me. I'll soon be worth millions and when I die I'll leave it to you. Maybe. Depends how you treat me between now and then. And mind, I don't figure on dying for a good few years yet."

She probably wouldn't either. I was beyond asking in depth questions.

"Bye, Auntie."

I put down the phone. *Memo: Check out the cost of top quality Old People's Homes.*

Could the painting really be genuine? The two old ladies might somehow have organised it. Had they conned their bosses into believing they'd turned over the genuine article when in fact they'd left it with Patsy? Giselle would easily paint several forgeries that were good enough to palm off to galleries and anyone else who wanted to buy one. Shit, it was possible. I hated to think what the conditions might be.

One thing for certain, Brian could search out current Picasso values.

I sat and stared at myself in the mirror. I felt like shit. I looked like shit but I had proved myself as an investigator. With any luck, Auntie would inherit a valuable painting. If she died of an aspirin overdose I'd push my brother off a cliff and so inherit Auntie's fortune all to myself. My mortgage would be paid off and life would be absolutely, one hundred percent, brilliant. As if. I laughed at myself as I filled up the jug. A nice, stupid, day dream. Not that I'd ever kill my brother and no way would Auntie die any time soon. And who knows, the Picasso, even if real, might only fetch enough to pay off mine and Pete's credit card debt. What did I want with money anyhow? More than anything I wanted to be in at the end of the Art Fraud Case and to discover who was Lucy's father. I could have that with or without a Picasso. Coffee. I needed coffee. Strong and sweet. Bucket loads of it.

TWENTY SEVEN

I was pulling on my navy trackies, the last pair outside of the laundry basket, when Pete knocked, announcing his presence loudly, presumably so I wasn't taken by surprise and took a pot shot at him. He swaggered down the hall like a small man with a big horse. My brother was no Clint Eastwood. The capture of a gang of criminals must have gone to his head. Promotion must be on the horizon. Parking himself on a chair he placed his order.

"Coffee. Strong, sweet and easy on the milk."

"Easy on the please as well, I note."

He'd never said please, even as a kid, so I didn't hang around for it. I put on the jug and piled yet more coffee into the plunger. Leaning against the sink I eyed my brother and realised I'd never tried to be close to him. Same mother, different father, was that the reason? Mum sure used to spoil him. Did he envy me knowing mum a few more years than him? Could be. I mused on the prospect that when Auntie died I'd have to split what was left of her Picasso money with my baby brother. Mind, as a cop doing dangerous work Pete could be dead before Auntie Gert. Come to think of it, so could I. Noisy miners jostled with each other over the nectar of the red bottlebrush outside the window

I poured boiling water over the Arabica. *Memo: Tell Pete it's good manners to say please and thankyou, even for a cop.* Pete scrutinised me, probably summing me up as a prosecution witness.

"Do you really have a gun, sis?"

I lied, with a very straight face.

"No."

"That's not what I heard."

"Does it matter?"

"I'm a cop."

"Who always tells the truth?"

Got him in one. He grinned.

"You always were the smart arse of the family."

I took it as a compliment.

"Thanks."

"So. Auntie Gert told you about the Patsy Dougherty picture?"

"She did."

"And the conditions?"

"She doesn't know what they are."

"Forgot already, has she."

I doubted that but let him rave on. I was interested in how Auntie stood, legally.

"So, she has definitely been left the Piccasso?"

"A copy. According to the expert."

"What expert?"

"All in good time."

Shit, men can be so irritating. I plunged. I poured. I pouted.

"Well?"

Pete supped, slowly. I thought of waving the Beretta in his face. Except he'd likely arrest me. Cop first, brother second.

"The expert we have is THE expert on Picasso. Flown out from London."

"Shit."

"Art Fraud is his speciality. He's been helping us."

He stood up and paced across the room.

"I'll fetch it. The Picasso. It's in the car."

"You left a Picasso in your car?"

He beamed an artful smile.

"Sis, I just told you, it is a copy."

Being so up himself he only just managed to get his big head through the front door. I poured the dregs down the sink and poured myself a glass of red. I was going to need alcohol more than caffeine. I wished Pete had found my Op Shop painting. Thrown in the river I should think. Too dangerous to keep after the murder. I'd liked it much better than Patsy's size ten naked woman. Pete entered, carrying the Picasso wrapped in a cloth.

"What about my painting? The one the murderer took."

Pete cocked his head nonchalantly as he parked the picture on my table.

"He's doing a deal with us. Not that we do deals."

"Of course not. And does the deal include my twenty dollar painting?"

"Don't recall he had a painting on him."

The way cops lie so natural made me reckon I'd have made a great cop. I was definitely wasted. Pete flicked back the cream damask tablecloth. Staring at the picture made me realise how good it was. Even if it was a forgery by Giselle there was something essentially sensual about it. It looked good enough to be the real thing.

"Are you sure it's not genuine?"

"You can hear it from the horse's mouth. He'll be here any minute."

"Who will?"

"The expert from the UK."

"Coming here?

He nodded nonchalantly.

"Pete, there's a sink full of crockery!"

"He's coming to discuss the painting not your housekeeping skills."

"And I look a wreck."

"Sis, you look fine. Well, okay."

"Thanks a lot."

"If only you'd lose weight."

"Like your size ten wife?"

"She's a size twelve."

"I like her more already."

"Good because she likes you."

"She does?"

"She does."

This was the most bantering we'd done for years. It felt good. There was a short sharp knock at the front door. I stood up casually. No pounding heart. No sweaty hands reaching for my bag of lethal weapons. My cop brother was with me.

"That must be him and Mario."

"Mario?"

"Yes."

"And me looking like this!"

Pete roared with laughter. Lucky for him my weapons were not close.

"Mario must be used to you by now."

"Very funny."

Only it wasn't. Pete's wife wore outfits from Rome and Paris and, worse, looked fantastic in them. Mario would shop in the same streets. Him supposed to be a journalist turns out to be a cop. Where did he get his money from? Family? Or was he a bent cop? Shit, all the deceptions. He could have been using me to get information. What other lies were out there? Was he married with ten kids? The next knock was louder.

"Are you going to answer the door?"

I slid down the hall, doing my best to smooth down my stained top and brush the lint off my track pants. My bare feet revealed toe nails painted alternatively orange and black. I'd forgotten why. Squaring myself up I flicked my hair back and planted a smile on my face. Mario gestured to the expert to enter first. He was around two metres tall, slim, late fifties and wore a stiped fawn and white shirt, complete with loosely knotted tie, a pair of fawn corduroys and a lightweight rust coloured cotton jacket. He looked very English. His hair, greying at the temples, bounced majestically as he strolled down to the living room. He was followed by Mario, all in black, walking just as majestic and then me, cringing like I was the maid. In my own house. I was very miffed. Mario turned to me.

"Holly, allow me to introduce Professor James Milburn, of the Royal Academy, London."

The man graciously held out his hand. I had to stop myself from curtseying. We shook hands firmly, he beaming a genuine smile. *Memo: A Pom giving me a genuine smile. A minor miracle.* The whites of his eyes were the exact shade of his teeth. Pleased to see somebody could afford a top dentist. His voice was the modulated tone of somebody who regularly had to explain things to people.

"I am very pleased to meet you."

"Likewise."

"I trust that our brief acquaintance will be of mutual benefit."

To what or to whom he didn't say. The two men found themselves a seat. Pete had stayed where he was, comfortable, watchful. He motioned for me to sit. The Professor, being a proper gentleman, whisked a small armchair from the corner of the room and brought it to me. I ended up sitting opposite the three men, like it was me on trial. Was Inspector Barnaby about to enter and announce the guilty party? What had I to be guilty about? Useless Aussie hospitality?

"Can I offer anyone a coffee? Tea?"

The expert gazed up at me. I expected he was wondering about the condition of my tea cups. I'd thrown out the cracked ones, so he was safe.

"A cup of tea would be wonderful. Milk on the side, if you please."

"On the side of what?"

Mario quickly came to the rescue.

"I'll help you, Holly."

I teetered into the kitchen. In one fell swoop I'd been stripped of my strong independent status. I was seething. I filled the jug, banged it onto its element and began rattling cups and saucers, literally throwing tea bags at them. Mario touched my arm.

"You would win everything on the hoopla stall."

I made the tea, ignoring his sarcasm which had quickly changed to sincerity.

"The Professor is a good man. Very clever."

"Oh?"

"He knows his business."

Pete marched in, pushed his hands in his trouser pockets and rocked on his heels.

"To business, I think."

Did he think we were having a quick shag while the jug boiled? We all moved back into the living room.

"Professor?"

Pete sat down. Mario moved to the edge of his seat. I sat perched on the edge of the armchair. The cups of tea sat steaming on the table. The Professor eased himself out of the chair.

"It seems, Miss Day."

Miss?

"It seems that the painting belonging to the late Mrs Dougherty, attributed to Pablo Picasso, is in fact a forgery."

"Shit."

I couldn't help myself.

"Sorry."

"Quite so. It has some value of course but relatively little by comparion to the genuine article."

"Auntie Gert is going to be mad as a cut snake. And that's putting it mildly."

"Ah. Quite. And who can blame her."

He sat down and leant against the cushion, his speech over. He graciously sipped his tea. Was that it? He could have phoned that in. Unless. Unless there was another motive. I'd become permanently suspicious. I stood up, arms crossed, chest heaving and glared at the expert.

"Is that it?"

"It is what I was asked to do. To tell you the truth."

My mouth ran away with itself.

"How do I know it's the truth. How do I know you're not part of a plan to cheat Auntie Gert. That you won't run off with the painting, the genuine one and sell it for your own profit."

The professor stared, his eyes blinking rapidly.

"I say."

Pete placed his arm firmly around my shoulder.

"Sis has been through a lot lately."

I shoved his arm away.

"Don't you patronise me!"

"Come on, Holly. The Professor has a reputation to uphold."

"What's a reputation compared to a million dollars, or whatever."

Pete moved away from me shaking his head from side to side. The expert and Mario spoke simultaneously.

"You are completely wrong."

Pete raised his chin to the sky and murmured that it was time to go. He led the Professor out. I heard them chatting in the hall. I was still suspicious. I was close to tears. Me and my paranoia.

"How am I going to tell Auntie Gert?"

This time it was Mario's turn to put his arm around me. I leaned against him.

"Listen, Holly. The only condition that Patsy Dougherty put in the Will, was that when Picasso's picture was sold, ninety per cent of the net price should go to UNICEF. She clearly imagined she had the real one."

"Great."

I was being stupid and selfish and unreasonable. All the things I was before I became a PI. I was mad with myself. Mario placed me gently on the sofa. Having seen the Professor off in a taxi Pete returned. He pushed a large glass of red under my nose. I gulped it down. I felt better. Well, less angry.

"It will still create interest among buyers, sis. What got into you?"

Frankly, I had no idea. I did my best to return to sensible and calm.

"How much would it fetch?"

Mario sighed.

"As a copy? Who can tell."

Auntie Gert would be disappointed, even mad, but she'd come round. Then I had another thought. I threw it at Pete.

"So what about the painting that was stolen from me."

"I told you we have the man."

I fumed.

"The painting? I liked it. Where is it now?"

Mario and Pete gave each other long meaningful looks. What now.

The task to explain was handed over to Mario.

"The professor is working on it, Holly. It's being tested. Modern technology can discover all sorts of things."

"Like how much a twenty dollar painting is worth?"

I felt like being sarcastic. Pete carried on.

"The bottom line is, sis, that there's a good chance that underneath that weird picture is a genuine Picasso."

"You what?"

They were humouring me.

"It could be the real thing, sis. Hard to believe, I know but."

"A genuine Picasso? That has to be the most idiotic thing I've ever heard."

My brain couldn't be expected to compute that information. A genuine Picasso? Impossible. I'd paid twenty dollars for it. Hey, that meant I owned it. Or did I? All too confusing.

"So who exactly owns it? Legally."

Mario grinned.

"The lawyers will have a field day."

I could imagine a line of them stretching round Sydney Law Courts battling to take on the case. If it was genuine and it was declared to be mine I could pay off the mortgage, get the Valiant done up, buy a chocolate factory and lease an office in town. 'Day and Knight, Private Investigators'. I could pay somebody else to shoot crims for me, in self defence of course. I smiled at the thought. The whole idea was ridiculous. A precious gem in it, fair enough, but a genuine Picasso. Never. And yet.

"Holly?"

"Sis?"

The sounds impinged upon my fantasies. I shook myself out of my reverie and stared at the two men who both gazed with affection at me. I loved them both, even though they both drove me mad at times.

"Sorry. Day dreaming."

My brother leaned over.

"You look a bit shell shocked, sis."

Too right but I'd come to my senses.

"So Giselle painted over the Picasso?"

"More than likely. No proof yet. Long odds."

"But…wouldn't that ruin it?"

Mario spoke with some sort of authority.

"Not if executed by someone who knew what they were doing. Which sealers, which kind of paint, which material to use."

Pete strutted across the room like a a man desperate for a cigarette.

"A painting over a painting. Clever. If that's what it is."

Pete admired clever. I thought of Tweedledum and Tweedledee. They would have organised it for sure. Them and Jimmie telling me to look out for it. It made sense now. If it was the genuine article.

"Any news on Jimmie?"

Mario slowly shook his head. Pete shrugged.

"Nothing so far."

I didn't want to think about what might have happened to him. Mario moved to the door.

"Sorry, Holly, we have work to do."

Pete joined him.

"The big boys to catch."

"Your uncle, Mario?"

Mario glanced my way.

"He means nothing to me, Holly."

So, *The Godfather* was wrong about family before all else. After several glasses of red and a couple of chocolate bars I was pretty philosophical about the Picasso. Experts were proved wrong all the time, especially in the art world. If there was money in it, great. If not, well, nothing lost. Apart from my outlay of twenty dollars. The big worry was Jimmie. I had to find out if he was alive and well. Only then could I continue with the Case of Lucy's missing father. I went back to bed and, in spite of the excitement and how bad I felt about Jimmie, I slipped exhausted into sleep.

TWENTY EIGHT

I shuddered. I turned on my back. I was floating on a bed of water lilies, the patchouli-scented flowers drifting into my nostrils. Somewhere The Beatles were singing *Lucy in the sky with diamonds*. Mum was humming along. I called her name. The music stopped. Then I saw them; Mario, Pete, Giselle, Harry, Lucy and Auntie Gert, all peering down at me, their outstretched hands hovering above my face, long claws scratching at me. I tried to move. I was stuck. I yelled. No sound came out. In a monotone chorus the visitation chanted, "We expected too much, we expected too much, too much." I jerked myself upright. I was on dry land, my bed. I opened my eyes and the nightmare vanished. The voices had been right, they had expected too much of me. Pete expected me to keep out of his investigation. Mario expected my body any time he wanted. Giselle expected me to find her daughter's father. Lucy expected me to make him a kind and honest and famous man. Auntie Gert expected me to confirm the painting was worth a million dollars. Harry, had he expected me to save his life? And Jimmie, what had he expected? My heart clunked slowly. I was exhausted. I was scared. I'd run out of steam. I'd trapped myself with my enthusiasm and my naivity. I'd expected too much of myself. I allowed myself to sob.

After a few moments I regained my composure, my strength of mind returning to near normal. I lay back as the sun began its daily journey, spreading a thin veil of light across my windows. Nearby a magpie stirred, heralding the first moves of his territorial tribe. *Memo: Check what a group of magpies is called.* The ceiling was just as beautifully white as ever and the heavy bowl shaped lamp swung lightly in the wind that whipped through the open bedroom window I'd opened some time in the night. I didn't recall doing it. I should have had everything locked up. The petty crims were all accounted for, but Mario and Pete had made it clear the big boys were still to be locked away. Who knew what they'd do to me. Or to Jimmie.

The thought of Jimmie made me get up. I checked my face in the mirror. No scratches. Just a red hot flush. *Memo: Early menopause?* Maybe I was coming down with something other than paranoia. I had to think straight. I'd helped solve the Art Fraud Case but there was still Lucy's father. He was still missing. I'd got nowhere with the DNA and who knew how many other men there were to find before I got a result. I chuffed off to the kitchen for my regular shot of caffeine and Mars Bar and began to plan my search for Jimmie. As far as the cops were concerned he was simply a missing person. To me he was a missing friend.

I drank long and hard and called Lucy to come over. Shit, if I was having nightmares I had to take hold of myself. I was a strong, independent woman who could sort out anything I needed to. I could find missing people, missing evidence, anything I put my mind to. I was a good PI. I'd have to get better but I was already pretty okay. No more doubts. No more inaction. The pep talk worked. I knew what I had to do.

Lucy arrived quicker than anticipated. I was hanging the washing on the Hills Hoist when I heard her car. I was wrapped in a towel, hair dripping, body smelling of frangipani. Lucy was in one of her varied black and red outfits. She raced over, face lit up.

"You've found him."

"Ah. Not quite."

Seeing the disappointed look on her face I almost dived back into helpless mode but saved myself by trippng over the garden hose left out from some long ago attempt at watering the garden. We both giggled like fourteen year olds as I let Lucy pull me up from my prone position, the towel falling away, my naked flab flopping about on the damp grass. Lucy stood over me, hands on hips, her eyes bright, her mouth wide with laughter.

"You look like a whale beaching itself. My best friend, a fucking endangered species."

"Very funny."

We walked back in. I got dressed. Lucy made and poured the coffee. I talked about finding Jimmie. My plan was to visit the one person who'd know for sure if he was still alive and if so, where he was. Lucy took a step back.

"No luck finding my father then?"

"No DNA matches yet."

"He's going to stay fucking missing, hey?"

I had no new leads. I shrugged.

"Did they catch all the fucking crims?"

"Not yet. The higher up they go the smarter they are at covering their tracks."

"Tell me about it. My boss could come up with the fucking evidence."

"I've already given his name to Pete."

"There goes my fucking job."

"Sorry."

Lucy pressed my arm.

"No worries. I was bored shitless. I can always earn a living."

That statement was a worry in itself.

"So what are we doing today?"

"Finding out where Jimmie is. If he's alive."

"He's fucking alive. Got to be."

I hoped so. If Jimmie had heard who her father was why hadn't he said?

Maybe that was the ace up his sleeve. If he had a sleeve left, outside of a block of concrete.

I rang the office of the so called people's representative and made an appointment to visit. I gave our names as Marion and

Stephanie Blair. At the duly appointed hour we turned up and sat in his waiting room, which had plush purple and grey furnishings and a size ten, very young, male assistant. No surprise there. The counter he sat behind was a gleaming mass of red cedar topped by black leather. It could have been plantation pine with a coat of varnish but I doubted it. Whatever, it looked flash. I gave the admin man a knowing look as I asked if Standford-Smythe was readily available. He smirked back.

"He is always readily available, to certain people."

We sat. We waited. The office door opened. We stood up. Martin SS strode out and, seeing me, snorted loudly.

"You."

"Yes. Me."

Martin SS glared at his assistant.

"Call my business partner. Now!"

"Which one, sir?"

His boss bristled yet remained in control, his shoulders back, his head up, his lips clipped tight, his flexing fists the only give away of impending violence. Good to have Lucy with me. He snapped back the response.

"The most important partner of course!"

The young man made himself busy looking up the number while his boss stalked over to us.

"You'd better come in."

He turned and marched into his office. I clutched my shoulder bag, packed with the usual weapons. We followed. Our presence at his office had shocked Martin SS. I hated to think what it would do to Mario and Pete when they found out. The phone call meant reinforcements. We had to be quick. My adrenelin kicked in. Lucy's had kicked in five minutes before. She was straining at the leash. I whispered in her ear.

"Take it easy."

The door was shut tight behind us. Martin pointed to two padded seats aligned at a slight angle to his large, rain forest timber desk. He sat. Lucy sat on the edge of her seat eager to pounce. I sat back in my chair, casually as I could, keeping my eyes on Martin's hands. He'd have a gun snuck in some drawer. His voice was deep, loud and authorative. I imagined he gave good speeches in The House.

"So. What is it you wonderful ladies require of me?"

"Jimmie."

His facial expression remained unaltered.

"Jimmie who?"

Lucy's voice was low and monotone.

"You fucking know who."

"Isn't it your job to find missing people?"

He was a cunning bastard. I answered quickly.

"So you're aware then that he's missing?"

Martin leaned back, confident of his safety against any charges, any event.

This man thought prison and poverty were for other people. He salted the wound.

"Do you require this Jimmie alive or dead?"

Lucy lurched forward. I held her back.

"So you know which it is?"

He crossed his legs and placed his hands together as if in prayer.

"Let me think."

He must pay his lawyers a fortune.

"Hmm. Dead or alive. Let me see."

It was more than Lucy could take. She bounced out of her seat and leaned forward, her face almost touching his. He did not flinch.

"Listen, you fucking moron, don't play games with my best friend. Right!"

He remained cool as a cucumber. He was a politician after all.

"Why would I play games? I am here to help people."

"You fucking arse hole!"

He checked his tie and glared at me.

"Do please control your Doberman, or whatever breed of bitch she is."

Lucy dived over the desk, grabbed him by the collar, twisted him round and had him in a headlock within seconds. His hand stretched out to a drawer. The gun. Or a security button. I jolted myself out of the chair and rushed over, Beretta at the ready. The more he struggled the tighter Lucy's grip on his body. I yelled in his face

"Now, the truth. What happened to Jimmie?"

He gargled a reply. I pointed for Lucy to loosen her hold. She did.

"Well?"

He brushed down his jacket and straightened his tie.

"You will not get away with this. I am a respectable citizen."

"And I'm the fucking Queen of England."

I laughed as I imagined Lucy wearing a tiara. She returned to her seat, satisfied she'd shown her prowess. Martin's hand moved to the drawer. I pointed the gun at his head. His hand stayed mid air.

"Really, Holly. Dobermans? Ancient weapons?"

"Jimmie?"

He relaxed, his hand settling on his lap, yet no doubt primed ready to make a quick move when he thought it safe.

"For your information, the Jimmie you speak of is currently being cared for."

I so wanted to shoot him right between the eyes but I'd be charged, even if I'd killed a known murderer. There'd be a cover up for sure, a man of his standing in the community, me with a record.

"So where is he?"

I was running out of patience. He was playing for time. I motioned for Lucy to do her stuff but as Lucy passed in front of me he flicked the gun out of his drawer. Shit, his aim would be better than mine. He stood, the gun trained on my head. Mine trained on his.

"Let me see. Two mentally ill women, definitely users of illicit drugs, it's on record, they enter my office and threaten me. One of them has an illegal weapon. What can I do but defend myself? That will be my story. What will yours be?"

My hands were sweating. Between my boobs a veritable waterfall was falling.

My brain had gone numb. My arm drooped with the weight of the Beretta. Lucy moved a few steps forward. He waved the gun at her.

"Stay!"

"You reckon you'd get away with that fucking story?"

"It has worked before, my dear woman. Several times as a matter of fact."

His gun wavered between my forehead and Lucy's. I needed a distraction. It came. A gentle knock at his door.

"Yes?"

The voice on the other side of the door was young and clear.

"Your business associate is here, sir."

Martin SS slowly lowered his gun towards his jacket pocket just as a loud scuffle was heard outside the office. A loud groan followed. Martin SS lifted up the Gluck just as Lucy threw herself at him and proceeded with her Martial Arts skills. His gun went flip-flopping to the other side of the room as he thumped to the floor. More noise outside, more groans followed by one loud thud and the door was flung open. Jimmie, like a Clint Eastwood hero, stood outlined by the office light behind him.

"Jimmie!"

He held a gun pointed at Martin SS. Shit, at last somebody was going to make my day. Lucy screamed at him.

"Shoot. Shoot the fucking bastard!"

Martin SS lay on the floor, staring in disbelief. Lucy leaned against the wall rubbing her hands with glee, as if she'd won the finals at something big. I walked over to Jimmie.

"You okay?"

"I am now. You've been lucky, Holly."

"I thought you were dead."

Lucy moved to the door.

"I'll call the cops, right?"

Jimmie grinned cheekily.

"They're here. Restraining a certain Bruno de Rossi."

Martin SS screwed up his face. I figured he was already working out what deal he'd make with the Prosecutor to lighten his own sentence.

"Your brother's here as well."

"Pete? Great."

"He'll be in here the minute he hands De Rossi over to another cop for safe keeping."

A guttural voice from the doorway cut across out thoughts.

"Put the guns down."

We all turned. It was a Detective. Nothing like Barnaby. A much harder face. A much leaner body. Cruelty in his eyes. Martin SS struggled to get up.

"See what I have to put up with, Kenny?"

Kenny? They were pals? A bent cop? Where were Pete and Mario? The man strode over to me.

"Put that stupid little thing down, you insane woman."

I was well and truly miffed. Even if this man was from Police Headquarters I didn't deserve to be treated like that, not after we'd captured a criminal. He walked in and calmly took the gun from my hand. Jimmie lowered his but refused to hand it over. The cop stared at him.

"I'll deal with you later."

Martin laughed.

"You tell them, Kenny."

Kenny turned to Martin and smirked like an evil angel.

"Sit down, Martin."

He sat in his leather chair, meek as a three year old.

"The rest of you, outside."

We paused. The grin was wiped off Martin's face.

"Let me out first, Kenny."

"You, Martin. You stay. The rest of you, outside."

He waved the gun at us and yelled.

"You hear? Move your butts. Outside!"

We moved our butts. Jimmie's gun was snatched from him as he passed Kenny. The door was slammed shut after us. The admin boy sat in a chair grizzling.

"They are all bad men."

We all knew that. Behind the door voices were raised. Kenny's was tough, cold, uncompromising. Martin's was soft and pleading. We crowded by the door but none of us dared open it. There was only one word we heard clearly.

"No!"

A single shot echoed through the building. A thud followed quickly after. Before any of us had a chance to react to the sound the door was swung open and the detective strode out. He threw the words at the sobbing admin boy.

"You, call an ambulance. Too late but call it anyhow."

I couldn't believe it.

"You've killed him."

Lucy moved in close to me.

"Fuck."

Kenny smirked at us. Innocents one and all.

"He had a gun. He was going to use it. Had to shoot him."

We gazed at Kenny as he marched out, then dashed into the room. Martin SS lay on the floor in a pool of blood. One shot to the head. He wasn't going to be dobbing in anybody, least of all a corrupt police officer. A moment later Pete rushed in. I exploded.

"Where were you! A man has just been shot! A man who could have given evidence against crooks and bent cops. That one who was here for a start."

Pete sidled over to Martin, checked his pulse and stood up.

"Politicians. They talk too much."

I was flabbergasted.

"You knew what was going to happen, didn't you?"

My brother pushed his way past me.

"How would I know that? I got a call to come over. I caught Bruno de Rossi on the way in. I had to hold on to him until assistance arrived. Now I have to check out this body. Any further questions?"

I watched as my brother the cop went about the business of checking the scene of the crime and, I hoped, collecting evidence and not planting it. Was he telling the truth? Or had it all been planned? Had part of a deal with Bruno de Rossi been to have his offsider shut up? I felt sick to the stomach at what I was imagining. Even street wise Lucy was trying to comprehend the terror of it. Jimmie stood silent, head in hand, as Pete bustled us all out into the street and towards our cars. He refused to look me in the eye.

"That's the way it is, sis. It's a tough game. You'll learn."

Jimmie pressed his sweating hand into mine as we waded out like zombies into the carpark. None of us could speak. I was choked with both anger and regret at my stupidity. Lucy trembled with shock. Jimmie shook with anger. My Beretta would be lost for ever. It felt like I'd lost my innocence for the first time. Perhaps I wasn't cut out to be an Investigator after all. I had to find Lucy's father though. I'd promised myself that.

TWENTY NINE

After a week of moping around the cottage I was ready to take on another easier Case. Lucy's father was on the back burner for a while. I needed a short break from the intrigue and the deaths. I was just summoning up the energy for the afternoon job when Mario phoned. He'd be calling round later. There was something important to talk about. So, the time had come, the end was nigh. I had it all planned. I'd cook dinner. I'd smile a lot. I'd wear the dress I'd worn at Pete's wedding. I'd worn it at his entrance into my world, so I'd make my exit wearing it. Lucy was right, good things never lasted.

After the call I postponed the Case. It could wait. A valuable pedigree poodle had gone missing. Whoever stole it would take good care of it. Probably have its own TV in its own kennel, with lashings of chicken and caviar for meals. More than third world country kids enjoyed. Or, it could be on the menu at a high class restaurant in Hong Kong. Interesting thought. Big business, I bet. *Memo: Check if pedigree dogs sell to restaurants for more than mongrel dogs do.* At least my reputation for finding missing things had got around. Once Bruno de Rossi was put on trial, together with all his associates, the media would go beserk. I'd get my fifteen minutes of glory. Worth a few years work I reckoned.

Mario turned up around six. I'd taken special care with make up, hair and outfit. I wanted to look good when I got the flick. Pride. Ego. Whatever. I'd made a Tuna dish, all cream and chives and pasta. His kind of food. I'd refrained from too many Mars Bars so I'd be well and truly hungry. Starving, more like. He hugged me real close and tousled my hair as if I was the missing dog come home. While he was pouring the wine his mobile went off. He answered it. Of course. He said it could be important, as if I wasn't. He chatted away as if nothing bad was about to happen. Still, I had to admit that what had kept us together was the Art Fraud Case. He'd go off to his next assignment and I'd continue looking for Lucy's father and do other Cases as they came up. We'd go our separate ways. Him a cop. Me a private investigator. That's how it would be. Shit happens. All quite rational. So, when I spent all night bawling my eyes out at least I'd have a full stomach and a decent hangover to wake up to. I'd hardly be upset at all. I had to believe it.

By the time Mario poured the third glass I was relaxed and resigned to the inevitable. I sat on the sofa, cool as a cucumber, armed to the teeth with acceptance of my Fate. He sat beside me. He put his arm around my shoulder. I took a deep breath. His face was dead serious.

"Holly, there are a couple of things I need to talk to you about."

I already felt like a martyr.

"Fire away."

"First, the Professor considers that a genuine Picasso is indeed concealed beneath the surreal painting that Giselle Knight did."

"Shit. Brilliant."

"More independent tests will confirm his opinion but it looks like you've had a genuine Picasso hanging over your bed for some time."

"I paid twenty dollars for a real Picasso. Shit."

"Rather a bargain. But of course the ownership will be contested."

"Do you know who took it to the Op Shop?"

It had to be Tweedledum and Tweedledee but no way was I offering him assistance. Let him do his own investigation.

"In theory it is the proceeds of a crime. Robbery."

"So I'll receive nothing."

"That depends on the top brass. And the lawyers. You were the innocent in all of this. I know a good lawyer. Paul Diston."

Wheels within wheels. Mario kept going with his speech.

"It could take years to settle of course.".

Bang went my hope of owning my very own chocolate factory next week.

"A good lawyer might substantiate a claim for a finder's fee."

"That would be brilliant on my CV: Holly Day finds missing things, including paintings by Picasso."

"Exactly."

Brian's research had revealed that Picasso was still a good investment.

"We're talking millions? For the painting."

"It will produce a great deal of interest at the Auction houses. Who knows what it will fetch. It may take some considerable time."

Nowhere near as long as my thirty year mortgage. He took my hand in his.

"You have told your aunt about her Picasso? The copy."

He was stalling. The coward was having trouble telling me. I shrugged.

"Not yet."

Auntie Gert would be disappointed as hell but like the trouper she is, she'd take it on one of her chins. She'd listen, go pink in the face, kick off her pink slippers and jig around the room. Then she'd drink sufficient Shiraz to change her face from pale pink to bright red, then sing every bawdy song she'd ever learned, and she'd learned quite a few down the Community Health Centre. She'd be off the planet for days. I pictured her floating around her house in her padded pants and pink everything. I had my own trauma to get through first.

"Shall I phone Auntie now?"

"Please, can it wait a while?"

Best face up to the next episode. I stood up and stared out of the window.

The sun was setting. Rays of gold and red streaked across the sky. It was a nice backdrop to the farewell speech I was anticipating.

"So what else did you want to tell me?"

"It's about Lucy's father."

I turned. Another line to put off the inevitable?

"I am afraid he's dead."

Relief flooded through my veins.

"Well, it was almost four decades ago. Who was he?"

I was hoping he'd been a kind, decent, possibly famous, man.

"You recall a Jonathon Squires?"

My memory flipped to Harry and his photos.

"I do."

"After further investigations we are pretty sure he was the father."

"His DNA matched Lucy's?"

"Yes."

I had no idea how and when he'd got Lucy's sample.

"Wait a minute. Jonathon Squires. The one in the photos. The one at the funeral. Isn't that the man you met up at your Uncle's?"

"There was a man who called himself Jonathon Squires."

"Called himself Jonathon Squires?"

Mario nodded.

"Squires is, in fact, dead. Murdered. Shot in the head."

"Lucy's father, Jonathon Squires, was murdered."

"According to the evidence."

My brain was getting overloaded with confusing information.

"So who is he? The man who calls himself Squires."

"Jason Mueller. Harry Mueller's brother."

"Harry? Hippie Harry? His brother, Jason? He died years ago. Didn't he?"

"Not according to forensics. There was a DNA match with Hippie Harry but not with the man whose body was exhumed."

"Harry was exhumed?"

"As well as the man in the grave where his brother was supposedly buried."

My mind was clogging up. The jigsaw had turned into a kaleidoscope.

"So. Jonathon Squires was killed and buried in place of Jason, who is still alive?"

"That is what it looks like. "

"Who killed Squires then?"

"That we may never uncover. Or why he was killed. Unless we get a confession out of Jason Mueller. When we catch up with him."

I began to wonder on the interviewing techniques of my brother and Mario.

"No doubt Squires and Jason Mueller were both involved in crime. Art or drugs, who can tell. They could have fallen out. It happens all the time. Perhaps Squires was double crossing someone. If it was my uncle, he would certainly have ordered the killing. We are awaiting his side of the story."

Deals would be in the offing for sure.

"Hippie Harry spent all these years thinking his brother was dead. While all the time he was alive and doing all sorts. Even maybe planning Giselle's death."

"Truth or fiction, yet to be discovered."

None of it made sense to me. My mind clouded over with pieces of information I'd stored in there for weeks. The picture I had begun to form was now shattered by all the new stuff.

"So when was he killed? And what about the doctors certificate? And wouldn't there have been an autopsy?"

"Whoa. Too many questions at once. We don't have all the answers yet but we will. De Rossi had many friends, in high places as well as low places. Money buys anything."

I was seriously beginning to believe it.

"To think he had the nerve to turn up at his brother's funeral. Shit, Harry must be turning in his grave. You have put Harry back?"

"Of course. We needed only a small sample from him."

I could have handed over Harry's beanie had I known.

"The other body we need to hold onto for a while, pending investigations."

It seemed like Hippie Harry was an innocent pawn in a dangerous game. Guilt squeezed my heart so tight I spluttered, which led to a fit of coughing. Mario rushed to the kitchen and brought me back a glass of water. I gulped it down, soaking away the lump in my throat.

"Holly, Harry's death was not your fault."

True or false it was hard to shake off. I pictured Harry in his doorway as I walked away from his shack. How many times had he stood there staring after his brother, or Giselle. I sighed. Mario's grip on my hand tightened. Framed in the light from the window he looked smaller than he'd ever done. I still lusted after him. He waited. I calmed myself.

"Do you think Harry found out it was Squires killed in his brother's place?"

"Maybe."

"And that's why he was killed?"

"We imagine so."

"Killed by his own brother?"

"That would be impossible to prove after all this time."

It was taking me a long time to finally accept the completed jigsaw.

"Lucy's father, a criminal, a drug dealer, a murderer. How to come to terms with that?"

"You must. For Lucy's sake."

He was right. One of the things I'd feared the most had come to pass. Ironically, her father could have been rich from his ill gotten gains and the tabloids would soon make him posthumously notorious, if not famous. However, he was definitely not a kind, decent man at all. I sat, unable to cry. Mario took me in his arms.

"Wait a while. Tell her when things have moved on a little."

I had nothing better to offer Lucy. I snuggled up to Mario.

I longed for his body and mine to be mingled as one. And yet, hadn't he yet to explain that our relationship was over? I stood up, unable to surrender my hopes and desires, determined to remain strong, calm, rational.

"What will happen to Giselle?"

"She will be charged for her involvement but will be treated lightly, if she gives evidence that helps put the rest away. She was, it seems, forced to work under mitigating circumstances."

Mario's phone rang. He smiled an apology, stood up and walked onto the verandah. Mobile reception was never brilliant in my cottage. One of the things I love about it. I shouted to him.

"I'll make coffee. I've some brandy."

"Fine. We both need one."

One? I needed a dozen. I wandered into the kitchen. Outside the magpies were giving robust enthusiasm to their evening chorus. Soon they'd all be tucked up in the tree tops somewhere. After dinner would I be tucked up in bed with Mario, for the last time. I'd had a few months with him. I was grateful for that. With some help from the cops, with their digging up of bodies, I was certain who was Lucy's father. The cops had been forced to change their plans because of me, and Harry was dead because of it. I had to forgive myself for that. Now it was all over. If it was over between me and Mario so be it. A mixed outcome. As an Investigator I'd have to get used to that statistic.

I strode back in with two mugs of coffee. I grabbed the brandy and a couple of glasses off the dresser. The front door was wide open. Mario was nowhere in sight. I raced back to the bedroom and got the pepper spray and the blade. Turning back into the hall I collided with Mario. The knife dropped to the floor. I gazed at it, panting heavily. He bent to pick it up and handed it over.

"I will not ask."

"I thought there might be danger."

I placed the knife and the spray on the table. Mario handed over a letter. I turned it over.

"This was on the verandah outside. Somebody must have delivered it."

I took it and turned it over. Mario cupped his mug, the steam rising to the warmth of his smile.

"Do you intend to read it?'

I recognised the handwriting. It was from Jimmie. I wasn't sure I wanted to read another note written in panic. Yet, as usual, curiosity got the better of me. I opened it. Inside was a 6 x 4 photo of a laughing Jimmie, wearing bright shorts, a floral shirt, a poncho and one of those big woolly brightly striped hats seen in documentaries from South America. On the back he'd written. *'Hello dear Holly. Here I am, happy as a pig in shit, in the amazing country of Ecuador. This is the place to be if the rest of the world does not want you. I've met some fantastic people. Good people. I have honest work. No more crime for me. If you and Lucy can ever get over for a visit it would be great to see you. Thankyou for your trust and friendship. Contact details later. Trust nobody bad finds me and I end up 'Making Their Day'. Out here they love Clint Eastwood movies so I swagger around and make them laugh. Take care Holly. In friendship. Love. Jimmie Claymore.'*

I dropped into a chair and wept. Gently Mario took the photo out of my hand and read the message. It took some time before I could speak.

"It's brilliant he's safe."

"Yes."

"Will you stay with me tonight?"

"I intend to stay with you for ever, if you let me."

Shit, what was he saying? He cupped my face in his hands and spoke quietly.

"Will you marry me?"

Marry him? It was like the final scene in a B Grade movie.

"I love you very much. Even in your flannette jammies."

We both had to laugh at that. There I was, prepared for a farewell speech, and what had I got? Love and marriage? Could

I cope with that? I liked my independence but I had to admit, I was closing in on forty, maybe it was time for sharing. *Memo: This emotional involvement is scarily great.*

"I love you too. I think."

That was as far as I dare go. We were real good together. We'd made it past the few weeks Lucy predicted. Not just the sex but the arguing and the disagreements and the fun and the kindness and the helping each other out. That's what friends and lovers do. But married people?

"I understand. It is a big step."

Big step? Shit, it was bigger than the moon walk.

"Can we leave the marriage bit and just live together? For a while."

"If that is how you prefer it."

"It'll give us a chance to, you know."

He grinned, lips closed, doubtful of my intentions. They were not all that honourable. Besides there was the tricky question of where we'd live. I couldn't stand his Unit for long. Would he get used to my untidiness? I glanced towards the kitchen knowing full well the sink was overflowing with crockery. And the only thing I colour coded was the hundreds and thousands I sprinkled on sponge cakes I bought down the supermarket. He was waiting for my next excuse.

"We could live at your place for, a while, then my cottage and so on. Sort of like doing shifts."

"A little complicated?"

"No. Dead easy."

It sounded like a done deal. As far as I was concerned it was.

"Right. And by the way that was the Professor on the phone. They are now one hundred per cent certain it is the genuine Picasso under your painting, and once cleaned up it will be as good as new."

"Whooppee! I think."

We hugged. He let me go and strolled to the window, his back to me, his arms folded, his eyes scanning something beyond my view. Was he already doubting his decision? Sometimes he went places I'd never get to. He turned. He looked as if he was about to confess to murder. He breathed deep and uncrossed his arms.

"My wife, Arlene, she committed suicide."

Shit, some announcement.

"That's why I became involved with the Drugs Squad. She was addicted to drugs, heroin mostly. She'd tried to kill herself a few times. She had nothing worth living for. Not even me. So, I failed her. Then one day, I came home and there she was, swinging from a rope. Of course, being a Catholic."

His voice trailed off. It explained his reaction to the rope in Harry's shack. I reached for him and rested his head against my big floppy boobs. A torrent of tears rolled down his cheeks. Shit, it felt strange me comforting a man.

THIRTY

We'd all gone up to Noosa to be with Giselle when she was released from hospital. Lucy had feverishly declared her position.

"If any dealer gets within a kilometre of my mother, I'll kick ass."

There was no doubting her sincerity. The McMansion was put on the market. Brian reckoned the security box in Amsterdam held the title deeds. In any case there was always another way around legal problems, according to a well informed Lucy. Giselle had rented a holiday home until the court case came up. She didn't seem overly concerned. The deals would have been set in concrete as soon as De Rossi was in custody.

She looked luminous in a bright cotton Indian skirt and gypsy top with the bangles and beads of old. Her memories were tied up with her hippie past and she seemed determined to remain in that world, a world before the drug addiction and its consequences. She and Lucy held hands and gazed at each other as if one of them could suddenly disappear again. Powerful stuff, mother and daughter.

I hadn't decided when and how to tell Lucy about her father. I wanted to query Giselle about Jonathon Squires. For my own satisfaction, nothing more. My chance came when Lucy wanted to go for a swim. Giselle was happy with her going. I joked that Mario ought to go with her to save the lifesavers any possible misadventures. Lucy grinned as she breezily pushed herself out of her black and red outfit and into the briefest size ten bikini ever. She looked deadly. *Memo: Lose weight.* With hard work and a starvation diet I might get down to a size sixteen. Not that Mario had complained, so far.

Giselle settled herself on the beach lounger on the back verandah. I noticed her slender fingers. They still held a fascination for me as she brushed them through her long, greying hair. She turned her elegant face to me.

"You have discovered who Lucy's father is?"

I had to lie for a bit longer.

"I think so."

"Ah, you only think so."

She stared out at the three storey holiday units opposite. They blocked our view of the ocean. Perhaps she was contrasting them to the native forest she'd lived in for a couple of decades. There was a sadness in her voice when she spoke.

"Holly, I honestly do not know who the father is. It is a terrible thing to admit. I am filled with such guilt. But that is how it is. I am such a terrible mother."

"No!"

The denial burst out of me like a bullet out of a pistol.

"You must never say that. Lucy adores you. Always did. Never knew how to show it but she did."

Her fingers probed the corner of her eyes.

"Thank you. Thank you for that."

I waited for the jaw to relax.

"Do you recall a Jonathon Squires?"

A hand shot to cover her mouth, as if she didn't dare say the words, but she did.

"It cannot be him. It cannot."

She'd basically told me what I wanted to know. How to handle it.

"You seem sure it cannot be him?"

"Not one hundred per cent sure, but as I said."

"Would it be so dreadful if he was the father?"

"He is the last person I would want. He did terrible things."

She clearly had no idea what had happened to Squires.

"He ruined people's lives. With drugs and violence. A bad man."

So that was it. She wouldn't want him as the father any more than would Lucy. My path was clear.

"You heard about Harry?"

She nodded, sadly.

"Poor, dear Harry, such a gentle man. He was like a brother to me. They were such happy days, for a while. A time of hope for love and harmony and, and peace. That is what it was meant to be. And it was, for some."

"But not for you."

"You think it is him, don't you?"

She bit her lip. What was I to say.

"There is still some DNA to check. Other men."

This time I felt the hole I was digging was an escape route not a trap.

"They tried several times to kill me, you know. When I threatened to expose them. But then I needed them too. Drug addicts become helpless as well as hopeless. That is what society does not understand."

She sighed loudly. Giselle faced me, her face drawn and tired.

"I regret now that I set this train in motion. I should have let sleeping dogs lie, so to speak."

I was beginning to feel the same way.

"The evidence is not yet conclusive."

One hell of a whopper. She placed her delicate fingers on my arm.

"Thankyou. And thank you so much for being Lucy's friend all these years. For looking out for her. Doing what I should have done."

Shit, I was about to bawl. *Memo: No emotional involvement! Right? Wrong. Impossible.* I marched to the kitchen and put on the jug. Tea, the universal panacea. Only it was going to be coffee. I brightened my voice up.

"Lucy is bound to come back with some food. Mario will bring wine. I'll lay the table."

Giselle settled back in the lounger and stared out at the consummate selection of freshly refurbished holiday homes parading themselves before the chattering tourists. A very different world was out there to the one she'd lived. What would others think of her life, I wondered.

Mario did return with wine, Lucy with half a dozen containers of Chinese food. We dined with different kinds of love wafting in the balmy air; mother, daughter, friends, lovers and good old plain lust. My body tingled at the thought of being in bed with Mario later. We'd booked into a Motel.

We took our evening stroll along the beach, talking of the wonders of Nature, how great it was for Lucy and Giselle getting back together and pondering on whether we'd stay first in his place or mine. I'd got what I came for. Giselle would believe whatever she wanted to believe. Of that I was certain.

It was in the after glow of fabulous sex that I decided not to reveal to Lucy who her father actually was. How could I possibly tell her he was a criminal, a drug dealer, a murderer. I had to lie. I just had to. Lucy was my very best friend. I'd do whatever was right for her peace of mind.

I stared up at the flickering fluoro light, and thought back to the diary entries. I swept my mind across the intitials. Should I make up a name from the intitials or simply pluck a name and a personality out of the air? Then I recalled the unnamed musician. Giselle had liked him. She hadn't said that about any other man. That was it. That was to be my story. As close to the truth as I needed to get.

Lucy's father was a musician, an American musician who's DNA had been found on...on something. Call him Mark. He'd arrived at the Festival as a student. He'd gone on to be a famous guitarist in America. He'd died in a plane crash long before his fame spread world wide. It was a private funeral. No media, although one report had cited him as being a good, kind, decent man. Only in-depth research by Brian had found out that much.

If I lied well enough, Lucy would be stoked by my version of the truth. Even if she asked Giselle about it she'd be happy to go along with whatever I'd discovered. Best thing was, Lucy could continue to imagine her father as anything she wanted. The kind of man, the kind of father, only dreams can command. It was a calm, rational, compassionate plan. I could rely on the silence of Mario and Pete. As for my integrity, I could live with it. I'd be doing the right thing for the right reason. It was the best gift I could offer my best friend, two parents to love. I was well pleased with myself.

Fruitbats flapped and squawked across the moonlit sky. I heard the ebb and the flow of the deep dark ocean and quietly allowed myself the comfort of a slow descent into a grey tinted slumber. I'd dream of the cottage I loved, with its trees and its flowers, with its casement windows that got stuck when it rained hard, with its polished timber floorboards and high ceilings with spiders parading themselves at every corner, free to spy on sexually active humans.

In that precarious moment between sleep and wake, between dream and reality, I reasoned that, back in the days of his innocent youth, Jonathon Squires may well have strummed a guitar. Lots of young blokes did back then. So, given a little poetic licence, Lucy's father could, by a fairly reasonable stretch of the imagination, have been a musician, of sorts. Sometimes a lie could be so close to the truth it served a higher purpose. I smiled to myself and rolled against Mario's firm, warm body. Life was good. That was no lie. I'd learned a lot about love and friendship. Important lessons for a virgin PI to learn. Next stop, what?

The end.